IRONCLAD

(RAVEN CURSED BOOK 6)

MCKENZIE HUNTER

McKenzie Hunter

Ironclad

ISBN: 978-1-946457-36-3

ACKNOWLEDGMENTS

Thank you for joining Erin's adventure. I truly appreciate readers for taking part in her journey.

Each time I finish a book, I reflect on how many people directly and indirectly helped me and I'm always humbled by it. I'm forever grateful to my friends and family for their encouragement and support. And to my alpha reader, beta readers, and editing team: Meredith Tenant and Alexa, I can't thank you enough for your hard work and dedication to ensuring I publish the best book I can.

CHAPTER 1

My anger made the room feel exceptionally warm and the fierce emotions that rampaged through me difficult to subdue. I took a deep breath and exhaled into the desolation. The tense silence felt surreal. Mephisto, Simeon, Kai, Clay, and Benton were gone. Fabian stood in front of me, smug with the knowledge that he and Elizabeth were responsible for their departure and sealing the Veil so that they couldn't return.

Fabian's lips curled into a genial, sympathetic smile that held a kindness I suspected he thought would soften my mood. I wanted to destroy him and Elizabeth. Make them pay for the pain, betrayals, and heartache I felt. My emotions made my magic erratic, and it pulsed in me. My hand rising to Fabian's chest, the roiling magic burst into him, sending him careening into the wall. Shocked, he hurriedly placed a protective field around himself. As I pressed my hand against it, an unsettling wry smile remained on his face along with that perceptive spark in his eyes that I'd come to loathe.

"You can't break it. Your magic is exceptional, and with more training you will become an unstoppable force. One that will compel people to take notice. Your undeniable power would demand people take notice. Despite your lineage, we would welcome you into the fold as one of us. You would be an incomparable asset," he admitted, his pretense lauding the significance of their acceptance of me. It left me wondering whose arrogance was more pervasive, gods or elves? Elves liked to believe they were a different, purer version of powerful magic. But from where I stood, they were the same side of a power-lusting, self-unaware coin. And both of that magic dwelled in me.

"How kind of you to allow me entrance into a collective of people who have worse ethics than the ones they claim to hate," I huffed. My anger was raw and unfettered. I wanted to show how disgusted I was with him. Especially at the smirk that inched over his lips as if I was inconsequential. I walked around the enclosure, hoping to feel a weakness in the structure or that my increased activity around him would be enough of a distraction for there to be a lapse in his magic. I just needed one moment of weakness. Even hubris could work in my favor. Him underestimating me could be his fall.

He was strong and focused, watching me through narrowed eyes. Fabian's smile relaxed and the cool indifference in his eyes melted away. They looked soft, entreating. A performance that I wouldn't fall for.

"You're hurt and you feel betrayed."

"Should I *not* feel betrayed by your betrayal? How foolish of me."

"It wasn't personal, Erin. You must understand that. Harsh, perhaps. I understand my methods could be perceived as cruel."

"You threatened Madison's life! That's beyond cruel."

"It was a necessary evil. I believe your judgment is clouded by your lust for that Huntsman. Once it passes, you'll see it was in your favor that the situation was handled this way. There is a reason they were in the Veil. It is where they belong, and the elves out here. Our paths never to

cross to avoid forcing our hands into proving who is the stronger power." The smirk crept back over his face. "Although I think I have proven who is." He waved the comment away.

"Erin, I do believe that after some time to reflect, you will appreciate what I've done. You have to know how dangerous it is for the Veil to be an option, for anyone. I've made this world safe. You've made this world safe, and you will see that the sacrifice isn't as great as you believe it to be."

Permanently closing the Veil had been a debate between Madison and me. The inhabitants of the Veil were more powerful, more ruthless, and immune to some of our magic, making policing them a challenge. But the Huntsmen were from the Veil, more important, Mephisto. And I wanted him here. I understood the unfairness of the situation. Most couldn't see the Veil, which meant they couldn't pass through it.

"Do you understand what we've done? The safety we've ensured and how effectively we've established our true roles here? You can't be angry with me for that, can you, Erin?" He'd mastered the art of persuasion. From the soft lilt of his voice, the entreating expression, and the unobtrusive posturing that made him seem less dangerous than he was. Fabian was no different than Malific or Elizabeth; he was just wrapped in a more palatable package. I despised him. Minutes slipped by as I imagined bringing him and Elizabeth down. Exacting my well-deserved revenge.

Taking my silence for acquiescence, he looked hopeful. He placed his hand against the protective field, waiting for my hand to meet it in a show of acceptance and solidarity.

Did this manipulative ass think I'm going to do some cheesy hand touch through glass scene with him? Even if some part of me agreed with him, I couldn't condone his method. He took away my choice. I was so tired of everyone taking away my choices for my "good," only to be screwed over by them. He had threatened Madison's life, and for that reason alone he could never be forgiven.

"Drop the field and we can discuss it," I suggested. Without any weapons on me, I didn't have a fighting chance, but I wanted one. The thirst for some retribution was making me impulsive and right then, I wanted to punch him in the face. Give him immediate brutal pain.

He studied me for a long moment. "I don't feel I have persuaded you to logic. I do hope after some time, you will see that the results did justify the means. We will revisit this soon. For now, I must return to the Havenage." Inching even closer to the thin illumination that separated us, he whispered, "Your father will remain under our protection."

Protection. He wrapped his threat in seeming benevolence. Nolan wasn't under their protection but had unceremoniously become his prisoner. I saw Fabian clearly: Behind his kind words, polite inquiries, and seemingly benign comments were manipulations and calculated cruelty. I would play his game better than he did.

"That's kind of you. Please keep him safe."

His lips twitched as they moved into a plaintive smile. "Erin, I'm not your enemy. Don't treat me as such. Your life will be better with me as an ally," he pronounced. "When you are ready to proceed, I will be waiting." He shimmered slightly, preparing to disappear. My attempt to break his barrier made it pulse and, to his surprise, undulate and stretch so much I thought it would tear. Fabian's confidence in it faltered. As his mask dropped, I got a glimpse of something he'd hidden before: concern. He had every right to be.

He disappeared before I could try again. I'd hold on to that anger and thirst for revenge. It might not be healthy, but it fueled my magic.

I was going to kill him. And Elizabeth.

———

No matter how strong the hate that dwelled in a person, a twinge of civility kept a person anchored to humanity, even if by the thinnest of strands. Which was why there was a part of me that felt guilt over my decision to murder Elizabeth and Fabian. I found my thoughts drifting to my sessions with Dr. Sumner. A little voice urged me to call him when I remembered how I scored on that damned test, acknowledged who my mother was and her role in what I could become, and my recklessness when I didn't have my own magic. That voice was urging me to reach out to him to steer me to a more civilized option. I didn't want to. Some cruelties can't be fought with civility. They had threatened my family. A jolt of pain shot through me, stopping me midstride as I made my way to Mephisto's room to retrieve my things. The situation could have ended differently, and I could have lost Madison, Sophie, and Keegan.

Fabian and Elizabeth didn't deserve leniency or even a second thought about it. Just cold, dark action.

As I gathered my things, I saw that I had a message from Ava, Mephisto's attorney, letting me know she'd meet me at his home within the hour. After our meeting, I planned to return to my apartment.

My overnight bag was at the door when Ava arrived, stepping into the house with a tablet in one hand and a cream-colored expensive-looking leather briefcase in the other. Her short hair was brushed back, more casual than I'd ever seen it, also giving a full view of diamond earrings. Completing her look with tailored burgundy slacks, silk shirt with large lavallière tie, and three-inch heels that she walked in with the ease of wearing sneakers.

"Hello, Ms. Jensen," she greeted in a neutral voice as she entered the house with purpose and strode past me, waving me forward. I followed as she navigated to Mephisto's office. Taking a seat at his desk, she directed me to the chair in front of it. Ava was silent for a moment, a frown deepening and relaxing as she scrolled through her tablet.

She turned it toward me. "This is just to confirm that you've been given the following items: code to the house, keys, access to the cars in the garage. There will be an over-ride code for his collections." Some of the tension eased in me. His collection of magical objects would give me an advantage in dealing with Fabian and hopefully reopening the Veil. Barely able to contain my surprise and satisfaction, it took effort to keep the emotions from my face. I could feel her eyes on me as I signed.

"What do you know about Mephisto?" I asked.

"I know he's my client and pays me well for my discretion. I only ask the most pertinent questions on what I need to do my job. And just my job." Ava's tight smile and sharp look warned me off further questioning.

The curious look she gave me vanished as quickly as it appeared. Upon our initial meeting, she'd voiced being unimpressed by me. When she was hired after River arrested me, her opinion didn't seem to have changed. Her curiosity was rooted in Mephisto's interest and probably only height-ened by the fact his contingency plan included giving me access to his home and collections. After signing more docu-ments that gave me access to all his funds, which I had no intention of using, and his plane, which may come in handy, I followed her to the hidden room that stored his collection of magical objects he had acquired over the years in his effort to find a way back home. She reviewed something on her tablet—I assumed instructions—before giving me fingerprint access to the room. Once I successfully opened the door, she stepped back to keep from seeing the items in the room. Her staunch professional demeanor dropped.

"Will he return?" she asked, her eyes searching my face.

Glancing at all the new magical objects available to me, my confidence heightened.

"Yeah. It may take some time, but he will be back."

She gave me another scrutinizing look, a wide smile curling her lips. The underwhelmed impression she had of me dissolved as she nodded her head.

"I don't know if that's true, but I get the feeling there's nothing you won't do to make it so." Ava reached into her purse, retrieved a card, and handed to me. "If you ever need help, just send me a message." She started to leave then stopped and smirked. "Even if it's legal counsel. I don't usually handle criminal cases, but I have a team member who can." Her gaze trailed over me. "I'm sure you'll need us."

She'd been hired when I was arrested and I didn't have a stellar reputation, so it wasn't implausible that I'd need her for criminal counsel. I held my snarky rebuttal. There was definitely judgment in her statement.

CHAPTER 2

Cory's hand scrubbed over the low dark beard shadowing his face. Looking more disheveled than I'd ever seen him, fear and apprehension had settled heavily over his features. Based on his appearance, when I called to tell him that Mephisto and the Huntsmen were gone and the Veil had been closed, he rushed over as soon as the call ended. My attempts to keep the pain out of my voice had failed. An incident at the Supernatural Task Force agency kept my phone call with Madison brief and unable to provide a lot of detail about what happened. I was grateful for the delay because I hadn't determined how much I wanted to reveal to her.

I didn't want to tell her how perilously close she and Cory were to being victims of an elven spell that would have systematically killed anyone with fae blood because of Fabian. And I wasn't in a rush to reveal that Fabian had used her as a bargaining tool.

My only solace was that the spell was linked to Elizabeth, and despite proving to be the monster she'd shown herself to be, I wasn't entirely convinced she'd sacrifice her life just to hurt me. I was certain Fabian would have and wondered if she was aware of it. Neither one of them could be trusted, but would it be a good plan to pit them against each other? Two powerful elves: one a full elf with extraordinary powers and the other elf/fae hybrid whose magical knowledge would make her a worthy adversary.

Seated on the sofa, Cory wiped a hand over the shadow of beard forming along his jaw. He grimaced. "You doing okay?"

"I'm fine."

"Liar," he whispered. He called me out on it as a way of letting me know it would be visited later, but he knew me well enough to know I needed time to process everything. A lot of emotions roiled in me but the most comfortable and profound was anger. I'd settled into it and welcomed it because it was the easiest one to handle. The rest of it was a perplexing mess.

"What are your plans? What happens now?" Cory's voice was tight, pulling me from my thoughts and to the painful-looking crease in his furrowed brows.

"Revenge." The word slipped from me in a venomous hiss, forcing his gaze to jerk in my direction.

His brow lifted. "And?"

"And what?"

"You want to reopen the Veil so Mephisto can return."

"That's a given," I offered, but the worried groove remained on his face.

"Is it, Erin?" His tone was conciliatory as he took a seat on the sofa next to me. His fingers traced small circles on my hand. "Don't let anger and desire for revenge overshadow what's most important to you. Everything about your vibe is giving off that revenge seems to be the priority. I see a hyper-intense focus and I fear it's misdirected."

He was wrong but I was determined to do both. The thirst for revenge and the desire to reopen the Veil held equal priority. I hoped.

"It won't overshadow my goals. One can't exist without the other. You think I won't have to deal with Fabian and

Elizabeth if the Veil is reopened? Elizabeth doesn't believe I should exist, and Fabian doesn't want a world with gods in it. They're both determined to make my life a living hell. Fabian's goal is to gain me as an ally to the elves, and Elizabeth will tolerate my existence because it will benefit her and help them obtain power. I don't think he'll hurt me, but no one around me will be safe. Everyone close to me would be a tool used to *urge* me into seeing things his way. It can't be ignored or go unpunished. I won't let it." Cory nodded but his pensive expression remained. "Even if I were to allow it, can they be trusted to behave? The absence of gods makes the elves the strongest magical beings around, and the only thing keeping them from exerting their will on others are their low numbers. But I don't think that will be a deterrent for long. Their magical knowledge is too great."

I wasn't dealing with the same pacifist elves that inhabited the Veil. They considered those beliefs a weakness they'd no longer subscribe to. It appeared they'd chosen an antithetical way of existing. No middle ground.

"How do you plan to deal with Fabian and reopen the Veil?"

It was a good question and one I couldn't answer. Telling someone you're going to be their worst nightmare and actually becoming it were two different things. It meant I had to improve my elven and god magic. Find a way to integrate them so that my magic couldn't be bested by either of them. Unfortunately, the very people who could help with the elven part were adversaries, and those who could help with my god magic were gone.

As if he could read my predicament, Cory gave me a weak smile.

"You now have access to the most extensive and powerful collection of magical objects known," he reminded me. Several of the objects were on the table in my living room, including the Mystic Souls spell book. After reviewing the spell book again, I'd realized that some of the spells I couldn't decipher previously were in Elven. There were still spells in languages that I assumed were archaic or from other species of supernaturals we had no idea existed. I could make out most of it, but my Elven was still limited.

"I need a way to put Palladium bracelets on Fabian and Elizabeth." I only had one. Since elves were considered extinct when I happened upon it, I thought it would be a collector's item and nothing I'd ever actually use. For a moment, I had suspected Mephisto was an elf. The irony that it turned out to be me wasn't lost.

"Are we sure it would work on them?" Cory asked, voicing a concern that I had several times. Myths and variances continued to exist in magic. We'd learned that the bracelet restricted elven magic, but without firsthand experience it was sheerly theoretical. If it wasn't true, using the bracelet as a defense could prove to be quite dangerous.

"Elizabeth restricted my magic with a spell," I pointed out. "If she could restrict my magic, I should be able to do the same to her. I just have to figure out the right spell."

Frustrated, I shoved my hand through my hair and blew out a breath. Cory's eyes followed mine to the three plants against the wall that I'd purchased. Same family as the ones Fabian had me use to test if magic on one could affect the others. He was able to perform the task; focusing on tearing the leaves from one plant caused the others to do the same.

"Any luck with that?" he asked, jerking his chin in the direction of the plants.

"I haven't tried," I admitted. My priority was talking to him. Going over everything aloud gave me more resolve and helped me put things in perspective.

He picked up the Mystic Souls book and started to slowly go through the pages with the same voracity he had when Asher got me one of the only two copies that existed. Mephisto had the other.

"I won't try any spells," he promised in response to my look of disapproval. Cory'd inadvertently released a fae with animancer skills who wanted to take over the fae court, causing a situation that could have easily made Cory an enemy of the Seelie fae and the Northwest Pack, because the malevolent fae was using his magic to make the shifters his own personal army.

The last thing I needed was another situation like that.

CHAPTER 3

Cory had fallen asleep, but I stayed up scouring through the Mystic Souls. With everything I'd been through, the elven spells I'd learned, being trapped in the demon realm, and skills I'd learned with Mephisto, I was now seeing the book with keener and more perceptive eyes. The veil of ignorance lifted. It was a double-edged sword; knowing the power and malevolence of the spells made me hesitant to try some of them. Especially the one I'd been reviewing over the past fifteen minutes. It was a good spell, but a dangerous one.

Fingers gliding over the words of the spell, I could feel the diablerie of it. *Venenum*. A paralytic spell where I'd serve as the host and would have to maintain contact with whomever I was subjecting to my magic. Maintaining contact was a feat in itself. I'd hope to accomplish two things: forcing Fabian to undo the *Necro* spell that closed the Veil, and release Nolan. It was an ambitious goal in which Nolan's release was the most likely outcome. That would still give me the advantage. Despite his magical limitations compared to Fabian and Elizabeth, Nolan had extensive knowledge of magic, understood how to read Elven, and because he was half-human, was often underestimated. Even by his sister.

Estimation of one's abilities was always an advantage. I wanted him with me. I wanted his presence, not just his knowledge. Despite our relationship being a labyrinth of complexity, I wanted him to be in my life.

Over-caffeinated and brimming with the need to master the plant spell, it wasn't until after several exhausting failures that I conceded and went to bed. When I awoke, I found Cory sipping on a cup of coffee, in fresh clothes, and a large overnight bag next to the sofa. Him planning to stay with me wasn't unexpected, no matter what I did to squelch the idea. Cory remained convinced that I wouldn't have to go to Fabian, that Fabian would come to me and try to force me into compliance. I disagreed. People who thirst for power tend to believe others feel the same and often base their decisions and actions on that. My alliance would work to Fabian's favor, whether given freely or coerced.

After breakfast, out of my periphery, I could see Cory cross-legged on the floor, a few feet from me, watching as the second snake plant twisted and bent, mimicking what I was doing to the first plant. Sweat glistened on my brow, my hand shook from fatigue, and I could feel the overuse in my jaw from doing this spell over and over. Watching the plant respond to me was a confidence booster. It wasn't the strength of the magic, it was skill. Rage and thirst for revenge still fueled my actions. I wasn't proud of it but reluctantly accepted it, because it wasn't misplaced. I wanted to give the plant spell another try in hope that it could be done with the *Venenum* spell, if I could successfully use it on Elizabeth and Fabian by simply gaining contact with one of them.

The plant hadn't torn, but it had shown the most disturbance of all my attempts. It was just a matter of time. However, I was short on time.

"How is this going to help with reopening the Veil?" Cory asked.

"It won't. This spell gives me more options for dealing with Elizabeth and Fabian. It increases my chances of abducting them and torturing them for answers."

Cory's sneer of disapproval lingered on me before he turned his gaze to his phone and the task of ordering food. I made my way to the kitchen and poured a large glass of water and took a long drink before sitting next to him to wait on the much-needed food delivery.

Turning in my direction, his tone somber, he said, "Seriously, what are your plans?"

"That's one of my plans. Why reinvent the wheel when I can just do what's worked for so many in the past? Never underestimate the value of violence."

His eyes narrowed and his lips pressed into a rigid line.

Crumbling under his judgment, my expression mirrored his. "Of course, I plan to practice diplomacy first." Knowing that the *Venenum* spell worked through my body, I wasn't in a rush for it to be my first option. But it was best to prepare for the worst. Step one: Try to speak with them without the use of diableric magic. Step two: Use it. Step three: Abduct one or both of them. Step four: Do whatever it took to get answers.

"Negotiation will be before or after you try to ram them in the gut with a sword?" Cory asked with a grimace after a careful study of my face as if he could see my plans there. A look of reproach darkened his eyes and condemnation was heavy in his voice. Guilt felt heavy in my chest; he was only aware of my plans to negotiate with Fabian and not the use of the *Venenum* magic from Mystic Souls.

"The karambit will leave a shallower wound. I don't want to kill them." *Yet* was implied. "I just want Nolan, and to strongly urge Fabian into undoing the spell that closed the Veil."

Apparently my attempt to remove the malicious intent from my words was unsuccessful because Cory's grimace deepened. Concern edged into his face. It wasn't the violence or the thirst for revenge that he feared. It was how acting on them would change me. We were aware of how often the goalposts moved in moments like this until the person eventually devolved into the loathsome and morally reprehensible person they wanted to defeat. I didn't want to become my mother, where violence and cruelty were her first and only option. But, feeling cornered and angry, it seemed like the most practical option.

"What spell did he use to close the Veil?"

"A *Necri* spell, but I couldn't hear exactly what he said to invoke the one that closed it. There had to be a trigger spell linked with it. Invoking the *Necri* spell initiated the Veil-closing spell."

Cory grabbed the Mystic Souls book. "If it can be closed, then it can be opened. We just have to find the appropriate spell."

"I'm sure there is one," I said. "I think this might be it." I pointed to a world-reveal spell written in Elven that I'd translated into English. That link to the spell and magic was probably the reason elves could see the Veil. Examining the words again, I questioned the accuracy of my translation. If done poorly, the results could be devastating. Spells from Mystic Souls needed to be accurate. Which contributed to my need to get Nolan released. If that was the only thing I could manage from the encounter, it would still be beneficial.

"You're uncertain about your translations?" Cory asked softly, looking down at my scribblings on the paper.

"I'm about ninety percent certain. I don't want to make things worse," I admitted. "If Nolan was here he could confirm my translations were correct."

It was the need for Nolan's assistance I continued to

think about when I retrieved our food. Cory joined me at the kitchen counter, taking a seat on one of the stools. I handed him his two burrito bowls without the rice, sneering at it and his gleeful look.

"It's a salad with steak," I pointed out after he started to eat. He gave my burrito, nachos, and tacos an equally derisive look.

"Your comment sounds judgy," he said, spearing a chunk of avocado.

"It is." I shoved my nachos in his direction. He declined, putting his bowl down and lifting his shirt to reveal the pronounced delineations in his stomach.

"I'd like you with abs or no abs. You'll always be beautiful to me."

"That's sweet. The sentiment is nice but I'm beautiful to everyone," he boasted. "This"—his hand waved over his body —"just makes people hate and love me. It's my toxic trait."

"Triggering a love/hate response from people is your toxic trait, and not your obnoxious arrogance?" I teased.

"Nah, that just makes me quirky. People find it endearing."

"That's not a quirk," I challenged.

"What are you, the quirk police?" he snapped teasingly, returning to his food and devouring it with the same voracity I did my food. Hungrier than I realized, we ate in silence. Occasionally, when I looked up from my food I found Cory's gaze on me. One of the disadvantages of knowing each other so well was that not many things could be hidden.

Food devoured in a matter of minutes, we returned to our work in the living room, although his intense studying of me hadn't eased.

"Erin, what wild, inadvisable plan do you really have? There's more to your intention than going to the Havenage and using the threat of violence to negotiate Nolan's release."

He sank into the sofa, his hand covering his face. "If negotiations don't work, you plan to break him out of there, don't you?" He frowned.

I nodded.

"Please tell me your plan is more tactical than charging into the Havenage demanding they release him or you're going to kick their asses? You can be quite convincing, even scary, but I don't think that tactic is going to work."

Before I could respond, he shoved a frustrated hand through his hair. "Maybe you should involve the Supernatural Task Force?" he huffed out. "Technically the elves have abducted him, no matter what flowery words they used. It's essentially an abduction. Elves exist and should be bound by our rules and laws of engagement."

"Technically they don't. They're considered extinct. No representation in the Supernatural Task Force or any governing agencies. Their anonymity has protected them in more ways than one."

Revealing the elves would be counterproductive because it would also expose me. I wasn't ready for the repercussions of the world learning of gods and elven magic, which was markedly different and more than currently known. It wouldn't be just other supernaturals I'd have to worry about but humans as well. Increasingly wary and apprehensive about every new discovery of magical beings, fringe groups used the information to advocate for the removal or separation of supernaturals. Between fear, admiration, hate, cautious curiosity, fetishization, and politics, the relationship between humans and supernaturals was a tenuous mess just one incident from chaos and conflict.

If that wasn't enough of a deterrent, making the elves' presence known with the pretense of holding them accountable wouldn't happen overnight. Even in the supernatural world, bureaucracy was slow and inefficient.

"I can get him released," I stated with an assurance that I thought would squelch Cory's doubt. Instead, it whetted it.

He rested one arm over the one crossed over his chest, using his finger to tap his chin at a slow methodic beat. "How? What would you offer? It seems like the only thing he wants is you." Insinuation lingered in his voice. Cory suspected that Fabian wanted more from me than my presence at the Havenage and being a useful ally for the elves. A magic purist like him would never see me as anything more than a tool.

"If not you, what do you plan to barter for them reopening the Veil and Nolan's release?"

"Their lives."

He blinked once.

"It's a one-time offer. I will extend leniency and mercy that they don't deserve. I had no intention of sparing their lives, but if they're open to fair negotiations their lives will be spared. That's all I'm willing to offer."

"You'll spare their lives if they honor your request?" he scoffed, shaking his head. "If nothing else, you have audacity to spare."

"Not just audacity but a plan."

I explained my plan to use the *Venenum* spell on Fabian. Since I wasn't proficient with the plant spell, it would have to be either him or Elizabeth. I liked my chances with Fabian better. He had more influence over the others.

"Nothing about that plan inspires confidence, Erin." Cory rubbed a hand over his hair, disheveling it. His lips pinched so tightly together his dimples peeked out. "The plan now is violent coercion, using very dark magic in which your body will be used as a conduit, and a side of torture?"

"It's extreme—"

"No, it's not just extreme. You sound like your mother," he snapped, icy steel vibrating in his voice. He stood, pacing, fingers scraping through his hair. Cerise tinged his cheekbones and the bridge of his nose. His short huffs of air filled the room.

"You can't become your mother. I'm always going to be there for you, but don't ask me to stand by idly while you become something unrecognizable because of your thirst for revenge. The *Venenum* is a dangerous spell. You're essentially using your body as a vessel for poison and dark magic. None of that concerns you?" he asked, his tone losing its sharp edge and becoming warm and entreating.

It was the beginning of an argument that I didn't have it in me to have. Not with Cory.

"Malific was terrible. I am her daughter, but I have no plan to ever be like her. I want— no, I *need* to channel the qualities that made her a worthy adversary to most. I'm the daughter of an Arch-deity with powerful magic and an elf. I'm going to use that power to my advantage."

"Quarter elf," he corrected.

I came to my feet, meeting his probing eyes. "Quarter is enough and gives me enough magical ability to be feared. There's power in what I am. As you've pointed out several times, Fabian wants me as an ally. To be part of the elves as a power broker. Do you think there isn't a reason for that? You didn't see his face when I nearly breached his protective field. The only thing stopping me from dominating them is limited knowledge of my abilities. Limitations that can and *will* be resolved. I'm resourceful, and it's only a matter of time before I'm proficient at my magic. He'd never come out and say it, but I know I'm a dangerous combination. I left my mother nearly dead in the Blose Chasm. A woman who violently destroyed entire communities. I did that." The confidence imbued in my statement wasn't faux bravado.

Closing the space between us, Cory pulled me into his arms and gave me a big hug. And sighed into my hair. It wasn't just to offer comfort but to help smother the flames of hate that ignited as I spoke. It helped, but he couldn't entirely squelch it. I needed the hate. I'd been underestimated too often, and it would be to Fabian and Elizabeth's detriment. At least they'd come out alive. They might not like the condition in which it was preserved, but they'd have their lives.

"Cory, don't worry."

"You're asking the impossible. I can't ignore you wanting to go up against the people who managed to close the Veil, a man who changed a demon to human and then aged him to death and taught you how to open the Blose Chasm. You're underestimating how dangerous they are."

"Whose blood was used to change that demon? I was the one who won the battle against my mother and left her there. Not one of them had that ability."

"It wasn't just your abilities. She willingly followed you. They wouldn't have had that advantage. It was her trust and power greed that made that so." Cory's pragmatism was something I admired and often valued, but it had warped into unnecessary worry.

"What's going on, Cory?"

"It's just me, you, and Madison against magic that we have very little familiarity with. With magical resources that outmatch ours. I don't think you've fully grasped the seriousness of this. The Huntsmen were an asset you no longer have. Elizabeth—the Woman in Black—is Fabian's ally and is thoroughly pissed off at you. I get you're trying to stay calm when dealing with this avalanche of problems, but I don't want you to underestimate them."

"I'm not oblivious to the seriousness of it. I don't have everything figured out. But I do have Fabian figured out. I have options. It's time for me to go on the offensive. Take charge of this situation. I won't be able to anticipate all his moves, but the *Venenum* spell is an advantage I have over him."

Silence stretched between us, the tension melting into a companionable quiet as I returned my attention to the spell books and magic objects on the table, opting for sitting on the floor rather than on the sofa next to Cory. I was running my finger over the markings on the blade Asher had given me that could be bespelled so that it couldn't be used against me when Cory piped up.

"I want you to start smoking weed again."

"What?" I choked out with a laugh, dropping the blade on the table.

"Take an edible if you want, but you need weed. I need you to have more chill." Although there was some levity in his voice, it didn't hide the strain of his worry.

"I'm tired," I admitted softly. "Choices about my life have been taken from me and the life I had was the result of machinations, lies, and magical interventions. Sometimes..." I wasn't uncomfortable being emotionally vulnerable with Cory, but the admission made it feel real and just added to the bereft feelings. "Sometimes I don't think I'm the authentic Erin. I was shoved into this world with so many lies and omissions. Just when I thought I'd have some semblance of a normal life—or my normal—puff, it's gone. I'm not being careless or deliberately foolish. Perhaps my plans are a combination of desperation and not a lot of fucks to give anymore. Nolan's gone. Despite the snags and complexities in our relationship, it was ours and we were just starting to find what's normal for us. I was starting to carve out a place for him in my life as part of my extended family. Now he's being held 'for his protection.' I don't think for one minute he wants to be there under these new circumstances."

Sucking in a ragged breath, I exhaled slowly, hoping to relieve some of the tightness. "Mephisto's gone. You've seen my past relationships. This one was the first time I felt seen. A person who not only accepted my flaws—" I shook my head. "I don't even know if he saw them as flaws but rather the sum of who I am. He accepted me for me. Call me out on my crap—"

"I was calling you out on your crap long before Mr. God was around," Cory teasingly pouted.

I flashed him a grin. "You are the original." My eyes traced along the markings on the knife to evade Cory's scrutinizing gaze. "I want a chance to explore a relationship with Mephisto. To be with him without all the obstacles in my life. I thought I had that. Had him and the option to be together until we made the decision to end it. That relationship was something else that's been taken from me. A result of more lies and betrayals. Performing the *Venenum* will be dangerous, but it won't be done out of being careless. I want a life. Erin's life."

"I get it." The smile in his voice had me glancing up at him.

"What?"

"You used a lot of words to say you think you're falling in love with M," he quipped, moving from the sofa to sit next to me.

"Maybe *you* need an edible," I grumbled, bumping my shoulder against his.

What I'd admitted to Cory stayed with me. Not just the choices that were taken from me but everything that had been done to everyone that had landed me in this place. My thoughts clung to my first meeting with my mother that culminated in me being bound to her. It was what led to Elizabeth's betrayal that gnawed at me.

"We need to go to Mephisto's home," I blurted, grabbing keys and heading out the door, Cory on my heels in a state of confusion.

In the car, I sped toward Mephisto's estate. "Elizabeth's betrayal," I explained, but that only added to his bewildered expression. "When we first met Malific, she injured Arius, forcing Elizabeth to make a deal with her to cure him. You said Benton had come up with a counterspell but wasn't able to use it. If he did, it's a spell that Elizabeth doesn't know how to respond to or counter. He has notes and books. Hopefully in his office among the things he left."

Cory smiled, noticeably relaxing. It was a safer spell able to be invoked without me having to be close to Fabian or even in contact. I just needed to make contact with Fabian. Malific had achieved it with an arrow; I'd do it with a blade.

Despite Benton leaving things out to be easily found, it still felt like a violation perusing through the wealth of information. I understood the importance of having a druid. He provided specific details to his spells, possible complications, and suggested workarounds. It was the most precise I'd ever seen in magic.

"Druids are another level, aren't they?" Cory commented. Neither of us had ever knowingly encountered one before Benton, so I didn't know if this level of detail was exceptional or typical. Once I'd found the journal with the counterspell, the spell to invoke it seemed to be easily reverse engineered. Although I continued to have a level of discomfort snooping through Benton's things, Cory's curiosity made him abandon all propriety. A quick perusal of the journals and a few spell books different than mine showed some same spells, although there were a few I didn't recognize. Cory had a green leatherbound journal in his hand.

"You're stealing his things?" I asked, shock and disapproval heavy in my voice as I gathered everything preparing to leave. Without Mephisto present, I felt more comfortable performing magic in my home.

"No, you're going to want to read this, *Raven*. It's about you."

Placing my load of books aside, I took the journal and scanned it quickly. It started out with a few musings, a documentation of Mephisto's interest, and speculations. Later, it switched to observational notes and theories of my magical abilities. The information was valuable, but it was difficult not to be unsettled by Benton's interaction with me being reduced to academics. A breakdown of Elizabeth's known abilities, cross-referenced with Nolan's, overlapping those of an Arch-deity. He did the same with my restrictions.

"It's weird that he made you into a clinical study without your knowledge, but we can't deny the usefulness of the information," Cory pointed out in response to every emotion that had undoubtedly displayed on my face.

"Yeah," I mumbled. "I wish he'd shared it with me."

"How do you know he wouldn't have? Everything you're feeling is just speculation. Some of the information had to come from Mephisto and the Huntsmen. They were at the information-gathering stage and probably weren't ready to present their findings."

"It makes me sound like a project."

Gathering the books again, I put the journal on top and returned to the car.

"No," Cory asserted before I could drive away. His finger at my chin guided my eyes to him. "Don't spiral. Nothing about this is typical. It probably feels ick, but this is good information. Neither of us ever thought to do this. Having this much knowledge about elves and gods as Benton has, and the theory references, is to your advantage. See it for that—and that only. Okay?"

"I'm not spiraling," I lied, which he allowed but noted it with a tick of his jaw. "It seems like I should be doing more. I have to do more." Anticipation, fear, and self-doubt whirred in me, but I pushed them aside. The most pressing was hope. Nolan's knowledge would be an adjunct to what Benton's journal had given.

After we'd returned to my apartment, Cory and I delved into mastering Benton's spell that reversed the spell Malific used against Arius. It had restricted Arius's magic, prevented healing, and couldn't be undone by Elizabeth or, more than likely, Fabian, either. I placed the spell on the knife and memorized the invocation for it. The beauty of Cory locating a spell to evoke the protection spell on the blade Asher had gifted me ensured that no matter how things worked out, the spell couldn't be used against me.

It had been a long day and I welcomed Cory's suggestion to delay returning to the Havenage until the next day. Dealing with Fabian and Elizabeth would require me to be at my best. Sleep was needed.

Preparing the sofa for Cory to sleep on reminded me how significantly my life had changed and that my meditation room was no longer a requirement and could now be converted to an office/extra guest room.

My phone on the table rang with Landon's familiar ring. In the past a call from him preceded a very good payday. Now it served as a reminder of the debt I owed him. He wanted me to help create a vampire family. I had no plans to help him produce the type of monstrous vampires my blood would create.

"Answer that," Cory urged. I had been ignoring Landon's calls for the past hour. By the time I reached the phone, the ringing stopped. As with the other calls, he hadn't left a message or sent a hostile text demanding a response. So I assumed they were just reminders of my obligation or an attempt to schedule more meetings of potentials.

I showered and was ready for bed when three consecutive calls from Landon gave me a moment of pause. After the notification of an incoming video call, I answered with a gritted smile.

"Come get your human," he demanded into the camera. Without waiting for a response, he ended the call.

CHAPTER 4

My human. After I quickly dressed, I headed out the door, giving Cory a rushed explanation as he trailed behind me wearing the sweatpants and loose t-shirt he slept in.

"Stay. I'll be fine. Your presence will only be an agitation. Keep your phone on. I'll text you if things change."

Reluctantly, he stayed back. Cory's relationship with Alex complicated things more than I would ever let him know. Cory wasn't just my friend and a powerful witch, he was also linked to the Pack's fourth. Indirectly, that came with the complicated power dynamics afforded to a ranking member of the pack. Cory coming with me would have added an unnecessary layer of dominance and testosterone flexing that I didn't have the patience to deal with.

At Landon's home a crowd of cars extended past the expansive driveway to the street. Great, a party. Vampires always had people willing to attend their indulgent parties even when they occurred during an off day of the week, like a Tuesday.

A statuesque woman answered the door. She had a martini glass in her hand, a silk shirt unbuttoned to just above her stomach, and no hint of anything covering her lady pillows. One quick move and I was going to get an up close and personal view of the girls.

This better not be a ploy for me to meet more potentials. She was regal in appearance but wouldn't be considered classically beautiful. Square jawline, aquiline nose, supple lips that made me wonder if they were the result of genetics or a talented doctor. Her jeans molded to her curves. Definitely human. A high-maintenance one and exactly what Landon would look for in one of his sired.

"Yes?" She gave me a judging toe-to-head look at my fitted yellow hoodie, which provided the pockets I needed, the white shirt that peeked from underneath, and leggings. With the impromptu visit, I hadn't had time to put any thought into an intimidating and protective outfit. Her eyes lingered at my lips, pricking an urge in me to tell her, like I had so many others, it was genetics. Most people didn't believe me.

"I need to see Landon," I told her. She waved me forward and I followed her until Elon stepped from a room to my right and blocked my path, skewering me with a look as he took in the pins in my hair and my ring. My other hand I had in my pocket, allowing easy access to the claw, courtesy of the stash of weapons I kept in my car.

"Erin," he purred. "Do I need to search you? You will behave, won't you?"

"Always do," I piped out, increasing my speed before he could rethink the decision. Guess there wasn't a need since he'd taken up the rear as I followed the woman.

"Your Erin is here," she announced to Landon who stood a few feet away in the dim, moody room that with a small casting of light from the sconces allowed safe navigation for humans. A woman's sultry croon played from the speakers, adding to the dark, seductive atmosphere. This was the vampire indulgence that scandalized humans. A den of sin. Various hues of gray made up the monochromatic room.

Thick charcoal curtains drawn closed looked heavy enough to prevent any hints of seeing the sunrise or any indication of the time of day.

Some vampires had coupled with a human to feed from. I rolled my eyes at the spectacle. They needed the human to satisfy a nutritional need that could easily be performed clinically and chastely. It was never that way with vampires. Meeting a vampire's feeding needs appeared to be alluring to humans. Vampires spurred it by making it an enthralling and enticing experience.

The vampires' hands moving slowly and seductively over the donor's body and the languid movement of their tongues over the bite site was nothing but obvious seduction of anyone watching. One person in the room I recognized as one of the potentials I'd warned Landon off because he'd definitely be vying for Landon's position as soon as he was mature enough. And I found his strong resemblance to Dallas icky as hell. The actual Dallas was nestled into a corner, intently watching the people in the room. As his eyes went to the potential, he didn't seem as put off by the resemblance as I was. I noticed his eyes tracking over the man several times.

Landon stopped his approach to pull a woman to him. A few whispers and she was baring her neck to him. His dark eyes fixed on me as he drew from his source and then continued his advance, relaxed, wiping away rivulets of blood with his finger, a smirk on his face.

"Erin." His voice was a satiny purr.

"Turn it off," I demanded.

Flashing me a miscreant grin, his tongue moved over his lips. "I'm so glad you came."

"I'm not here for your *party*, Caligula," I asserted, casting a glance at the spectacle that wasn't far from delving into hedonism. His smile widened as if to remind me that I was often a participant.

"Of course. Not today."

"Where's Sumner?"

"Ah, the human." He moved past me, reaching his hand back for me to take.

"I can follow without a hand-held guide."

He was inches from me in a heartbeat, his eyes tracing over the features of my face with a darkly cruel, amused expression.

"Follow me." He led me past several doors into a sitting room lit only by a candle and moonlight ebbing in from the glass sliding door that led out into the expansive backyard. Dr. Sumner's eyes were closed and he lay on a modern-looking boucle chaise. Rushing toward him, I looked for signs of breathing.

I got to him, to check. Landon was next to me, watching me as I examined every visible inch of him for signs of feeding, relaxing back on my heels when there weren't any.

"He's asleep," Landon informed me.

I whipped around to face him. "You drugged him and left him in an unattended room during tribute to Caligula?"

"I don't have to drug him, just compel him to sleep, which I did."

Didn't like the idea that he'd compelled him, but at least he wasn't drugged. Trying to ignore how close Landon had positioned himself to me, I attempted to shake Sumner awake. Landon grabbed my hand, tugged me to stand, and then linked our fingers in a manner that was too friendly and intimate for my liking.

"He should awake in an hour. Some potentials are here. Why don't you mingle a little and get to know them? Perhaps someone will pique your interest and be more to your liking."

"I don't have time to mingle," I told him, pulling my hand from his and returning to my position to stir Dr. Sumner awake and help him off the chaise.

"Erin, just an hour of your time. That isn't too much to ask?" The barbed coolness of his tone left no room for declining.

"Right now, it is. It's late and I just want to get my—" I stopped midsentence, refusing to adopt such a dehumanizing term for Dr. Sumner. "My friend home."

"He won't awake until the time I commanded has ended. The introductions could take up some of the time."

"Why is he here?"

"The better question is why is your friend so intrigued by me? Have you not warned him about the cost of curiosity?"

"What was he curious about?"

"He seems to be under the impression that he can help me navigate the difficulties and challenges of my new role and that I pay him with vampire blood."

Landon smiled at the hiss of breath I inhaled.

Dr. Sumner had made a name for himself after treating a few misbehaving shifters and vampires, although the correlation between their recovery coincided with the intervention of the Alpha of the wolf pack and the ruling vampire. He accepted the accolades, which led to him treating many of the supernaturals who were sent to Stygian rather than to our prison. Shifters tended to keep a tighter rein on their pack; vampires didn't. But if a vampire became a big enough problem the punishment was severe. Examples were often made of the offending vampire. It wasn't Dr. Sumner's intervention; it was the threat of reprisals that led to any improvement.

He'd only had surface-level access to our world. It was me being in his life that had submerged him deep enough to the point of drowning. He was afraid of it and its occupants although he wouldn't admit it. Him wanting vampire blood and the benefits afforded by it confirmed what I long suspected.

"People believe us to be selfish because of the caution we

take with doing such things." Landon turned to me. "Do you believe it selfish or protective of the humans?"

"If you're offering benefits then I don't think you are as cautious. It gives you a currency you enjoy exploiting. I'm not obliged to believe it's to protect humans from their addiction to it. You just don't find what they offer worth it."

A slow curl in his lips was a playful indication that I was right. I ignored his extended hand. "Please," he said. "Let's enjoy the party until he awakes. Let's go find our family."

I hated every word of that statement, including the spark of joy in his eyes as if he believed we were going to be some weird happy family. I followed him as he headed out the room because it wasn't wise to take Dr. Sumner away from the person who'd compelled him, in case there were problems. I hesitated. At my hesitation Landon pulled out a key and locked the door.

Returning to the gathering, I accepted a flute of champagne from one of the servers and took a small sip, staying at Landon's side as he surveyed the room with satisfaction.

"What is your fascination with those two?" I asked as Landon's eyes followed mine to the Dallas-copy and another potential he'd introduced who wore his unearned confidence like a fragrance. We caught each other's gaze and a spark of recognition flitted across his pale eyes. The woman he was chatting with was unceremoniously ignored as he made his way toward me. The last time we'd met, I'd told him that if he displeased Landon or caused any problems for the vampire family he'd be punished and could end up in the dungeon. The threat would have had me running from Landon like he was wielding an axe with the intention of using it against me. This man seemed unbothered. The Dallas-copy had taken control of the situation, where a vampire was attempting to seduce him into being his meal. The vampire was hanging on to his every word, her eyes fixed on his lips. A coy smile curled his lips as if he was unaware of the effect he had on her.

Mr. Confidence stood in front of me, flashing a wayward smile that I was sure worked to disarm people. Very often.

"Erin, so nice to see you again," he said, extending his hand to shake mine. I attempted to make it a quick shake, but his hand covered mine in an effort to seem warm and inviting instead of calculating and arrogant.

"I don't believe we had a full introduction before. I'm Tegan." The partial introduction was because he hadn't deemed me important until he discovered I was his pathway to vampirism. He continued to study me with stark interest, unable to hide his curiosity regarding my importance to Landon.

"I'm delighted my warning about the dungeon didn't scare you away." My reminder of the vampire's chamber garnered me a slitted look of anger from Landon.

"I appreciate it." Tegan jerked his attention from me to put it on Landon. "The cruelest of punishments would be readily accepted if I ever did anything to displease Landon or embarrass the family in any manner deserving of such behavior modifications."

He was good. Landon devoured the sycophancy like the most decadent of desserts. Tegan was the walking embodiment of the arrogance and indulgence of vampires. His striking features would bode well for Landon as an acquisition, as if his parents' genes were irrelevant. He'd abuse his affluent position as Landon's sired.

Feeling Landon's weighted gaze on me, I allowed my eyes to meet his. A small smile had settled on his lips. I followed his lead as he excused himself and moved to the opposite side of the room. Settling into the darkest part, he looked over the attendees. I suspected he was still assessing them as potentials.

"What's his name?" I asked, referring to the imitation

Dallas. The original Dallas stood on the other side of the room, putting very little effort into obtaining his meal for the day. His deceptive and effortless charm had the tall curvy woman inching closer to him, preparing to be his food source or more for the night.

"Peyton," Landon provided.

"Despite my warning, you're still interested?"

"It is because of your warning that my interest remains piqued. You underestimate me. You do not believe I'm capable of positioning myself in a manner such that he would never consider deposing me. All the things you said I should be mindful of, I knew all along. You must admit he is quite beautiful."

"And he's quite aware of it," I pointed out. Tegan's interest in the vampire who was trying to lure him into a blood donation earlier lost, he moved throughout the room, enjoying the attention lavished on him by the various vampires who wanted him for a meal or perhaps more. He kept them at arm's length. It didn't take an expert in body language to see his manipulations.

"So, you're looking for a dysfunctional family. Got it."

With a dark chuckle, Landon took a drink from the glass of wine that I missed him getting. It bothered me how quick and inconspicuous vampires could be. I looked at the time on my phone; only twenty minutes had passed. It seemed like longer.

"You are welcome to stay after your *friend* awakes. I will have someone take him home."

Of course Dr. Sumner hadn't driven.

"I can't. I'd like to see him home." Turning to look at Landon, I said, "Please don't take any more meetings with him."

Landon's lip quirked. "Are you asking me to be inhospitable?"

"You don't seem to have a problem when it suits you."

"Are you in a position to continue requesting favors?" The galvanized edge to his question implied that I wasn't.

"It's not a request for a favor. I'm asking you not to taunt him. You have no intention of giving him what he wants."

Landon grunted a sound, then took a long draw from his glass before returning his attention to the crowd. "Why won't you stay longer? I'd really like you to get to know some of the people here. Mingle. After all—"

"I can't. I have pressing business I need to deal with," I inserted, not giving him time to mention that they could be my family. He had an image and expectation that I felt was cruel to continue to let him have.

"Business like what, Erin?" He leaned down until his face was just inches from mine. His eyes grew darker as they studied me.

"Just business."

"Business. Would it involve your magic? When will you go into further detail about that? I'm intrigued by it." If he didn't back up he was going to feel it. In the past I had managed to keep from displaying my magic with him. "Everyone's so secretive about it. Even your human struggled to keep the information to himself, even under compulsion. I thought he was going to crack his jaw he clenched it so tight to keep all he knows about you to himself."

Dr. Sumner kept my information to himself under compulsion? Impressive. Our complicated and inappropriate relationship had its benefits.

Landon appeared to share my admiration. "He's a strong human and protects those he cares for," he said quietly. I didn't like the sound of longing in his voice.

"He's not up for consideration," I said firmly.

"Well, that's not up to you. To be honest, it's not up to him. He could be persuaded."

"Not an option," I ground out.

He made another sound, but I couldn't determine if it was

reluctant agreement or dissention. "Walk with me. I'd like to introduce you to your potential daughters." Everything about this process was disconcerting, but I had time to waste until Sumner awoke.

Landon made the introductions, but this time I kept my assessments to myself. Initial impressions mirrored those of the others I'd met, but one thing they all shared: dark cynicism and hints of hegemony, and that would be a problem. It didn't concern Landon because those were qualities he sought, and I'd be responsible for making vampires who could enforce those beliefs.

That consumed my thoughts as he guided me outside to his exquisite backyard. There was a beautiful flourish of trees and a garden of exotic and common flowers lining the house. No one was taking advantage of the manicured lawn and comfortable seating area to take in the cool night air and the coziness from the illumination of lights in the trees.

Our departure prompted the opening of the drapes. Elon looked in our direction but immediately moved away at a dismissive flick of Landon's hand. But the drapes remained open. As we watched the gatherers, they didn't seem to have noticed Landon's departure. Elon was no longer at the sliding door but kept a watchful eye on us from across the large room. It didn't escape me that Dallas had eased his way closer.

"What did you think of the potentials?"

Taking another small sip from my glass, I sighed. Adding a disgruntled Landon to my long list of problems wasn't something I wanted to do, but drawing this out was going to create more issues. Hope and impatience pulsed off him, and either Tegan or Peyton was going to be his sired son. One of the potential daughters had made an impression on him. He made an attempt at hiding his favorites.

I was silent too long for Landon. "Your agreement with my choices is just a courtesy, not a requirement." His harsh directive prompted me to handle this sooner than later. This was going to advance, so I needed to handle my refusal as diplomatically as possible.

"They all have the qualities you are looking for. But I can't be the one to help your family," I asserted in a low neutral voice, not wanting him to take it as a sign of defiance but one of practicality. "You are in a new position of power and you're being watched by all sects. The last thing you would want to heighten their concern or put the other vampires at risk is to create vampires with a death mage." He knew I wasn't one, but it got the point across. "I'll help negotiate the use of a human or witch to help with siring your family. That wouldn't be atypical and would go under the radar and wouldn't create reason for concern."

"That wasn't the agreement. You are breaking our agreement?" he asked, a sharp edge to his voice as he used his thumb to wipe away the sanguine liquid that had spilled from the glass in response to my statement.

"No. I'm making modifications."

"Yes, and it seems those modifications are not in line with our initial agreement," he pushed out through clenched teeth.

This situation had the potential to be explosive and I needed to deescalate fast. I drew in a fortifying breath.

Landon flung his glass against the far side of the house. Shards of glass spread and the sanguine fluid darkened the stone on the house. The smell of blood and wine wafted between us. "What was the agreement, Erin?" he demanded angrily.

"Landon—"

"No, what was the agreement, Erin?"

I repeated it verbatim. Shame made the words sticky in my throat.

"Prior to helping you, I confirmed the conditions of my help and you agreed," he reminded me. As if I needed it.

"My friend was dying. You were the most reliable

chance he had for survival." There was a quiet plea in my tone in hopes of appealing to a humanity that he'd long discarded. I attempted to remind him of the desperate place I was in. One that brought on tears. Tears that he'd wiped away.

"Then it is settled. You must abide by your agreement," he snapped.

"Landon, I feel inclined to prevent the world being made worse by my existence," I said, making another appeal to whatever smidgen of humanity he'd retained. An urging to see it from an ethical point of view. Based on his sneer, I was being too optimistic and naïve. "I won't carry the burden of creating vampires more dangerous than those that already exist."

"It won't be yours to carry."

"Yes, it will. Any acts of malice, any problems they cause would be a result of me assisting in creating vampires who may not be able to be subdued."

His brow rose with interest. "You're not a fucking mage. What the hell are you, Erin?" He devoured the minute space that I'd managed to put between us.

"I could be your ally or your worst nightmare," I offered, a little too snidely for the situation I was in, but Landon, being the peculiar enigma he was, found amusement in the comment. A small smile lifted his lips and unbridled interest overtook his expression.

"So many secrets. There shouldn't be any between friends." A cloying satin tone replaced the anger.

Desperation made everything so tenuous, and dealing with a mercurial vampire like Landon added to the challenge. I took another breath, holding it for a few beats before I softly breathed out, "An elf-god hybrid."

Landon's mouth parted. He looked wistful. There wasn't any humanity, just greed and a desire. "They aren't extinct," he whispered. "You are quite the delightful find." After several moments, his lips pulled back, revealing his fangs. "I can't release you from your—"

I slammed magic into his chest, sending him back several feet. He quickly recovered only to find me gone. Slowly turning, he lifted his nose to the air and inhaled. He'd located me but before he could react, the pins from my hair pressed into his chest. Hard enough to feel and know I wasn't to be messed with.

"I guarantee, this will be in your heart before they can get to me," I whispered. "Dallas and Elon think I'm gone." I didn't risk a look but made an educated assumption. "This is just a mere taste of my abilities. You don't want to be on the other side of my anger."

"You don't want to be on mine."

"Are you sure about that?" I pushed a little harder. "What do you know of gods and elves?" Despite his many years of living—or rather vampire living—his knowledge would be surface level. Being a hybrid would only ensure he'd never know my capabilities. "I can assure you, everything you think you know is wrong. Do you understand how little effort it would take for me to end the existence of vampires?" The bluster was strong, but necessary.

Needing him to see my face, I dropped the cloak and revealed myself to him.

"I appreciate you saving Dr. Sumner. I will be forever grateful, but I won't help you make more vampires. Find another way for me to repay you."

Turning my back on a vampire was a risk. Turning my back on Landon was asking for trouble. But it served its purpose in making him question how powerful I must be that I'd done just that. Walking through the door, I could feel Landon's presence and was aware of Elon eating up the distance between us in a blink. I kept my expression neutral, proud of the level of bravado I displayed and how convincing it was. I was the scary anomaly; Landon didn't need to know that my human side diluted some of my magic. Or me wiping vampires off the earth was probably impossible. Vampires didn't have magic other than their immortality and ability to Wynd, limiting their knowledge of magic. They relied on witches and mages for that. I suspected he'd be visiting one for more information.

Elon's eyes were daggers as they looked at me. The crowd continued to mingle, oblivious to the growing tension, and I steadied myself for having to handle them. The pin from my hair still in my hand, I returned it and settled for the claw in my pocket. I split my attention between Dallas and Elon.

In a cautious glance over my shoulder at Landon, I found his brows drawn together in careful thought. He held my gaze, his lips pursed. Speculation lingered in his eyes. Could I actually end the vampires?

I eased toward him. "I promise you I will satisfy my debt to you. It will not be with a family, but it will be to your satisfaction."

Without a word he headed out the room. "Help her with her human," he instructed Elon. By the time we got to the room, Dr. Sumner was starting to stir. Elon held his face in place, examining his eyes and his response to commands, then he escorted us out of the house, although it felt more like we were being tossed out.

After Dr. Sumner was in the car, I remained standing until I caught Landon's eyes as he leaned against the door frame. I mouthed a thank-you to him but couldn't get a true read from the smirk on his face. Had he allowed me to renegotiate the terms, admittedly brutally, or was he just allowing me to believe I had? I knew for certain that I did have days of reprieve while he researched everything he could find about elves and gods.

But for now, he remained the least of my worries.

CHAPTER 5

The silence between us was tension filled. Dr. Sumner looked out the car window, his fingers lightly drumming on his thigh. As the minutes ticked by, my mind flooded with all the ways the situation could have escalated.

"What were you thinking?" I asked through clenched teeth. His embarrassment put a bright rose color along his cheeks.

"I wasn't," he admitted, running a hand over the short hairs of his beard.

Quiet settled between us as I figured out how to broach the situation. "I get it," I said softly once we were close to his home. "I wish I hadn't gotten you injured. You were so close to death, and you don't want to experience that desperate vulnerability again. But taking vampire blood won't make you invincible or change the fact that you're human. Making deals with Landon or anyone else isn't wise."

When I pulled into the driveway, I turned to face him, waiting for a response that he'd avoided the entire drive to his home.

"It may not be wise, but it's a good trade to feel less vulnerable and weak." He rubbed his hands over his face with a sigh. "It's embarrassing to admit, but that day, I felt like I could comfortably and safely exist in both worlds."

"It's just an illusion. You'd still be vulnerable in my world. We live together and have to interact, but you'd never been truly exposed to the supernatural world. You were treated to parts of it. I bear the burden for that exposure."

"It's not yours to bear. You did nothing wrong."

"I know. It was circumstances. But it was a result of the circumstances of me being in your life. I think it's time for you to step away. You're a great therapist and your skills will better serve those you have more in common with."

Pursing his lips, he made a face, opened the car door, and got out. "Come in, let's have a cup of tea."

I considered declining but needed to make sure we were in agreement and that he'd stay away from Landon. No, not just Landon but all vampires. In his house, I followed his example and left my shoes under the bench near the door. I eyed the small table where he had two pairs of his prescription-less glasses. He gave me a sheepish grin before heading to the living room. I wasn't surprised by his minimalist style. I'd expected his home to have an industrial or austere modern appearance that made me self-conscious as to where to sit, so I was surprised by the plush dusk-gray cloud sofa placed opposite the fireplace and the framed television. Soft-looking blankets lay on the side chairs that looked just as comfortable. His home was warm and welcoming.

"Where's the guitar?" I inquired with a smirk, stroking the blanket that felt as soft as it looked.

His brow rose as he returned the look. "That's presumptuous, Erin."

"It is. Where is it?"

"I don't have one. But I do have a room full of vinyls and a turntable, want to see?" Something about the enthusiastic glint that moved over his eyes reminded me of Cory when he discussed classic movies and made it abundantly clear that a visit to the room would devolve into him going into depth about music and the acquisition of the vinyl.

"Another time," I suggested.

At his polite knowing smile, I figured I hadn't hidden my lack of interest as well as I'd thought.

"Make yourself comfortable," he said, heading toward the kitchen and a cabinet where he took out a canister of tea. After sinking into the sofa, I was grateful for his reappearance with the cup of tea. With the onslaught of the day finally wearing on me, I was moments from falling asleep.

He sat next to me. I warmed my hands around the cup.

"I don't agree with your suggestion of only treating humans. Perhaps a break from dealing with the magically inclined is needed. I'm willing to do that," he acknowledged. His intense gaze bored into the side of my face as I kept mine ahead, fixed on the art on the TV.

"Erin," he urged. "Talk."

I shook my head.

"I'll step away from the others. Not from you." He added in a low whisper, "I'm not sure I can."

When I turned, crossing my leg under me, he did the same. Face to face, he waited patiently for me to speak.

"My mother is dead and I'm the reason why."

"Malific?" It was probably disconcerting for him to view her as my mother when I spent so much time distancing myself from her having that role. She contributed half my DNA and magic. That was it. Or rather, that was all I wanted it to be.

I nodded.

"Okay," he breathed out. "Go on."

Dr. Sumner's face remained impassive as I delivered the waterfall of information, only stopping to answer his requests for clarification.

"They would have killed the fae to rid the world of gods," he said in a low whisper. I could hear the thread of grim revulsion in his words. I'd exposed him to another nefarious layer of the supernatural world.

He urged me to continue, and despite how he felt about Fabian and Elizabeth's action, no approbation was directed at me. There was never judgment in his tone as he continued to question me. Even my intentions about Fabian and Elizabeth were met without critique. Once I finished, I turned away from him and slumped into the sofa, placing the nearly untouched cool tea on the side table before directing my eyes to the ceiling. "That's everything."

"You were dealing with this and never called me?"

"You're not my therapist."

"If I were *just* your therapist, Landon wouldn't have called you about me."

"If you were just my therapist, I never would have found myself indebted to him. Our chaotic hot mess of a friendship has made things complicated," I huffed, accepting another complex situation that I'd have to learn to manage.

He grunted something and relaxed back on the sofa, too, his arm draping over his face. "How does this make you feel?" he asked.

"Me on a sofa, speaking to my former therapist? Like I'm stuck in a cliché movie," I shot back.

He chuckled. "Yeah." His head lolled to the side to look at me. "The setup is quite the cliché. But it doesn't make the question any less valid."

"I wish I could just stop it all. Pluck the nefarious and complicated magic from this world and make things simple. I've never had simple and I yearn for it."

He exhaled a shaky breath and offered me a sympathetic smile.

"I hate that most of the magic and ruthlessness seems to only be directed toward me," I went on. "I understand Elizabeth's, albeit hypocritical, view of me. My magic is complex and possibly problematic. God magic is fear worthy. The Veil should be closed. But the elves' cruelty, magic, and abuse of power mirrors my mother. How can I accept their existence in this world and not gods?"

"And you believe this behavior isn't seen in the human world?"

"It is." But when magic was involved, it made things more dangerous.

"My home was burglarized last year. I've cared for a person after they were shot. Talked down a suicide attempt, counseled people whose sole purpose in life is to destroy someone who they feel has wronged them. I don't think the cruelty, politics, thirst for power, and odd determination to maintain the purity of one's lineage is confined to the magical world. It's just enacted and enforced differently. Although I'll never invalidate your concern for me in the magic world, I'm no less in danger with them than I am with humans."

Dr. Sumner's sabbatical from the magical world would be short lived. He seemed unreasonably drawn to it.

"Do you want to be a vampire?" I asked. The question was met with a long moment of silence. Too long. His introspection became worrying when seconds became minutes.

"No," he finally said. "I don't want to be a vampire. Their immortality doesn't appeal to me, nor does the absence of their humanity. I've dealt with mages, witches, shifters, and fae but no one seems to be missing their…" He struggled with the right word. "Humanness. It allows you to function in both worlds almost seamlessly. Landon doesn't seem like a terrible being, but even when he makes an attempt to seem human, it seems off. Mechanical. Rehearsed as though he's mimicking it rather than actually feeling it. I don't know if that tradeoff is worth it."

His response lifted a weight that I wasn't aware I was carrying.

"Then you have to stay away from him. All vampires.

Please." Standing up and heading for the door I left no room for further debate.

He gave a slight head nod into the agreement. "And I'll see you next Tuesday at three?" he provided before I could exit. His defiant smirk was shored up for a challenge if I declined.

"Next Tuesday at three," I repeated.

"Erin," he said before I closed the door, "the magic you inherited from Malific is stronger than any other magic, correct?"

I nodded.

"And the magic from your father can't be undone by anyone but elves, correct?"

I confirmed it again with a nod.

He considered the information. "I'd leave the plant spell alone. I don't think it will ever serve you. *But,* I'd investigate further why Elizabeth sees your existence as such a problem. I think you are the solution to an issue they don't want fixed."

The entire drive consisted of me mulling over Dr. Sumner's parting words and Benton's dossier on me.

I couldn't agree more. I was the solution, but to which one of the innumerable problems that now existed?

CHAPTER 6

Arms crossed over his chest, Cory's breathing was sharp and measured as we drove to the Havenage. After returning home, I'd quietly slipped into my apartment without waking him, thereby avoiding the discussion about what had transpired between me and Landon. I didn't have that advantage in the morning. During our preparation to visit the Havenage, I was able to ward off the questioning. In the car, I had no other choice but to discuss it with him.

"Now you have to worry about Landon?"

"I don't think so. He's upset but he'll get over it."

"That's exactly his personality. He's definitely one to get over an attempted assault. I'm sure he's pondering what type of gift basket to send to thank you for putting his life in peril. Maybe you'll get jewelry," he spouted back.

Despite the potential for the situation to escalate, I didn't think Landon would do anything soon. His curiosity about me and desire to change my mind would hold his interest long enough for it to be a problem I could deal with later. Or at least I hoped it would be.

Cory dropped further discussion so I could pay closer

attention to the roads and navigate back to the Havenage from memory of the directions Nolan had given me.

The surroundings were familiar and kindled the feeling of hopeless desperation I'd felt after learning that other elves existed and the anticipation of meeting more. Parked a few feet from an enclave, we got out of the car. Cory's face strained from the repulsion spell; it appeared stronger than I remembered. Instead of the violent illness I'd felt on my first visit, this time it was a feeling of shocking fear. Magic twined around me, dark and chaotic images flooded my mind, and my body burned. Sweltering heat created droplets of sweat at my brow.

This was the cruelest repulsion spell I'd ever experienced. Cory remained at my side. The nullifying spell I performed to counter the intensity of the spell required a great deal of energy, but quickly the images receded, the nauseous feeling stopped, and the dank smell in the air was replaced with the hints of evergreen that denoted elven magic.

"Your magic is stronger than before," Cory pointed out. It was stronger but it also had changed since my mother's death. I couldn't quite put my finger on the difference. Fabian had taught me to separate my warring magics, but now they seemed to complement each other. They had melded together to form something entirely different than elf magic and god magic. It brought Dr. Sumner's comment to the forefront of my thoughts.

"Fabian, we need to talk," I said into the ether in the same manner Nolan had notified him of our presence during the first visit. Nothing. Moving closer to the magical barrier, reaching out, I felt for the familiar magic to indicate where the ward began. I whispered a spell to break it. The borders of it pulsed with violent undulations in its effort to hold its position. Repeating the spell again, my magic pushed harder, battering against the ward as it delivered equal resistance to uphold itself. Steadying myself against the new feeling and the onslaught of stronger magic, out of my periphery I viewed Cory's mouth open in surprise. My magic was rampaging through me. I was about to rip away the wards and leave the elves exposed, with no place to hide.

"Erin, don't destroy the place," Cory urged. I couldn't read any more than the look of caution on his face.

"How may I be of service to you, Erin?" Fabian's soothing tone filled the area as he emerged a few feet from me. Whipping around to face him, I dropped my assault on the barrier, leaving it intact and the occupants of the Havenage hidden. I refused to keep my back to him. He was still stronger and more skilled with elven magic. Magic and spell casting were like a muscle; the more a person practiced the less energy they expended.

Fabian's gaze dragged over Cory with derision before returning to me. As he took slow measured steps, his pinched moue relaxed. His brow rose, urging me to answer.

"I'm here for Nolan," I told him when he was just inches from me. The cold amusement that skimmed over his deceptively gentle features heightened my irritation with him.

"He's under our protection. Do you not want that for your father?"

"Nolan doesn't require protection. Let's call it for what it is; an abduction."

A vulpine-like mask wisped over his features, revealing the dark intent he'd previously concealed. "You're a unique half-caste that he is responsible for creating. Although I see the value in your existence, not everyone will. Including your involvement with the Huntsmen and being responsible for the shifters' magical immunity on this side of the Veil. As does his daughter, Nolan has his share of enemies. His human bloodline isn't giving him the advantage that his sister has. She's elf and fae." It was a caustic reminder of her using her familial link to the fae to threaten Madison's life. "His protection is necessary. Will you take that from him?"

"You're right, I have my share of enemies, but you do, too." I devoured the distance between us. "I'm at the top of that list. The very reasons people may hate me are reasons they shouldn't want me as an enemy."

His lips twitched trying to suppress a smile. His amusement would be short lived.

"You claim to see value in me and would like an alliance. Consider my request an act of good faith. I trust Nolan. He's been a good counsel for me and can see the good in the elves and the Havenage, whereas I see no value in either," I said.

Fabian dragged his attention from me and glared at Cory who had wandered closer.

"That's close enough, witch," he snapped. The sharp glares they exchanged would have ended both of their lives if looks could kill. Ignoring Fabian's command, Cory continued his advance. It wasn't until I gave him a reassuring look that he stopped.

Fabian grumbled his dissatisfaction before returning his attention to me.

"I want my father with me, and for the safety of the elves and the anonymity of the Havenage you should want that as well."

"If he is returned to you, what will we gain?"

I could see Cory's distress. He still wasn't on board with the chosen barter or the use of the spell. I'd admit, the barter was a ballsy move, but a necessary one. "Your life. As things stand, when the issues between us are settled and over, I have no intention that you or Elizabeth remain alive. I'm extending a one-time courtesy. Reopen the Veil and return Nolan to me."

"I'd easily trade my life to keep the Veil closed, but I don't fear that is something I must worry about. Regarding Nolan..." His eyes trailed over me and to the ward that I'd nearly destroyed before returning to me. "I concede that him with us is to our advantage. As I said before, I protect mine at all costs and by any means. Even in opposition of Malific's daughter. He stays with us until you start to understand where your loyalty must lie." He inched closer, his head canted slightly, smugness wafting off him like scent. "You are part of the collective and should feel duty-bound to protect our kind," he whispered, paraphrasing what he'd asked me to agree to. I didn't like the cult-like language then and still didn't now. He was demanding blind loyalty.

"I asked that of you before. Do not make me force—"

He choked on his haughty demand when I engaged the miniature blade from my ring, poked my free hand with it, and then stabbed it into his arm, spilling his blood. Taking hold of him, I recited the *Venenum* spell, causing him to convulse and seize in pain. I expected the spell to feel dank and toxic like demon magic, but it was worse than I imagined. My heart raced, my body warming to inferno levels. And if death had a taste, I'd devoured a large serving of it.

Fabian's legs were the first to go. He crashed to the ground. To maintain contact with him, I followed. He whispered spells in rapid succession but they failed as soon as recited, the air swallowing his words and its power. He gasped out ragged breaths, desperation a landscape on his face. If he felt like he was dying, I was knocking at death's door waiting for an invitation. The spell did its job, but it cost me a great deal.

As his magic continued to fail, he resorted to physical violence. pounding and clawing at my arm in an attempt to break the contact. With my waning energy, it was only a matter of time before he'd succeed. Through blurred vision, I got glimpses of Cory approaching. I concentrated on maintaining contact with Fabian, waiting for Cory to get close enough to collect Fabian and usher him to the car. Cory was just inches from me when there was a blast of blinding bright light and Arius appeared, Elizabeth's condescending red-skinned imp companion in his natural form. His dainty horns now extended and curved to resemble a ram's. His leathery skin stretched over a massive body that made injuring him difficult. His razor-sharp claws quickly put you on defense to prevent them making contact. That's what Cory was doing, dodging the imp's blows that came at him too quickly for him to break concentration to perform magic. I divided my attention between him and Elizabeth, who'd appeared at Arius's side. I suspected they had a magical link that allowed him to use her magic to transform. I assumed it would limit her magic, although the pelts of magic she thrashed into me felt like they were at full force.

Between her attack and Fabian's efforts to break my hold, my grasp on him started to slip. I snatched the blade from my ankle sheath, stabbed it into his left hamstring where he'd feel it the most, and said the invocation. He shrieked and glared at me as a slit in the barrier opened and two elves came out, yanking him from me and pulling him into the Havenage. I whipped around to Elizabeth who had jerked her attention to Fabian. At a shake of his head, she and her shifted imp retreated, disappearing into another opening into the Havenage.

Aware that they were in the Havenage, removing the knife and failing to heal Fabian, I gave in to optimism and waited. How many unsuccessful spells would it take before they gave up and sought my help? Twenty minutes passed before I accepted that I wouldn't see Nolan accompanied by an elf and for negotiations to start. Instead, they responded with resurrecting repulsion spells.

"That didn't go as expected. What's the next plan?" Cory said, sliding into the driver's side and adjusting the seat. I needed rest. Sinking into the seat of the car I was still driving on loan from Mephisto, it forced my thoughts to him.

"Not as expected but I'm confident it worked. I invoked a spell he couldn't counter. The wound in his leg won't heal, and after they spend the day failing, they'll come to me. Then negotiations begin."

"I saw his face during the *Venenum* spell. It scared him when he couldn't counter it. He fears you. Erin, fear is a bad motivator. I'm concerned he'll care more about getting rid of you than an alliance, let alone a negotiation."

I shook my head. I'd dealt with power-lust countless times for work and seldom was I wrong with my predictions on behavior. "I'm not wrong. He saved Elizabeth's life because of her knowledge. I just demonstrated that I have access to spells they've never encountered. He has an injury that a full elf won't be able to heal. I did that, and when he discovers I'm the only one who can undo it, he'll want me at his side more than ever. He's angry with me, undoubtedly despises my actions, but he wants to be a power broker and sees me as a means to it. He will release Nolan. And possibly reopen the Veil."

Cory frowned. "You may get Nolan, but I'm not sure they'd reopen the Veil. If it's about power, right now they're positioned to be the most powerful on this side of the Veil. Only you possess more. If he wants an alliance with you, I don't see him opening it for you to access Mephisto or the Huntsmen." His conflicted emotions moved over him like a shadow as he exhaled a heavy breath. "I don't know if we're underestimating who they would sacrifice to maintain that power. Is their desire to have Fabian whole enough leverage?" His last question seemed to concern him the most.

"Regarding the Veil, I'm not confident," I admitted. "They want Fabian. He was the Havenage—the lead. He's a good leader, one they want. Elizabeth knows that and she will stress it. It's just a matter of time."

Cory seemed convinced. And even his short interaction with Fabian when I was hospitalized had spawned a dislike for him. It was probably the quiet ruthlessness that Fabian attempted to hide. I would have to give him a taste of the same.

CHAPTER 7

"Tell me again that you don't have to worry about Landon?" Cory asked as we stared at the bouquet of black roses placed upside down at my front door that greeted us on our return from a visit to the grocery store. The paper wrapped around the flowers had a seal of the vampire's crest. It should have secured the paper closed but it had been torn in half. An innocuous presentation that left plausible deniability to the threat it certainly was. With the vampires, any gift turned upside down, crest torn meant you were a target. It was a warning no longer commonly used but it had the greatest impact. Old school. A reminder of retaliation and cruelty that vampires no longer participated in—or rather did a better job of concealing.

Despite this being a known threat, the presentation was so innocuous it ensured it would never be taken seriously. Report it to the SPF and you would look utterly ridiculous telling them that you received haphazardly discarded blooms with a torn emblem. "What, you don't like black roses?" "Sounds like a personal problem?" "They were upside down?" "Don't blame Landon, it's the delivery person's fault."

I cursed under my breath, surveyed my surroundings,

picked up the roses, and opened my door. I removed the seal and examined it and the paper for more messaging before tossing everything in the garbage. In the two days that I'd been waiting for a response from the elves, I'd filled that time with practicing magic and thinking of alternative methods to force their hand, allowing the situation with Landon to slip far into the recesses of my mind. This was his reminder that he was an ever-present issue in my life.

"Can we stop pretending Landon's not a problem?" Cory asked, looking out the door and assessing our surroundings before closing it and placing the bag of groceries in the kitchen.

"He's showing his displeasure with me. Things are fine." I didn't sound convincing to myself, so I knew Cory wasn't buying it.

"I'll talk to him," Cory offered, heading toward the door. I quickly grabbed him before he could leave.

"Nothing you say will change anything. It will only exacerbate the situation and he'll consider it a challenge to his position and power." I plopped down on the sofa, cradling my face in my hand. My mind became a whirl of images cataloging every magical item I had, spell I knew, and contact I'd made for something valuable enough that I could offer Landon to persuade him to give up on the idea of me giving him a family.

Each time I looked up I found Cory typing away on his phone.

"What's wrong?" I asked.

"I'm canceling my plans with Alex," he said. "You need me."

"You will not!"

"I can't leave you now."

"You can and you will." I stood, went to the cabinet, and took out some scribing chalk, then made the markings for a magic neutralizing spell, *adligatura*.

"It's for when the elves visit. I don't want them to have magic during negotiations," I provided in answer to his inquiring look.

He nodded but remained reluctant to leave.

"I'll call Madison over later. I promise. And if I get a whiff of danger I'll call you. Okay?" Hopefully she'd be able to get away from work. The situation she'd been dealing with left her unable to talk to me for any length of time and her response to my texts were just a few words and the promise to chat later.

It relaxed him some, but he still looked uneasy. Glancing at his phone he said, "Alex and I will have time to talk to Landon before the play."

"That's a big no. Bring the shifters' fourth in the pack with you and the conversation will just devolve into a jiggly bits measuring contest."

Cory's lips quirked. "Really? 'Jiggly bits'?"

"Man stick. Boinking pole. Bulbous pool stick and balls. I can do this all day."

He groaned. "Please stop." He gripped his lip in thought. "I think you're wrong."

"No, I'm not. You on your own would be an issue, but approaching him with Alex would definitely be viewed as a challenge. And it would cause issues for Asher."

Cory understood the rules of propriety as well as I did but seemed to throw caution to the wind when I was involved. I loved and hated that about him. It put me in the position of defending and upholding unspoken rules that I often found ridiculous.

"I'll handle it later. Believe me, it's fine."

Arms crossed over his chest. "Yeah, because you're going to handle it. You've staked him, given him the finger, and on more than one occasion pretty much told him to bite you—and not in the vampire-y way. Oh, and let's not forget you threatened to stake him two days ago, and you think *you're* the one who'll have a more productive session with him than Alex and me?"

His shoulders relaxed a smidge when I flashed him a smile. "It works for me because I'm just sugar and spice. I'm cute."

"Yeah, I'm going to ignore this alleged cuteness you seem to believe you possess. I'm sure while you were hovering over him with a stake at his chest, promising to destroy him with your unique brand of magic, *she sure is a big bowl of sugar and spice. Where can I get me some more* was exactly what ran through his mind."

I made a face before slipping off the ring I'd used on Fabian earlier and placing it on the table.

"Everything about you screams sugar and spice, a little vanilla, whipped cream, and sprinkles," he grumbled.

Pulling him into a hug, I pressed a quick peck to his cheek and guided him to the door. "Go have fun with Alex and we'll chat tomorrow."

"Tomorrow? I'll be back later today. I'll bring more clothes."

"Roommates? No thank you." I was remembering his snide remarks earlier when I awoke to the scent of freshly brewed coffee. He looked freshly showered and dressed. Blanket folded and pillows neatly stored. Overnight bag tucked away in the corner, and the washing machine in use. We had two entirely different morning processes. I'd simply rolled out of bed, brushed my teeth, and headed for coffee.

"As much as I'd love to wake up every morning to chaotic bedhead and your rumpled bed-chic look, my presence will be temporary. You have no need to worry about me becoming your roommate."

"I feel judged. Don't judge me. This morning I was rushing to coffee and breakfast. Besides, I have perfected the effortless morning-shambolic look. It's cute."

"First, that's not a thing. Second, I believe you are using

cute wrong again. Really wrong. For the love of fates, I urge you to look it up," he teased, bundling me into him. It made me wish he'd worry about me a little less. At least one of us could have a somewhat normal and fun night.

"Whatever. Promise not to fall for me."

"No, I'm going to just toss neat, handsome, urbane Alex aside for you and all your glory," he shot back.

"All I heard was if you weren't gay, you'd be *so* into me because my quirky ways are cute."

"Yeah, it's the *woman* part I'm turned off by. It has nothing to do with your numerous other… Well, I'll give you quirks," he said, pulling away and rolling his eyes. "I'm leaving," he said, backing away slowly, his face strained. "Don't answer the door for anyone until I come back."

"I'm not agreeing to that," I told him, returning to the neutralizing spell. "No one will enter my home with magic, and I have no intention of entertaining any vampires. If the elves come, I'll talk to them. But it will be with them magicless. I'll have the advantage. Magic and …" I waved my hand over the apartment where an assortment of weapons could be easily accessed if needed.

After moments of consideration, he nodded and left.

With Cory's departure, I completed the *adligatura* and wondered if I'd receive a visit from Fabian, or Elizabeth on his behalf, or someone completely different. Sanaa seemed the most reasonable choice. Two days, they had to be desperate. While I waited, I put away the groceries. Then I devoted the rest of my time to reading over Benton's dossier and what he'd observed of me and his constant speculations around questions about me that remained unanswered. The one mystery he seemed determined to solve was, could I borrow magic as I once had? He'd circled the question and repeated it several times throughout the dossier, along with scribbled notes in the margins with symbols that looked like signs of concern and distress. His information, along with what I'd witnessed with my magic now that Malific was dead, had me questioning whether the opposite of what would have happened with her magic, occurred with her demise. Malific wanted me dead because my existence siphoned away her powers. Now that she was dead, had limitations on mine been lifted? The uncertainty washed a feeling of loneliness over me. I couldn't even test my magic against other gods, and to my knowledge, there wasn't anyone around like me. The urge to canvas the city looking for someone like me had me pacing the floor until I gave in to the impulse to test my magic again.

Pulling a leaf from one of the snake plants, I placed it on the table. Gave myself a pinprick from the many pins I kept in a bowl for convenience, the spilling of blood being the foundation of my most powerful spells. I rested it against the plant and recited the spell and watched as the roots thickened, pushing forward buds that flourished into leaves at an uncanny speed. The plants continued to grow, some replications of the parent and others splitting to form entirely different offsprings of life. Using Google Lens, I discovered they were in the same family.

After terminating the spell, my table along with a significant portion of the floor was covered with snake plants, corn canes, spider plants, and plumosa ferns. The original plant had also produced a selection of yuccas and bluebells. Garden plants. The asparagus stalk that managed to sprout from the same root as the original plant as the result of a prick of my blood didn't require any debate about whether I'd have it for dinner. There was no chance in hell.

I'd created life. Plant life, but life nevertheless, and without the help of another person.

Feelings of triumph and overwhelming fear had me backing into a corner, surveying my new creations. I needed a different distraction to keep me from dropping into the rabbit hole I most certainly was about to drop into. I willed an elf to knock on my door.

Nothing. I suspected they were working overtime to undo the spell that kept Fabian injured as he limped around, each step a reminder of an injury their magic couldn't heal.

No one came.

My next task was to Wynd. Each attempt in the past had turned me into a cat. With a room half-filled with new life that I'd created, I didn't feel the need to discard my clothing on the off chance that I'd shift into a cat. However, I was concerned where I'd end up. With the knowledge gained from each previous attempt and to minimize the chances of error, I attempted to Wynd from the living room to outside. Minutes later, I was looking at the outside of my building. Fully clothed and human. Not a cat. I'd had a sliver of concern that I'd Wynd and be a shifted cat on at my new location. But I'd done it. Yelping out my excitement, I pressed my lips together. I'd Wynded. It was an achievement that I wanted to celebrate with Mephisto. I wanted to see the small look of amusement he'd given me at every attempt turn to the same excitement that was now in me. I wanted to share it with him, explore how much my magic had changed. But I didn't have an option as simple as calling him on the phone. Nothing.

The emptiness that moved through me became unbearable and I brushed away the tear that I couldn't blink back. I missed him. Recalling the last moment with him filled me with desperation and anguish. The sense of loss was just as painful as it was that day.

Before I could return to my apartment, the familiar earthy scent of elven magic permeated the air. Quickly scanning the area, I didn't see them but I felt their magic, scented it, and knew they were coming. I dashed into the house and checked the sigils of the *adligatura*. Confidence in my magic was higher than it had ever been, but I still didn't want to negotiate with a magical elf, especially one who was full caste, or Elizabeth and her exceptional magical abilities.

Without time to put away the cornucopia of plants emerging from the same parent plant and the lonesome asparagus, I did my best to shove them out of sight at the knock at the door.

"Come in," I said, stepping away from the circle that covered the entrance and half of the landing. I could be near the door without risk of smudging the chalked sigils.

Sanaa and Elizabeth looked diametric and analogous of each other. Elizabeth's high-collared shirt was a stark contrast to her cobalt blue slacks. A decorative belt and stern frown of contempt at my presence completed the outfit. Sanaa's jade-green billowy blouse had the similar high-collar look they both preferred. The long flowing skirt moved at a different rhythm to her stride as they entered the house. When they were centered between the sigils, I engaged the magic neutralizing spell, earning me a sneer from Sanaa.

"What did you do to Fabian?" she demanded, bypassing any greetings or pleasantries.

"We know what was done to him. A nefarious spell and groundless violence. She knows no other way," Elizabeth added with a hiss and grossly unaware hypocrisy. Disdain darkened her eyes as they swept over the sigils.

"I'd like to hear it from her. I don't wish to paint her with the broad stroke of being the monster you so willingly ascribe to her." Sanaa moved as close to me as the spell would allow. The sharp intensity of her appraisal ebbed away, softening her, entreating civility in a situation where Elizabeth had chosen an opposite path. Elizabeth's glare proved that the neutralizing spell was the only thing preventing this situation from devolving into a hostile display of magic.

Sanaa's voice was low and gentle, which made it difficult to treat her with hostility. Which was precisely the point.

Being aware of the tactics people used didn't make me any less likely to initially fall for them.

"She feels backed into a corner and we are responsible for making her feel that way. Erin would not deliver such harsh penalties to a man who holds her in such high regard. Who was instrumental in bringing her into the Havenage and made it his sole responsibility to teach and guide her with her elven magic. I do not believe her to be heartless enough to reward such generosity and kindness with death."

She was slathering the BS on rather thick. Even with the most generous leeway I couldn't let her get away with such florid characterization and liberties with the truth.

"Death?" I scoffed. "He has a little boo-boo on his leg and it's making walking difficult. He'll hardly die from it. He has a limp, big whoop. It would heal…" *But you can't do it.* A smug smile of satisfaction tugged at my lips, but I fought it. "I'm assuming that's why you're here. You want him healed, correct?"

"You shouldn't have done it in the first place! Healing him is the least you can do," Elizabeth snapped. "Unprovoked cruelty is the foundation of your being. You are your mother's daughter."

Her response roused a blaze in me that I had a tough time controlling. Close to the sigils, I was ready to break the spell and punch her in the face. But that was what she wanted. My auntie knew exactly how to push my buttons. It wasn't just her insults; they didn't bother me as much as her hypocrisy.

"You killed Malific. Are you not satisfied? Or is it both of our deaths that you want?"

The gleam of hope that flitted across her face answered in a crueler manner than any words. She looked euphoric at the possibility.

"I killed your mother? I'd love to hold such an honor. But I'm not the one who killed her. It was a kindness on my part to end the suffering from the state her daughter left her in."

She choked out a jeer. "How poetic, the child she had in order to release her from her prison is the reason she's dead. Such a fitting end."

Flashes of my fight with Malific and the injuries I'd inflicted prior to fleeing with my own injuries that left me in hospital ran through my mind. A part of me thought she'd heal, live her well-deserved magicless existence in the Blose Chasm. Although the likelihood was slim, if anyone could have achieved that it would have been Malific. I was curious to know more about Malific's last moments, but I wouldn't give Elizabeth the satisfaction. There was no way she ended her suffering with mercy.

"Erin, daughter of Nolan, explain yourself," Sanaa said, redirecting the conversation and pulling my glare from Elizabeth to her.

"I need to explain myself? I'm not naïve or foolish enough to believe you don't know everything Fabian has done to me. You're quite talented at making him seem like a martyr. The altruistic, compassionate elf who is now suffering from an unprovoked cruelty. He's not innocent and my retaliation was well deserved. If you want my help in healing him, bring Nolan to me and reopen the Veil."

"It's not the Veil that you want, is it, Malific's daughter?" I hated when Elizabeth called me that. Assigning nothing but the heinousness of Malific's existence to me. It took more effort than I wanted to admit keeping the hurt from showing. "You want the Huntsmen, more specifically Mephisto."

Elizabeth's icy dagger eyes held mine. "He has shown you quite a beautiful face. The other face he keeps hidden from the world, as if doing so could make us forget his atrocities and the atrocities of the Huntsmen, just because they hold the honorable claim of keeping the peace and punishing the most monstrous ones that exist in the world. Make no mistake, he and his ilk are the same as Malific. As you. I always wondered what he saw in someone like you." Her speculation was never silent and when she'd abducted me to trade to Malific, she'd voiced her curiosity. "Affinity for his likeness. He couldn't help but be drawn to the very person that reflects him the most. The Alpha still baffles me. Perhaps the feral beast will find a woman not far from it, charming."

"If you don't stop with all this flattery, I'm going to fall a little in love with you," I shot back, causing anger to flare in her expression. "Are we going to spend the day exchanging insults or can we discuss what needs to be done to make us both whole?"

"You want Nolan and you want the Veil reopened. Your expectation is for this to be done while Fabian's injured and unable to perform magic?" Elizabeth rebutted.

My eyes widened on her then moved to Sanaa, who would not make eye contact with me. Insulted by how incredibly stupid they thought I was, it took a moment to gather my emotions and handle the situation amicably to meet my goals. "If he was able to do the spell, then it can be done by another full elf. After all, you were the person who created the spell. He just brought the magic. Sanaa can do the same."

Sanaa's jaw clenched, making it more challenging to hide my offense at their assumption that I lacked basic knowledge about elven magic and spells.

Elizabeth licked her lips and slowly roamed the boundaries of the circle. Her voice methodical and low, she said, "My brother is the root of many problems among the elves. When he had the chance to kill Malific, he had a child with her. Instead of giving her a well-deserved death, he opted for her to live a weakened existence and gave her an avenue to escape her prison. She did, because of you. Arius was injured because of her, and she died responsible for countless deaths after a reign of terror marked by torture and immeasurable cruelty. The fact that my brother is still alive is nothing but grace on the part of the elves. Their extension of kindness and understanding demonstrates the benevolence of the elves." She looked up and locked eyes with me. "I love my brother. I've made accommodations for his misguided love of you. I have even played a role in helping him keep you safe. Helped him with his foolish paternal acts of affection when none should have been given. Nolan was a failure and brought dishonor to the elves. Now he's being used as a tool for their demise." She inched closer, leaning into the magic boundary as much as it would allow. "Make no mistake, I see you as that. If we give in to any of your demands, we deserve our annihilation." She frowned. "What you've done is quite impressive and the mere fact you've managed this potential for harm can't be ignored. I never underestimated what you'd be able to do. The others did. They saw you fumbling through your magic, but I knew it was only a matter of time before you would harness it in a way that would make you a danger. My niece, that is where we are similar. I am quite resourceful." Her lips twisted into a caustic smile; keen eyes narrowed on me. "You are getting tired. Keeping up the *adligatura* is a challenge. It's linked to your elven magic and you don't have a lot of that, do you."

The spell had wavered a little, but I had a lot more fight in me.

"We aren't going to negotiate with you to help Fabian. When I discover a way to undo the spell, he'll be more accepting of my initial apprehension about you. Nolan will not be released to you. I must accept the measures that must be taken to protect the elves and will keep the Veil closed indefinitely. It is heartbreaking that my brother's life will have to be sacrificed so that he can never be used as a bargaining tool on your behalf."

I gasped out a breath. It was a sucker punch that I would never ever be prepared to take, and nothing in me was able to tamp down my emotions enough to prevent Elizabeth seeing it. The sly smile proved that she enjoyed it. I blinked back tears. And chastised myself for thinking I'd be the worst monster in the room. When Elizabeth occupied it, I'd always be second.

"You hated Malific because she was just a preview of what you are. It had to be uncomfortable seeing yourself in someone you hated."

She didn't care about the insult. It meant nothing. I'd shown my cards and she'd revealed hers. She was willing to kill Nolan for what she deemed as the survival of the elves. I was willing to do what it took to save him because of the affection I had for him that she appeared to have abandoned.

What I felt must have showed on my face because Sanaa and Elizabeth both took several steps back. Magic wasn't required to open the door, which they did and exited without another word. Elizabeth's face was a landscape of shocked horror when I Wynded in front of her, grabbing her by her hair and ripping out a fistful. With the flash of movement from Wynding, I was back in my apartment, her shriek still ringing in my ear. I tossed the strands on the table. There were spells I could use it for, as well as track her with it. Blood would have been better, but time was limited. The more rewarding part of my acquisition was that she knew there were innumerable spells I could do with her hair, and that was going to keep her up at night.

CHAPTER 8

"That's not a few things." I pointed to the large suitcase Cory pulled behind him and the smaller tote Alex carried as he trailed behind.

"And those weren't there when I left. Look at us, we're both observant," he spouted back, tucking the case in the corner. Alex followed, placing the tote next to the suitcase before taking up a position beside Cory and staring at the collection of flora on a table I'd found in storage. Alex moved closer to the plants and touched the asparagus that lingered at the tail of the hybrids.

"What happened, Erin?" Concern was heavy in Alex's voice.

"Me," I explained cryptically. Before I could elaborate, Cory had launched at me and pulled me into a tight hug. My breath whooshed out.

"I have no idea what you did, but I feel like it's badass," he said.

"You're crushing me," I sputtered.

"Sorry." He made another sweeping look in the direction of the plants and sat on the sofa waiting for me to give details.

It all came tumbling out in a flurry of excitement that I'd denied myself earlier. Alex kept a careful eye on Cory, whose enthusiasm quickly faded when the topic moved to my encounter with Sanaa and Elizabeth. Elizabeth's threat against Nolan had Cory pacing the length of the room, disheveling his hair as he ran his fingers through it. The messy spikes were a contrast to the meticulous fit of his clothing, which led me to believe that his plans with Alex were more than just casual. Alex's worried eyes tracked Cory's every movement. His demeanor was calculating and protective as his gaze moved between me, the flora, and Cory.

"They plan to kill Nolan?" Cory asked.

The response got stuck in my throat. I wanted to deny Nolan's life being in imminent danger, but I wasn't certain.

"I don't know," I admitted.

Cory growled a low curse. "You want to get him out, don't you?"

"I have to. If they won't send him to me, I don't have many other options."

Cory's attention returned to the plants. "Don't you?"

Surprised, my eyes widened and Alex's mouth gaped briefly before snapping closed.

Holding his hands up to halt our responses, Cory said, "I'm not being heartless. Look at what you're able to do, what you've done. Yes, Nolan can help you improve your elven magic, but his life is only in jeopardy because they see you value him. You care. The threat of his death is being used as revenge against you." He moved closer and everything in me wanted to shove him away. Tears of anger pricked at my eyes despite knowing he was right.

"I can't fucking win, even when I have the advantage!"

The strident silence compounded the feeling of helplessness that was rearing its ugly head. The only thing that kept me from spiraling was the bag of Elizabeth's hair on the table next to the Mystic Souls, several other magical books, and the notebook full of spells that I'd been practicing weaving.

"I'm going to take their magic," I announced, picking up the notebook. Relief swept over me as I flipped through the pages. The definitive plan brought me some relief, but it forced Cory into silence. The room filled with ragged, labored breathing.

"They sent Mephisto and the Huntsmen away and closed the Veil to ensure no one has magic that rivals theirs. Nolan was threatened because I'm challenging their plans. All of this was done to protect their magic. They care about power and their magic. They can't have the power without the magic. If I take their magic, they'll be distracted trying to get it back or they'll just leave me the fuck alone in hopes that I'll return it. But either way, I get rid of them. If Elizabeth was able to make the shifters immune to magic, what's stopping me from taking their magic?"

Cory was gearing up for a debate and I was preparing to counter it when I got a text.

"Madison's on her way," I told him. He snapped out of his deep thoughts and smiled with relief. I was almost certain my plans to remove the elves' magic would be the first thing she heard about in his effort to persuade her to side with him and discourage me from going through with it.

It wouldn't work.

Cory discussing anything was quickly shelved when Madison entered the apartment looking as if she were Atlas carrying the world on her back.

"What's wrong?" I asked when she turned off her phone and placed it on the table. She shrugged off her jacket and tossed it aside before taking a seat. With a heavy sigh, her head dropped back. Madison was growing her hair out from its short, relaxed style. Now she sported a short mass of coils revealing her natural color of deep sienna, which she got from her father. She nervously ran her hands through the curls. Professionally dressed, she was still on the casual side and wearing running shoes instead of her typical flats. The scent of forestry and flowers clung to her, which meant she was pulling from them heavily for magic.

"Fae business." A pronouncement like that typically meant she wasn't going to disclose a lot of information, but this time she appeared desperate to unburden herself. Sensing it quickly, Cory and Alex said their goodbyes and left.

"I know you can't tell me everything, but share what you can." I was worried. She'd never look this stressed— No, it wasn't stress. It was a combination of fear, frustration, and stress. She'd leaned forward and was gnawing at her nails, her brow furrowed. I gathered she was sorting through information and determining what she could disclose.

Growing up with Madison a fae, and me considered a mage, "fae business" was a source of contention, but we knew there would be parts of fae lives that wouldn't be open to me. Their fae name being one of them. It was a part of her life blocked off from me. Aware of the seriousness of knowing a fae true name, I never wanted to be in a position where I could compromise my second family by exposing the name to another person. So I'd never pushed to know it, and when Madison offered to give hers to me, I'd declined.

People always have the best intentions to never reveal a name or use it for harm against them. But having it always came with the risk of that knowledge being exploited or someone trying to attain it. If I didn't know it, I couldn't reveal it, even under the threat of harm or torture. I never wanted to be responsible for anyone gaining control over Madison's autonomy. Fae names were valuable; I'd even heard of them being sold.

"Adalia is missing," she admitted, her frown deepening. Frustration and concern radiated off her. The heavy distress in her voice prompted me to ask questions. The struggle of her navigating what she could disclose placed an apologetic frown on her face.

"Neri doesn't have Adalia," she blew out after a long pause.

Prior to them marrying, Neri had been a mercurial nightmare who bucked against any rule for the fae, continuing to illegally bind humans to deals. Although they weren't forbidden to use glamours, they couldn't do so for deception. A rule he'd ignored. Manipulation of the weather was strongly discouraged. He found fae antics entertaining and appeared to find chaos and the attempts to reprimand him entertaining. His union with Adalia managed to curtail some of his behaviors to manageable. Rules were enforced and his attendance at meetings with the state and Supernatural Task Force were productive. He wasn't making an appearance just to be a cog in what he'd deemed an unnecessary machine. Essentially, he became more tolerable. Tolerable by fae royalty standards. Adalia needed to be found.

I waited patiently for Madison to continue.

"It's not that she's *just* missing. He said she went to bed and he said he went to the bedroom an hour or so later and found her gone. We can't manage his anger. He's threatening to burn down the city if she's not found. I don't think he means metaphorically."

No one thinks he means metaphorically.

"Is she missing, or did she leave?"

There wasn't a history of divorce or separation among the fae, but if anyone was going to wake up one day and say to hell with this, it would be Adalia. The denizens limited their interpersonal dealings, being more concerned with keeping up to date with the power players. They interacted enough to keep the peace. They knew the ones with the razor-thin temperaments who could potentially be a problem. The heads of the magical community understood that the knowledge wasn't just about survival but also how to appropriately damage control in order to maintain the tenuous relationship they had with humans.

Whether Madison had considered Adalia leaving on her own, or my questioning had opened the door to more speculations and questions, it was clear she wanted to change the topic. She asked me to tell her what had occurred with Mephisto and the Huntsmen.

"Everything. Unabridged," she requested.

I relayed it all, including my interaction with Elizabeth and Sanaa earlier and their threats against Nolan.

"They seem to want to threaten everyone in your life, don't they?" A dagger's edge was in her voice. She'd taken Fabian's threat of killing off the fae to coerce Mephisto into completing the spell that sent them away better than I imagined she would. But the emotion played over her face. Irredeemable hate. "If they're prepared to be cavalier about the lives of people you care about, perhaps you should have the same approach about theirs."

Oh shit. I reared back at her response. Had finding out her life and the life of her family was threatened, the possible abduction of the fae queen, and the closing of the Veil depleted her of all empathy? Cory wouldn't find an ally in her, or someone to help dissuade me of my plans. She wouldn't care if I took the elves' magic—or even worse.

"Clayton made it seem as if he'd only be gone temporarily." An anguished tinge threaded through her words. "I wish I could have seen him to say goodbye."

"Their departure was a chaotic mess. I would have liked more time, too. But everything happened so quickly and Fabian wouldn't negotiate for longer." The panic and desperation I felt that day washed over me and was quickly replaced by anger and the thirst for revenge. Grabbing the notebook with the woven spells, I perused them with new determination.

"They'll be back. I'm going to make sure of that," I asserted.

"If anyone can do it, you can. *We* can."

I hadn't realized how emboldened I'd feel with Madison's approval. I didn't want to fight with her and Cory. Encouraged, a productive hour with Madison yielded a list of objects I needed to look for in Mephisto's collection, several more spells we'd found in the Mystic Souls, and several more woven spells. With her limited experience with them, they weren't the top ones to try. We even dipped into armchair psychoanalysis of Adalia's state of mind. In the end, we were more confident that Adalia was more likely to tell Neri she was done than just leave without informing him.

Before returning to her search, Madison lingered at the door, watching me. "Removing the elves' magic will more than likely mean the loss of yours. Is that a sacrifice you're willing to make?"

It had to spark memories of my struggle with not having magic. Everything that accompanied it. I shrugged.

"I'll still have magic, just not the same."

No longer able to deny the frown, it darkened her concerned eyes as they traveled to the plants. "Your magic will change again. It will be like starting over."

"I'll adapt. I didn't have the magic before. I think I'll be fine without it."

"You always do." Her face brightened and she came over and hugged me. "I love you," she whispered.

Hearing more in her words than the simple declaration we'd made so many times, I pulled away and looked at her. "Love you, too." I studied her mask of misery and guilt. "You know that situation with Fabian wouldn't have been handled differently? I didn't even have to consider it. I do care about

Mephisto and hope we'll have more time together. But I choose you. Always."

"I know. It infuriates me that these choices have to keep being made. I'm tired of you having to give up so much constantly."

I refused to sulk about it. "The desire to make them suffer and to think twice about ever threatening mine is worth the magic I'll sacrifice."

"I get that. When I learned of the elves' presence here, I was happy for you. I thought that you'd have a community of your own for protection, resources, who possessed similar magic. I know it's not a necessity, but it would have been nice. I hate that you don't have that," she admitted. Sorrow resonated in her words. Something she attempted to hide. She gave me an apologetic smile. I wanted it for myself, but it was hard to mourn something I'd never experienced. It was nothing more than a thought that never grew to fruition.

"I have that, just not the way others do. Remember when I thought I was a mage? They didn't want anything to do with me."

The load that Madison carried upon arrival seemed to have lifted. She took a deep breath, exhaling it slowly.

"I'll check on you later," she told me before opening the door and shrieking in surprise.

CHAPTER 9

"Erin," Madison called from the door. "You have a situation here."

Approaching the door, I was prepared for any number of things: a demon circle; a cadre of elves demanding Elizabeth's hair back and to heal Fabian; Pearl the snow leopard, who was quite fond of the god who could speak to her, searching for him; Ms. Harp making another escape from accountability. At this point, I wouldn't be surprised by anything.

"Damn," I ground out through clenched teeth along with a slew of other curses at the wolf shifters and one lonely fox in the back, crowding the hallway. Frowning, I bypassed Madison and was attempting to force a path through them when a familiar wolf, Daniel, whom Asher had sent to guard my home before, nudged me back.

"Do it again," I warned. He bared his teeth in what must have been an animal version of a smile, met the challenge, and pushed me back and gave Madison one for good measure.

She snarled at him. He returned it and the others added their low growls of support. Except for the fox who appeared to be there for entertainment. It had taken several steps back, its beady dark eyes looking over the small pack then darting to me followed by a sound that could be mistaken for a chortle.

"I have neighbors. You're blocking their path," I pointed out, although it wasn't true since Ms. Harp's departure to one of the pack's homes closer to Asher, and the Northwest Pack's acquisition of my apartment complex. They didn't seem to be in a rush to fill Ms. Harp's vacant apartment. They weren't blocking the path to the only neighbor, who lived upstairs. They were my annoyance, not others'.

"Move," I demanded louder, lowering myself until I was eye level. It was difficult holding eye contact with shifter wolves; the more dominant they were the bigger the challenge. It reached you at a visceral level. Daniel snorted. Another wolf padded next to him, thankfully forcing me to break eye contact without it being viewed as surrender.

"Listen, I'm not part of Asher's pack nor am I his responsibility. I don't care that he sent you, I'm telling you to go away. This is the only time I plan to be polite about it. Move, or I'll make you move."

The collective sounds of amusement that were between snorts and growls just added fuel to my irritation. Madison looked out over the crowd of obstinate shifters and groaned. Hearing the defeat in it irked me. *We aren't giving in to them this easy.*

"Fine, whose ass do I need to kick to get you all to listen?"

"Mine," Asher said, coming into view from the side of the building, the shifters moving out of his path as he approached. My eyes narrowed on him, his bemused wayward smirk and the self-confidence that was laced in his brand of arrogance. *Good. He needs to be taken down a few pegs.*

Once at my doorway, he nudged his chin in the direction behind me, asking for entrance. I moved aside. He unbuttoned his sleeves of his shirt and rolled them up his forearms.

Made a production of stretching his neck, arms, and bouncing from one foot to the other as he flashed Madison a smile. She appreciated it as much as I did.

"What else do I need to do to prepare myself for this ass kicking I'm about to receive?" he taunted, assessing his folded sleeves.

Now he's moved into comedy. A jack of all trades.

"Move your vermin," I demanded.

He looked back at the closed door and pulled an exaggerated pout. "That was uncalled for. They can hear you. You're hurting their feelings."

"Asher, they can't be here. Tell them to leave. I have things to do. We"—I moved my hand between me and Madison—"have things to do."

"Yes, you have plenty to do, and it seems like it's been quite dangerous for you. So dangerous that Alex has been uncharacteristically on edge because of how worried Cory is about you. Do you know how that is affecting Alex? He's part of my pack? So guess who has to be involved now."

"Deal with him. He's the one in your pack, not me. It's his safety and health that you're responsible for."

He nodded slowly, taking in my words with his resolute expression unchanged.

"Are you being intentionally obtuse?" he asked. "He's a great fourth but he's highly affected by what happens to Cory, his boyfriend. Now that Cory's my issue, then indirectly so are you. Even if it didn't concern Cory, I care about your well-being. When you're in trouble, I want to help. Take the help." The latter a command as if I were part of his pack and not at liberty to decline.

It wasn't just *help* but a takeover. Knowing that his intentions were good, just him being him, I tempered my frustration. "Asher," I eased out.

"Erin." Madison noticed my hands balled at my side and my struggle and moved between Asher and me.

"At this time," Madison said to Asher, "she's declining your assistance. I can assure you, if she needs it, she won't hesitate to ask." It was the most diplomatic she'd ever been with Asher whom she'd described on many occasions as insufferable. "If your wolves don't move, you're keeping her here against her will. There are laws against that, Mr. Sullivan." She flashed her badge as a reminder of her position with the Supernatural Task Force and not just my sister.

His brow rose in challenge. Raising his hands, he exposed his wrists to Madison. "Am I about to be arrested?"

Madison glowered. Asher flouted the rules when they didn't serve him, and having the best attorneys in the world, he rarely suffered consequences. When he was assisting me, it was an attribute that I welcomed and appreciated. When I was working from the other side of those advantages and privileges, it was a pain in the ass. A true annoyance.

He took several steps away from us, his eyes slowly roving over me and then Madison. Head canted to the side, his eyes were intense with question. "How did you think I became the Alpha?" he asked. "Because I answered the contestants' questions the correct way? Was it because I was the loveliest person in the room?" His hand swept over his body. "Although it's true, I'm not sure it was taken into consideration. Perhaps you believe it was because I'm unbelievably charming?"

The rhetorical question pierced the quiet.

"Spoiler, I am." He flashed a smile that was far from charming.

I wonder how charmed he'll feel with a kick to his Good and Plentys.

He moved closer, his sharp predator gaze directed at us, giving us a peek at the side of him I had the honor of not seeing often. And for good reason. It was a scary look into the apex predator he shared a body with.

"It's because at any given time, more likely than not I'm the biggest asshole in the room."

"That's not the flex you think it is," I grumbled out.

"Truly," Madison cosigned.

"I'm an indomitable ass," he preened.

"You don't need to convince us," Madison pointed out and was met with his darkly amused grin.

"I'm consistently the most resourceful and connected in any given situation. And when it is necessary, I have the ability to bring most to their knees. Metaphorically and literally. I get results despite rules or obstacles. So I care very little about whether I'm liked. Being the biggest asshole *is* the flex that I think it is. The only thing that matters is protection of my pack and the people I care about. I care about you, Erin. You may not appreciate my methods, but you can't deny my results. I don't know the entire situation, I'm just speculating. It seems like you are way over your head and I'm offering my help."

I could feel Madison's eyes on me as she waited for me to respond. She found Asher insufferable. An opinion she shared freely with him, his team of lawyers, her coworkers and anyone who cared to listen, but she never denied his effectiveness as the pack's Alpha. In fact, it seemed to be the only thing she liked about him.

The situation was so messy and complicated, I had no idea if he could help. The pack's assistance came with— Well, it came with Asher. He was indomitable; it was the essence of being an Alpha, but it also meant it was easy to be swept into the force that was Asher. I didn't—couldn't operate that way.

He studied me, surely assessing the internal debate I was having. "Erin, this is your situation. I'm offering help because you need it and I have a bad feeling you're not going to come out on the other side of it whole. That is unacceptable for me. You are not without options. You have two. Accept the help of my pack." Then silence fell as he looked at me with a raised brow.

Did he forget how to count? "What's the second option?"

"Oh." He shrugged. "Whatever is going on, you accept the L. It's a loss you take on the chin, learn from it, and do what you can to return your life to as normal as you can make it."

"That's not really two options."

"It is. Just because you don't like the second option doesn't exempt it from being one."

I sneered at him. Madison shifted closer to me, giving his taunting smirk a similar look.

"It's the arrogance for me," she grumbled quietly.

Chuckling, he gave an exaggerated bow. "Let me rephrase. Ms. Jenkins and Ms. Calloway, will you please give me the great pleasure of being of service to you? I'd be ever so grateful."

His sarcasm hadn't moved me, reality had.

"Okay. I'd like your help. Please." My acquiescence warped his self-assured smile to a gape that he quickly recovered from.

I plopped onto the sofa, resting my face in my hand. "Everything about this situation is a certifiable mess, Asher," I said. It was that admission that made me slightly embarrassed by my ambitious goal of taking the elves' magic, despite Asher and his pack and their immunity to magic being proof powerful spells like that existed. With her fae duties a priority, Madison reluctantly left after I gave her a nod of reassurance.

Time ticked with Asher standing in front of me, his hands loosely shoved in his pockets, his face a blank landscape as he waited for me to share the situation with him. I'm sure he expected an edited version, but I had no intention of doing that. His immunity to magic gave him intimate knowledge to the spell that achieved it. Elizabeth made a point of not sharing it with me and I thought it was in protection of her knowledge rather than a show of disdain, which she consequently had no issues displaying.

In telling Asher my plans, I had to face the inevitable: What happens if it failed? I was guilty of not always having a plan B. My plan B was very similar to the same one as before. How blunt should I be about disclosing that my plan involved variations of torture to get information from the elves, and possibly murder? How could Asher not place me in the "bad guy" category? When this concluded, I wouldn't have the moral high ground. Ever.

I told him everything, fighting past the twinge I felt revealing what Mephisto and the Huntsmen were. Me killing my mother—or partially killing her and Elizabeth completing the task. Fabian circumventing the oath I'd made with Asial. I watched as horror and rage crept into Asher's expression as I detailed Fabian's plans to kill the fae if Mephisto and the Huntsmen hadn't left.

He nodded slowly. "Are you sure your mother—"

"Malific," I interjected.

"Malific is dead? Only thing you know is that your magic returned."

I pointed to my creations as evidence. Although it wasn't concrete, my only other option was to open the Blose Chasm and check. That wasn't a possibility because I wouldn't have anyone to reopen it to let me out. The pleasure on Elizabeth's face when she detailed the situation was evidence enough.

When I shared the exchange with Sanaa and Elizabeth, including it prodding my decision to take the elves' magic, I asked Asher if he could provide any insight to the spell that gave him magical immunity.

Vibrating with excitement, I grabbed my notepad and scribbled down everything he rattled off with such precision it was as if he had eidetic memory. When he described a magical object Elizabeth used, I gave him the notebook to draw a replication of it because I couldn't envision it. Despite his poor artistic skills, I had a direction to look. And the spell she used. Because no matter how low Elizabeth spoke, it wasn't quiet enough to prevent a shifter hearing.

I was infinitely closer to my goal and the only thing that kept me from launching at him and giving him a hug was his brow knitting together and his cool assessment of me.

"What's wrong? Your breathing is much faster and your heart is racing." He leaned closer, inhaled, and stepped back giving me more withering looks. "I don't like the way you smell."

"Thanks, you charmer. Are you flirting with me?" I teased.

"No, it's a lot of emotions and it's…" It was confusing to him. The uncertainty coursed over his face. I couldn't identify them, either. Because I was feeling them all.

"I don't know what to feel," I admitted, realizing things were a lot more concrete than before. I was feeling a lot of things that I couldn't describe. Fear was one I could identify.

"Sort them out because there are some things I need to know." The grave intensity of Asher's words pulled my attention from the notebook.

He sat next to me and gave me a considering look as he ran his thumb languidly over his downturned lip. "What is acceptable collateral damage for you? And casualties. Whose life are you prepared to sacrifice?" he asked.

Shocked into silence, a blink was my only response.

"You have simplified this to you just taking the elves' magic away. It's not. This is essentially a declaration of war. I guarantee they will retaliate in kind. Go into this fully aware that there may be casualties. I know Madison and Cory are nonnegotiable. What about Nolan?"

The answer stuck in my parched throat. "I won't accept my father's death, either. I don't want anyone to die."

He nodded. "No one enters war wanting death. It has to be something you must accept. Top priority is to minimize the risk. What can you do to decrease the chances of Nolan dying, Erin?" he asked softly. I eyed the floor as I considered the question. He placed his hand on my thigh and gave it a squeeze, prompting an answer. I knew the answer, just hated what it would entail.

"I have to get Nolan out of there."

"How? When you take away their magic, the wards in the Havenage fall along with the repulsion spells. He will be magicless, and so will they and thirsty to make you pay in the most vicious way possible. You know how those with magic respond when it is bound. If you go in without subduing their magic, can you handle them all?"

I was emboldened by my new skills but not foolish. Fabian didn't have magical ability right now, but the others did. I'd be going up against true elves with powerful magic.

"I need to think about it," I admitted.

As we fell into a long silence, I could feel his attentive eyes on me. "Is this sacrifice worth it?" he asked. Positioning himself so that we were face to face, the intensity of his hard gaze became difficult to hold. "Elves are the only ones that have a chance against gods, and you are taking that magic away. I understand why you want to do it. It is warranted, but can you live with knowing you have gods who can't be checked by any other magic?"

"Gods can be killed like anyone else. They're not as invincible as they seem. They have weaknesses as well."

His lips slipped into a smirk. "What are they?"

"You're immune to their magic, so why do you care?"

"Curiosity."

"All curiosity doesn't need to be satisfied."

Noticeably unhappy with the answer, he nodded. Feeling the weight of his gaze, I turned to look at him. His lips pinched into a tight line, he exhaled a deep breath. "Wars are ugly, Erin, even after they conclude, even when there's a clear winner. Losses are inevitable. And not just loss of life."

"I know." My intentions for Elizabeth and Fabian hadn't been as cavalier as he'd let on.

"Is he worth it?' he asked softly. "You never struck me as the type who'd go through so much for a man."

"He's not a man."

He gave me a wry half smile. "Right, a god," he said with breezy derision. "One that was trapped here by your mother and is now trapped in the Veil because of Fabian. Such a powerful being seems to be rendered powerless rather often."

"We all have our weaknesses. You're quite powerful yet you and your pack were rendered nearly powerless by a fae with animancer magic."

The memory of it made his confident smirk waver, although it quickly reasserted itself.

"And I helped you. Not because I'm more powerful, but because I was in a position to do so," he said. Helping now left me open for elves to assign blame to me if they ever abused their magical immunity.

"I'm not sure if Mephisto will find a way back. Since I'm in a position to help, I will. I care about him and want him back. So, the simple answer is yes. He is worth it."

"And the complex one?"

"I'm worth it, too. I want Mephisto here and the spell lifted from the Veil, but I deserve not to be threatened into joining a community who only want to use me. The loss of my father's life used as punishment for declining. I deserve better than worrying about the elves trying to kill my friends and loved ones with a spell whenever they want to put me in my place. I want a life free of people who hate me and believe I deserve retribution for being something I had no control of. I am going to war, but they declared it on me first."

He nodded, a smirk turning into a smile of understanding. "Think about your plans, Erin, and we'll discuss it tomorrow." He stood up and headed for the door.

"Asher, thank you for being the biggest asshole in the room," I teased.

He smirked. "It's not nearly as difficult as it looks."

"Once again, that's not the flex you think it is," I volleyed back.

"It's not the insult you believe it to be." He opened the door to the shifters. "Who do you want to shadow you? Daniel is probably the best choice since you all have history."

"How cute. You're making it seem like the history doesn't involve you leaving that massive wolf at my door." He gave me another unbothered smirk. "I choose none. I'll come up with a plan, we can reconvene tomorrow to discuss, or I'll call. We'll go from there."

"Look who's being cute now, thinking she has a choice. I've compromised to just leaving one shifter. That's as much as I can give. Daniel or someone else?"

I pointed to my creations against the wall as defense; he offered a look of appreciation.

"Very impressive. Daniel?"

"Remember Cory, the badass witch? He's staying with me for a while."

Asher looked around the room. "Is he invisible? I don't see or smell him."

"Ick, stop with smelling people. It's really gross."

"I don't sense his magic, either." An addition to their abilities that accompanied their immunity. One that Asher seemed to be actively trying to diminish. I figured with their other heightened senses, it had to be too much stimulation.

"He'll be back."

"Daniel will leave when he does."

Before I could respond, Asher left. I heard him murmur but couldn't make it out. A tactic they adopted often. Because of their exceptional hearing, they spoke at volumes others couldn't hear. I figured Daniel was instructed to stay and the others relieved of their duties.

When I went to check, an enormous wolf was snoring at my door. I invited him in.

CHAPTER 10

Daniel had watched with wide-eyed fascination as I performed the spell on the vined tomato, also creating three duplicates and the growth of a bell pepper that emerged from the cluster of nightshades.

"Do you think it will taste any different than the natural versions?" he asked. That wasn't something I'd contemplated. Nor did I have any intention of finding out what magically made food tasted like. Malific had created an army that moved, behaved, and had the higher thought processing of humans. They were essentially normal. The nightshade fruit looked normal, too, and probably tasted that way as well. But it seemed different than harvesting from a garden. It was a magical creation.

"They're not real," I pointed out.

He grinned. Not sharing my reticence, he plucked a tomato and bell pepper from the cluster. "They look real to me." He headed to the kitchen with confidence and the smooth grace of movement shifters possessed, demonstrating no self-preservation instincts. Instead of running from danger, he just sprinted toward it. And eating magically created food seemed to fall in the category of danger.

As he proceeded to the kitchen, I watched with a similar look of awed fascination he'd given me earlier. He retrieved eggs from the fridge. After washing the food, he thoroughly examined them.

"It feels and smells normal," he provided after running his fingers over the skin and taking a whiff. Cutting a slice from the peppers and tomato, he chewed them slowly before reporting. "Very flavorful. Like they came from a garden," he reported.

I don't care if they taste like ambrosia made by Gordon Ramsey, I'm not eating my weird magic creations.

After his test of the tomato and pepper he went on to prepare an omelet under my deep scrutiny.

"Are you afraid?" he asked, his eyes flicking up from the pan.

"Of what?"

"Your new abilities? They haven't been seen before. At least not here. You have to realize that once they're discovered, people will be quite wary of you."

"I'm not afraid."

"Hmm. It'll probably be to your advantage if you become a better liar. I hear the uncertainty in your voice." His eyes flicked up to meet mine again, offering me an affable smile that made it hard to imagine him as a Mackenzie Valley wolf. I knew behind the docile golden-brown eyes lurked a person far more deadly than presented. He wouldn't have been Asher's choice to stay if he weren't.

"Stop listening," I snapped.

His eyes lit with suppressed laughter.

"I'm not afraid, just concerned. People were intrigued and fearful of my magic before. But I didn't have magic unless someone lent it to me. I was a potential threat, not a true one. That's not the case now. I don't want to be considered such a large threat that they feel the need to eliminate me," I admitted.

In a polite and civilized world, we all pretended such things didn't happen. But threats and issues that couldn't be contained were eliminated. It was the sacrifice that was made to live a *polite and civilized* existence.

Sliding the omelet onto a plate, Daniel kept a steady eye on me as he took a bite. I waited in anticipation. Nothing.

"Magic doesn't work on you, so I don't think you're a good tester," I pointed out.

He took several more bites, then became motionless except for the twist of his mouth. His head snapped up and he looked in the direction of the door and walked toward it, to open it. He mouthed that it was Cory. Shifters were better than cameras.

Cory slid past Daniel, his head lowered in a dramatic maudlin display of regret. Lifting his head slightly to display sorrowful puppy dog eyes, he said, "I didn't think I'd be the reason Asher got involved."

Someone needs acting lessons. He may not have wanted to be the reason, but he was definitely happy with the intervention.

"It's fine. I'm glad to have the assist," I admitted, unburdening him of whatever guilt he may have felt for being the catalyst. Cory stepped back from Daniel who'd invaded his space while handing him the plate with the omelet and a fork.

"Taste this?" he requested.

Cory looked at me for an explanation, but Daniel beat me to it. "It's made from the vegetables she made."

Cory looked at the plate. "Peppers and tomatoes are fruit." Based on Daniel's eyeroll, he didn't appreciate the correction, which only ensured that Cory would do it whenever possible.

Without hesitation he cut a piece and ate it before I could object. He took another bite and handed the plate back to Daniel. Several moments, I watched him. We both did.

"What? Did you expect me to turn into a frog or some-thing?" he asked, moving farther into the living room and eying the rest of the fruit.

I wasn't sure what to expect since I was still reconciling my new abilities and what the real implications were of what I could now do. Daniel finished the remainder of the omelet, gathered his things, and before leaving reminded us he was a phone call away if we needed him.

As soon as he was out of earshot, I handed Cory the sketch Asher made. "I need to check Mephisto's collection to see if he has this."

Cory took it, stared at it for a moment, frowned, and turned it in all four directions. "I have no idea what this is," he admitted.

"Me neither, but I'll need it for the magic removing spell."

I quickly relayed my entire conversation with Asher, him giving me the spell and drawing the object needed for it. Cory made no effort to hide his discomfort about the decla-ration of war.

"Erin, this is a real concern. Asher isn't wrong, Nolan could be a casualty."

"I have no intention of that happening."

"Erin—"

I interrupted. "Cory. I have no intention of that—"

The door blasted open, sending me into the opposite wall and Cory to my right. We crumpled to the ground. Strug-gling to regain my footing, I blinked at the sight of Fabian's lithe buoyant strides toward Cory. Not a hint of any injury. How was he here? With magic? Without injuries? I knew the answer. Elizabeth. Feeling the weight of failure and fear, I forced myself to stand to get to Cory who had stood and was hurling defensive magic at Fabian. Probably still disoriented from his crash, so Fabian dodged it with ease. His swift unre-stricted movements were met with me lobbing an orb at him. It slammed into the protective field. The field erected and

dropped as he moved toward Cory who was rendered ineffective against the field. Fabian mocked me with a contrite
smirk at my efforts to return fire in the microseconds he let
the field break. Anger flared in me each time my counter-
magic smashed into the field and dissipated into the air. At
my next retaliation, Fabian gave me a onceover with slate-
cold eyes before snatching it from me to redirect it at Cory.
The shield dropped and ice pelted Cory in the chest at a
rapid fire, hammering him until he retreated and slumped
against the wall. One of the icicles cut Cory across the face.
Fabian's assault on Cory gave me an advantage and I
slammed magic hard into Fabian's side, sending him
careening to the ground and barely missing falling into the
adligatura circle. He recovered quickly but I was able to shoot
off another round of magic that he dodged, jumping the side
closest to Cory and erecting the protective field.

"Coward," I barked.

Unaffected by the jab, his smirk darkened. Who did I hate
more, Elizabeth for circumventing the spell, or Fabian for
being the beneficiary?

Each time he moved, I hated the reminder of his lack of
injury and debilitation. We kept keen, cautious eyes on each
other. Cory, who kept sucking in breaths, obviously injured
from the ice pelts, maintained a perceptive eye on Fabian,
waiting for the chance.

It came. I unleashed a sphere that clipped Fabian on the
shoulder, unbalancing him, but his lips moved rapidly and a
black cloud moved over Cory who made an ineffective lunge
at Fabian before collapsing to the ground. His eyes shut
completely. I waited for a rise in his chest to show he was
still breathing. It never came. My heart raced. Please, Cory,
breathe. Please breathe. I darted toward him and came to a
stop when Fabian hovered over Cory with a knife at his
throat.

Fabian enclosed himself in the field again. I hated how

deft he was with its use. He continued to be a coward in my book, but I begrudgingly acknowledged the level of skill.

"Will he remain sleeping, or will it be death you choose for him? The decision is yours."

"He doesn't look asleep," I challenged, my hand balled so tight, my nails cut into the palm of my hand. If Cory was dead, so was Fabian.

No breaths came from Cory, but my ragged ones filled the room. Cory's lifeless body still had coloring. But from my position, I couldn't see any other indication of life. Rage tore through me as I scanned his body, searching for signs of life through blurred, furious eyes. Fabian pressed his hand to Cory's chest and after a brisk movement of his lips, a surround sound of life-sounds filled the room: the steady thump of Cory's heartbeat and the slow rhythmic swoosh of breath. It was intrusive and overwhelming to hear at such intensity, and it made me more sympathetic to shifters and vampires.

Fabian's brows rose and I knew he was inquiring if that was enough proof of life. It was doubtful I'd get more. Another invocation and the sound disappeared.

"Sleep or death, Erin?"

"You know the answer, don't be obtuse," I snarled.

"Do I?" he challenged. "I have no idea how you think and your true beliefs. You claim to care for this witch, but do you? Your words don't appear to have value, nor your promises. You agreed that it was your duty to protect the collective, which you violated. You are an elf—"

"A quarter elf." Something that was typically important to them seemed to be suddenly inconsequential.

Contempt furled his lips. "You attacked us without any consideration to your duty or any thought of how we'd respond to such betrayal. Surely you were aware that your witch could be the cost?"

I returned his glare. "What did you think *your* betrayal would cost? Do you believe it should have gone unchecked?"

His glower deepened and the glare he'd fixed on me sharpened. "Shall the witch sleep or die, Erin?"

"Sleep," I pushed out through clenched teeth.

He stood, straightening his shoulder. He directed his full attention to me, but I couldn't keep mine from going to Cory.

"That's not a typical sleeping spell." *Not one I'd seen.* Cory seemed to be in a state closer to death than sleep and I didn't want him that way too long.

"You've only had the use of inferior magic. Of course it will look different. If you hadn't gone rogue, you could have learned so much from me."

"With that narrative, I'm sure you do see yourself as the victim. You threatened my sister and sent Mephisto and the Huntsmen away. You were the first to break your promise, and now you're angry because I retaliated? What about your duty to me?"

His smirk reached his eyes, darkening them. "The collective. You have an obligation to the elves. When you failed to do so, I did what was necessary. Instead of appreciation—" He frowned, I assumed recalling my earlier attack. "You chose violence against me."

One I was ready to finish. His eyes slid to my fist balled at my side, the only thing helping with restraint. Spells cycled through my mind; I wanted the deadliest for him. But without a complementing magical object, there weren't any deadly spells.

"Can you agree to a truce?" he asked.

No, I didn't want a truce with him. I wanted to hurt him. Kill him. Do violent things to him and force him to tell me how he circumvented my spell. I wanted violence. Untethered violence. I didn't want civility, but it was what was needed right then. Reining in my emotions, I took several measured breaths. Nodding, I was unable to put words to his request because it was a lie.

I'd listen to him and the moment I had an opening to retaliate, I planned to do just that.

"That was quite an efficient spell you used on me. Elizabeth and the others had no way of countering it." His smirk reached his eyes. "Elizabeth's failure was unexpected." His admission was tinged with a cool disappointment. "Finding a way to undo it challenged my skills in ways I never expected. Left magicless, I had to rely on Elizabeth to perform the spell." That earned me a scathing glare.

He did it! Fabian had killed a demon by making him human and aging him to death. I should never underestimate his abilities. I wouldn't make that mistake again.

"I'm intrigued by the many ways you challenge me."

I'm intrigued by the many ways I want to punish you. Although I managed to keep the comment to myself, I was unable to keep it from my expression.

He made a sound at whatever he saw on my face before being pulled into his thoughts, his gaze dropping to the floor. When he looked back up at me, his eyes were assessing and full of speculation. "I'm assuming you had a way to undo the spell, or did you plan to leave me in that state forever?"

I nodded.

He grunted. "Of course you did." His tongue moistened his lips as he inched closer to me. His covetous interest intensified, flattening the lines of his smile. The effort he put into softening his eyes wasn't lost on me, but I saw the deception. "Should we share notes?" he asked. On full display were Fabian's abilities, which had proven to be better than Elizabeth's. Curiosity was getting the best of me. I wanted to learn his strengths and his weakness. Erroneously, I'd believed spell-weaving abilities and limited magic knowledge was the reason for his interest in Elizabeth.

"Share," I urged.

A shadowy smirk overtook his face. "Of course I'll share. But only if you agree to give me the spell you used to invoke it?" There was no way in hell I planned to share that information with him. Me acquiring the information from Benton wasn't something I wanted to share, either. Fabian was cynical and thorough enough that he wouldn't accept a made-up spell without testing it. I had the same apprehension about him.

He didn't have the original spell to reverse engineer it or do a reversal, so his spell weaving was more impressive than I'd ever admit to him. There was a great deal I could learn from Fabian, but it wasn't worth the sacrifice it would entail.

His smirk deepened. "The lack of trust between us will be our defeat, won't it?" he acknowledged.

"You set the foundation for that. I can't trust you. I won't trust you."

With a look of consideration, he nodded. "A sacrifice must be made to earn it," he admitted. I watched him carefully as his moments of silence became a stretch of deliberation.

"You and Elizabeth will never be allies," he pointed out softly. "She is quite talented and knowledgeable, but I see something in you that I don't in her. You're not driven by thirst for power, are you?"

"I'm not driven by it, but you are."

He shook his head. Finally sheathed the knife and held his hand up in placation. "I see how you'd believe that. You know of our history and your mother's role in our near extinction. My desire to prevent true extinction makes me seem like a monster, I see that, but perhaps I can get you to see things through my eyes. Can you be openminded enough to listen?"

I inched closer, taking in his gentle look of repentance and the way his body relaxed at my approach as if it was a surrender.

"Go ahead," I urged.

"I broke the oath you had with the demon, didn't I?" he reminded me.

"Yes, through deception and the use of my blood. That was something I should have known beforehand. Instead, you tricked me and the demon."

"Perhaps. But I understand that there always needs to be someone willing to bear the burden of cruelty and immorality in order to give the people they care about peace. To protect them from such things. You saw that as an act of malice when it was quite the opposite. I'd be foolish not to admit that I've underestimated what you could bring to the collective. I made a mistake in my value assessment."

The BS is quite high here. I remained silent as he slathered on the compost with the delusion that I was naïve enough to fall for it.

"What assessment of value did you underestimate?"

"Yours. My most important goal should have been to protect you at all costs, even from Elizabeth. I should have held your friends and family in the same regard as you assign to them. I'm willing to do that now."

He studied me, waiting for me to speak. I had to temper my anger and disgust with his clear attempt to manipulate me, and the little effort he put into it was fucking insulting. Was I supposed to bend to his gentle tone, fake displays of self-awareness, and platitudes? I fought the urge to see how punchable the defined lines of his face were.

"And what will that newfound position among the elves be? What will it require of me?"

"Nothing. No sacrifices from you, but from me. Elizabeth. If I must choose between you two, I choose you."

My mouth gaped and a fresh wave of disgust moved through me. I stared at him with wide-eyed shock and abhorrence and not with the sense of awe and flattery he apparently mistook it for. Fabian was far more ruthless than even I'd suspected. Snapping my mouth closed, I sucked in a breath and swallowed my insult, letting a small smile feather over my lips. My effort was convincing because he returned it.

"The others won't see this as betrayal?" I asked.

After moments of contemplative silence, he spoke in a warm, honeyed tone. "You may not have taken the oath you made to protect us seriously, but the others did. I've been charged with our safety and our transition to living among the others who have magic. Our ability to remain efficient in our protection is my priority. We will not become prey and complicit in our demise as the other elves were. Hard decisions must be made. They won't see it as betrayal but rather as a necessary evil."

Despite my efforts, some of my emotions showed, pulling a frown from him.

"For someone as close to the shifter pack as you are, I'm surprised you still possess such naiveté. Alphas do whatever is necessary to protect their pack. I've seen it firsthand and have heard countless stories of their ruthless commitment to that. Do you think that their pack members look at them as betrayers?"

He'd inched even closer during my plaintive silence. I appeared relaxed and fully engaged in the conversation. It made his posture relax along with his tensed expression. His head canted as if he was studying my acceptance. Shooting furtive glances at the knife sheathed at his waist, I assessed for any vulnerabilities I could exploit. I stiffened when his finger grazed over my hand and inched to the pulse of it. A gentle, entreating touch that prickled my skin. The warmth in his eyes slithered over my skin. I stepped back a few inches. He extended a bashful smile that invited understanding.

What was he imploring me to understand? That he was a seedy, corrupt, manipulative piece of garbage? I understood that well.

"Erin, please answer me? Do you think that their pack look at them as betrayers?" Fabian was intentionally conflating two different things. I couldn't imagine Asher or his pack betraying one another for any reason. The shifters did it for protection; Fabian was doing this for power. It was not the same. He moistened his lips as he waited for an answer. Every ounce of brash cruelty had disappeared, and if I didn't know better, I would have been fooled by the warmth of his expression, his body language, and the gentle timbre of his voice. Instead, I saw him for the smarmy master manipulator he was.

Avoiding his question because I couldn't answer it without calling him out on his trite BS, I posed my own. "Am I part of that necessary evil? Surely choosing Malific's daughter over Elizabeth may be of some concern?"

"Not at all. There's something quite symbolic about Malific nearly making us extinct and her daughter being the reason we become a force among others." His voice softened. "For that reason, I ask you to understand that I'm making the sacrifice of Elizabeth. Can you make one that's less costly but just as significant? Will you leave the Veil closed? Only then can we truly flourish."

The very idea sent a pang through me. I missed Mephisto, and Fabian asking me to stop trying to reopen the Veil was too much. Even if I was optimistic or naïve enough to agree to his proposal, I couldn't agree to that. His expectant look just flamed my anger because he was the reason Mephisto was gone. He took a part of my life away that I hadn't gotten to fully explore. I felt bereft.

"Leave Mephisto and the Huntsmen trapped?"

He shook his head. "Leave them where they belong. There are no more elves in the Veil. The Huntsmen are there with complete power. Happy in *their way*."

"Here, you will live with complete power," I added.

"*We*. Erin, you know what the Huntsmen are capable of. Is it wrong for me to want the comfort of safety?"

"They lived here without bothering anyone. Why do you think that would change?"

"History."

A chill ran through me when I looked over at Cory's motionless body. If Fabian hadn't allowed me to hear his vitals, there was no way I'd think he was alive. "How did I hear his respiration and heartbeat?"

"A spell. I will give it to you." Another attempt to manipulate me. He disclosed the spell and I performed it and quickly became overwhelmed by all the sounds around me. Once I homed in on Cory's vitals and felt comfortable they were normal, I ended the spell.

"You know a great deal of magic, but there is still more I can teach you. We can help each other and improve the skills of the others," he urged. "We could be a team."

He turned to look at Cory. A dark cast fell over his face that he quickly removed, returning to the faux-genteel smile that made me despise him even more. "Cory and Madison will be held in the same regard as we hold you."

"I'll pass on your regards." I jerked his knife from the sheath and slashed at his throat. His response was quick but not enough to ward off the shallow cut across his neck. He vanished, reappearing just a few feet from the door but outside the parameter of the *adligatura* sigils that I'd managed to preserve even with Cory and Daniel passing over it. Fabian slid his foot over it, breaking the seal, while he wiped at the trail of blood running down his neck. His lips trembled with anger. A dangerous, cold expression was in full force. And if looks could kill, I would have died a thousand times.

"You've made your decision and I intend to make it one you regret. I offered our alliance freely, now you will beg for mercy." He was gone before I could respond.

CHAPTER 11

I ran to Cory and attempted to undo the sleep spell. It took several variations of a reversal spell before he awoke. Sluggish and lethargic, he remained on the floor, his back resting against the sofa. Skin pallid and cold.

"Right now, you and Nolan are the only elves I like and I fucking hate Fabian," he grumbled after a few minutes of rest as I explained everything that transpired between me and Fabian. His disgust and anger were palpable, viewing Fabian's willingness to betray Elizabeth with the same reluctance and animosity I felt. Fabian could not be trusted.

It took nearly an hour before Cory and his magic had completely recovered. Making sure he hadn't suffered any lingering effects, he spent another hour moving objects around the room, erecting wards that mirrored the appearance of my living, and aggressively smashing pillows and soft objects into the wall. I suspected he wished it was the dubious elf visitor who'd bespelled him that he was sending careening into the wall.

"It's too bad you didn't kill him." Anger reverberated in his voice like a growl.

"I tried," I admitted. The shame for our true dark desires went unconfronted because our priority was to find the necessary object to remove the elves' illusion.

On the drive to Mephisto's house to search for the object in Asher's sketch, I made a mental list of any other people who might have it.

Cory kept rotating the picture, squinting at it. "I like that this picture is a complete and total mess," he admitted when I drove up the driveway.

"What?" I choked on the laughter.

"Let's admit it. Sometimes it's annoying that Asher's a little too… He seems too perfect."

"Perfect? Arrogant, domineering, criminally inclined, ruthless—"

"Is he really ruthless?" Cory interjected. "He literally tells people exactly what he's going to do. Shamelessly. *Hey, I'm about to break this law to protect my pack. You can try to do some-thing about it if you want. I applaud any effort you make to do so.*"

"The level of confidence in his wrongdoing is not an attribute. It's pure arrogance and self-entitlement."

Cory's mouth twisted as he considered. "Maybe. I think dating Alex is making me have sympathy for the devil," he admitted. "His admiration of Asher is rubbing off on me."

"He's very capable and his abilities are why I might be able to succeed. I need to *always* be clearheaded with the people I deal with. I know what Asher is capable of and right now, I'm on the right side of it. And reaping its advantages. But if I'm ever on the other side of it, he would be the ulti-mate problem. I can't forget that."

"The same with Landon," Cory reminded me. I might have attempted to dismiss Landon's threat, but Cory hadn't. I gave him a look. He held up his hand in protest. "Okay, I'll drop it for now. But, Erin, ignoring his threat won't make it go away."

"I know. I'll figure out a way to fix it. One problem at a time," I said, letting us into the house and heading straight to the room with the magical objects.

After an hour of searching, we had everything that resembled the picture stored in a tote. Asher would have to identify the right one. I'd considered allowing him into the room, but it felt like a violation of Mephisto and his privacy. It felt invasive into my world with Mephisto.

"What is she doing here?" Cory asked when we saw Wendy walking back and forth in front of my door, periodically knocking as if there was a back door I could magically enter the apartment from. In the few minutes we watched, her knocks became more frantic and persistent. She had knocked more than a dozen times by the time we got out of the car and approached her.

Without her theatrical cloak and air of arrogance she didn't quite look herself. She was dressed in a simple puffy shirt with a coverlet neckline and a pair of flat-front cerulean blue ankle pants, and she looked like a woman on the edge. At our arrival, she pushed her dark round glasses up her nub nose. She blew out an exasperated breath and scraped away her shaggy dark hair. Her face was flushed.

Wendy's anxiety-ridden expression muted when she caught sight of the bag Cory had shouldered. She rose slightly to her toes to get a peek at the small opening left from the overstuffed bag. The woman was a ride-or-die opportunist.

Cory made sure the magical objects were concealed.

Wendy might have looked innocuous at my door, but I wasn't going to forget the self-proclaimed "Maestro of Magic" practiced dark magic while brokering deals with demons, had blackmailed Landon for several million dollars, and had attempted to do the same with Asher. She was a menace.

"Wendy, did you need something?" I asked, redirecting her attention to me, opening my door to let her in although she shook her head to decline. Cory slid in to remove the distraction of the tote.

"I need you to come to my house," she rushed out in a low, panicked whisper, casting anxious glances around as if she suspected she was followed.

"Why? What's wrong?"

"I have to show you." She started toward the parking lot and had gone several feet before realizing I wasn't following her. We didn't have a relationship where I followed without question. "Erin," she snapped, her voice blade sharp. "I helped you out of the demon realm without question."

That was an interesting play on the truth. She helped me after a series of pleas from me begging for assistance, and she had made it blatantly apparent that she expected a favor, maybe even *favors*, in return. A powerful avaricious witch with questionable ethics wasn't someone I was going to follow blindly.

"What is it?" I repeated, my tone rigid enough to leave no room for her to deny my request or think it was negotiable.

"It's not something I can describe. You have to see it." There was a long pause. She looked around, frowned at the door. You're not expecting the fae, are you?" she asked, inquiring about Madison. The tinge of reluctance in her voice made it apparent she was hoping I wasn't.

My eyes narrowed on her. She moved quickly toward me, doing another full sweep of the area. "You have to give me your word that you'll leave her out of this. Under no circumstances can she be involved."

"Does this have to do with the fae? Is it illegal, Wendy?"

"I need your word."

I took this as a yes. Whatever the situation, it was now a determination of how bad it was. My mind was awash with all the things this constant practitioner of dark magic could get me involved in.

Great. As if I don't have enough problems.

"I can only promise that I'll do my best to keep her out of this, but my help satisfies all debts I have to you. You will never come to me again for help. We will be done."

"No, you have to fix this. Then the debt is satisfied," she said. "And everything—and I do mean everything—that day will be dismissed." Her subtle threat hadn't gone unnoticed. Despite not wanting the world to know what I was, I knew the discovery was inevitable. But I wanted it to be on my terms.

"Your request has been heard." The coolness in my voice served as a warning. I didn't need to collect more enemies, but I wasn't going to be blackmailed by her or allow the information she possessed to be a cudgel that she wielded freely to get her way. "I'll follow you." I stuck my head into the apartment to invite Cory along.

"You can leave Cory where he is, too," she demanded before breezing to her car.

For someone who needed help, she was pretty damn selective about where it came from. Her desire to keep him out made me believe that a witch wouldn't approve of the situation, either.

Wendy couldn't be described as anything less than needlessly dramatic. And once we entered her home, she adorned her accoutrement of a cloak. It floated behind her with balletic theatrical movement as she guided me through her tidy two-story home. Magic, tannin, salt, and verbena coated the air. I followed her up the stairs. She flung open the door to what I assumed was her guest room and my eyes widened at the woman resting peacefully on the bed.

"Why the hell is Adalia in your home..." My words trailed

as I stepped closer because I couldn't detect a rise in Adalia's chest to determine if she was breathing. There wasn't any movement as the queen of the Seelie court, Madison's court, lay motionless in Wendy's house.

"What the fuck, Wendy?!"

"I awoke three days ago to find her like this," she rushed out in a tremulous voice. Her cool veneer gone, panic and fear were etched on every inch of her face. It appeared that all the restraint she'd used to keep her emotions at bay had been ripped to shreds. "I don't usually keep my doors open, so whoever left her like this broke through my wards and placed her here undetected." She was nearly incoherent.

I nudged the queen. She didn't move. But I could see small incremental movements of her chest, and her pulse was weak but present. She was alive.

"She's in some type of sleep state. I've tried every spell I can think of to break it, but it's not witch's magic." She started to pace the floor. "I even used enhanced magic." Her evasive way of saying dark demon magic. I had to figure out a way to restrict her from doing that anymore. She needed to be reported. Nothing good could come from that practice. If the Veil could be closed permanently, then the demon realm could, too.

Looking at Adalia's comalike condition made me think of the *Medul* spell I'd seen in the Mystic Souls. There were two known books; Asher had one and I had the other. How did someone get hold of the spell?

"I've used everything that I had access to. Everything." She pointed to broken aqua-color glass. "It has the ability to mimic most magic. I thought it could undo it." Her voice had risen an octave in panic. "It was destroyed during the invocation, preventing me completing the spell. There's a protection spell on her that destroys anything used against it." She gently took the queen's arm, turned it over to reveal the forearm, and did a spell. An interlocking crescent symbol lit up and then disappeared.

That was definitely a protection spell.

"What do you need from me?"

"I know they've been looking for her. Take her. Tell Neri she was found in your home. I cannot be linked to her disappearance. This would be the beginning of a war with mutual destruction and my coven would disavow me and leave me without any support or defense. The fae will kill me."

It was apparent I was missing many parts of this story. The fae weren't the nicest people to deal with—they had an arrogance problem that rivaled the vampires'. But they weren't unreasonable, either. Most of the time. "I'm sure if you told Neri what happened, he'd be understanding as long as you offered your help."

Vigorously shaking her head, her lips pinched tight, making them disappear as color drained from her face. It was discomforting seeing this side of her; she was usually so haughty and obnoxiously self-assured.

I glanced at Adalia. Even in sleep she displayed a regal beauty.

"I can't be linked to this in any way." When Wendy's hands covered her face, I expected tears. She only let out a long desperate sob. I pulled her hands away and locked eyes with her.

"Wendy, if I'm going to help you, I need to know everything."

She beckoned me out the door and I followed her downstairs to the kitchen where she shrugged off her cloak. Her shrewd mien had sloughed off and in her current state, it was doubtful it would make a reappearance.

"Tea?" she asked, slipping into her English accent that seemed to come and go whenever the mood hit her. I nodded and watched in silence as she took out the loose leaves and steeped the green tea.

When she joined me at the table with the tea, I could see the editing of the story in her features. She took a sip then looked out the sliding window at the garden as if I'd be so fascinated by it that I'd forget the question.

"Wendy?" I prompted.

"A Levox came into my possession," she said. I'd heard of them; they worked like a magic diffuser and responded poorly to strong magic. It was more like a party favor of magic. The last time I saw one in use, a witch was teaching a magic class for humans and used it to convince the attendants they were performing magic as they used their fingertips to make swirls of glitter-covered words in the air. Cute but harmless. As far as magical objects were concerned it was rather innocuous. Levox were never on the restricted list of magical objects and were so fragile most magic rendered them unusable.

I shrugged.

"They aren't really anything to fear, but I found a spell that maintained its integrity and would allow me to infuse iron in the air. No other element, I tried them all."

I could feel my lips dragging into a judgmental frown. She averted her eyes.

"You just happen upon the spell or did you spend a great deal of time coming up with it?"

"Magic intrigues me. I'm good at spell weaving and I have extensive knowledge of it. I will not allow you to shame me for it."

"I'm not shaming you for your curiosity, just pointing out that in the past you've used it to cause harm." She was also greedy, manipulative, and treated blackmail like it was a personality quirk. "What does this have to do with the fae, Wendy?

She pressed her lips together. I skewered her with a glare demanding a response.

"Iron restricts their magic. It seemed like something the

fae wouldn't want me to have possession of, so I gave them the option to buy it from me."

I cursed under my breath. "How much?"

"Four million," she whispered then rushed out in defense, "they can afford it."

"You didn't learn anything from dealing with Landon? You nearly died, you realize that? He was going to murder you. Why are you like this?"

"The fae are more civil than the vampires and they have the money."

I had to unlock my jaw to speak and ball my hands into my lap. Violence shouldn't be the answer, but giving Wendy a good smack seemed like the answer to something.

"They refused and went on a search for all the Levox. There aren't that many. I believe there are three others. I have the fourth. It's not just the object but the need as well." She took a sip from her cup. "They wouldn't pay it. Not even negotiate a lower price. And"—she waved her hand toward the stairway leading to the guestroom—"were absolutely unreasonable, expecting me to hand over the spell and never speak of it again."

"Have you not heard of basic common courtesy?" I stood, leaning into her. "What you did was absolutely abhorrent."

"Abhorrent," she snapped. "That's extreme. The amount I requested wasn't unreasonable. The fae can afford it."

I scoffed. "It won't just affect the seelie, it would be all fae."

"They're the strongest and the court is in a position to meet my requests."

"Requests? That wasn't a request. It was extortion." I stood and walked around the room to expend the energy pulsing through me. Shoving my hand through my hair, heat radiated from my scalp. Anger pulsed through me from dealing with another person who had placed Madison at risk.

"I'm not assuming responsibility of Adalia."

"I can't break whatever spell has her in that state. I've tried everything. You have far more resources than I do. And"—her face flushed—"Mephisto isn't returning my calls."

"Why are you trying to get in contact with him?"

"He's a collector and quite connected. I was going to barter the spell for assistance."

It was easy to read between the lines on that BS. When the fae declined to pay her, she was going to approach Mephisto for it as she had with the Amber Crocus, which could be used to kill vampires and which she created to blackmail them. Refusing to give her any room for deception, I called her out on it.

The smidgen of shame and remorse she'd shown for a fleeting moment was gone, replaced with indignation. "I'm talented and knowledgeable. Why shouldn't I profit off it?" she spat out.

"No one said you shouldn't. But I'm going to speculate that you didn't come up with the spell alone. You've been practicing dark magic. So you're not that talented, you're reckless and immoral."

"Yet I wasn't the one trapped in the demon realm," she shot back, standing up and getting in my face to drive in her accusation.

"Good luck with this situation," I said, stepping aside.

"Neri is going to kill me if I'm linked to whatever is going on with Adalia."

"Most certainly. It will be torturous, too. He might try to find a way to bring you back just so he can have the pleasure of killing you again. If she dies your coven will have a war to contend with. You coven may win, but you will certainly be banished from it."

I had other things to worry about than a witch with the ethics of a rogue mafioso constantly practicing dark magic.

"Please," she said when I opened the door. Holding my

hand tight, she lowered her head in a submissive gesture that made me uncomfortable. Wendy was desperate. Desperate people did thoughtless things to save themselves. I didn't want her desperation to lead to her selling or bartering the spell to whomever could help her. Nothing good could come from that.

"I'll help, but it will cost you. I owe you for releasing me from the demon realm, but what this will entail more than satisfies any debt I have to you. Not only will this satisfy the debt, but I want the spell and a blood oath that you won't make any other spells that would harm any of the other denizens. You won't summon any more demons for any reason. You will only practice natural magic."

"How I practice my magic isn't up to you to dictate." The remaining sliver of her arrogance and self-importance indignation showed.

"Ordinarily I wouldn't give a damn about it, but you're a menace and you're unscrupulous—and this is coming from someone who's worked with the shadiest of shady. And you're still pretty damn terrible even among them."

The insult didn't land. Like most people, it only hurts if you care about the source. Wendy probably didn't like me any more than I liked her. I was just a means to an end.

Her lips pressed into a tight thin line as she fought back everything she wanted to say to me. It raged in her eyes and sparked with menace.

"Are we in agreement?" I prompted.

Giving me a considering look, she contemplated my conditions so long, I thought she'd decline and take her chances. If it were the other fae, she might have risked it. But Neri's adoration for Adalia was well known. I was surprised that he wasn't setting the city ablaze looking for her.

Her head barely bent into her nod of acceptance.

"I'll need a video of the markings and she'll need to stay here. Cory and I will return for you to sign the oath."

Irritation flooded her eyes as she sneered at me. Did she think I'd start working on this without a signed oath? She wasn't a person I'd ever enter a handshake agreement with.

It was an extreme agreement, and I didn't feel good about exploiting her in her time of need, but the direction she was heading, I was saving her future problems. And maybe her life.

CHAPTER 12

On my way out of Wendy's home, I looked at my phone to check the numerous notifications of ignored texts and calls. There was even a voicemail notification. All from Madison. Short concise texts: "Where are you?" "What's going on?" "Call me!" "I can't stop this situation." What situation? Cryptic messages sent clearly in a rush or under the scrutiny of watchful eyes. Stopped at Wendy's door, my body ran cold at Madison's distressed voice warning me that Neri believed I was involved in Adalia's abduction and that the fae were coming for me. So many questions ran through my mind of how I was implicated. Had Wendy done it to prevent herself being a suspect? I wouldn't put it past her.

Before I could return Madison's call, I heard her. "Wendy Hoffster and Erin Jensen, I need to speak with you." Madison's professionally stern voice accompanied the pounding at the door. Grumbling a curse under my breath, my only thought was to attempt to Wynd with Adalia. Despite the uncertainty of it working, I started to head toward the guest room.

"Erin, come to the door." The pleading in Madison's voice the subtle request not to make things worse.

"Wendy, open the door or it's coming down," Madison commanded when the door remained unanswered.

Wendy looked at me for an answer, which made me realize she hadn't implicated me. She was just as confused as I was. My eyes darted to the back exit, but I could see a shadowy figure through the curtains. Escaping wasn't an option.

"Answer it," I mouthed.

She moved at a turtle's pace as the coloring drained from her face when Neri's voice demanded the door be brought down. It was said with such tangible cold cruelty, there was no room for any doubt of his awareness of Adelia's presence in the home.

Wendy dragged open the door a crack, giving me an obstructed glimpse of Madison and Neri. He pushed the door open farther and fae uniformed guards flooded into the room. One aimed an arrow at Wendy's chest; another aimed one at my head. Neri's dagger-sharp gaze moved over me then to Wendy. His body tremored with poorly restrained violence. Madison and members of the Supernatural Task Force spilled in after, commanding the fae guards to lower their weapons. They didn't comply.

Magic and violent tension inundated the room.

"The request won't be made again," Madison said to the guards. Neri nodded and they lowered their weapons, allowing the STF to take lead. The STF magic wielders' hands were posed to use magic to subdue me. Two Supernatural Task Force shifters stood erect, undoubtedly struggling between any commands they were given by Asher and their duties as STF officers. Worn heavily in their expressions was the task of dealing with Neri's team, who were teeming to unleash their wrath solely at me, and the STF objective to find whomever had abducted Adalia, and probably Asher's request to protect me at all cost. I didn't envy their situation.

"Where is she?" Neri demanded through clenched teeth.

"Who?" Wendy responded with a level of innocence that would have fooled me if I didn't know the truth. I kept my eyes trained on the people in front of me to keep me from staring at her with awed incredulity. Wendy possessed a sociopathic ability to lie. She was a bigger menace than I'd suspected.

"Neri, you cannot question her. You want this done the right way?"

Madison cringed when he directed his ire at her. "Erin and this witch are involved with Adalia's abduction. You've protected Erin too many times. When she's involved, how can I trust that you have given this your full effort? It was my sources who found Adalia's location."

"I was happy to help," Elizabeth's cloying voice offered as she glided into the room. My hands clenched so tight my nails dug painfully into my palms. My stomach curled at the reverential bow she extended to Neri. Little did he know just days ago she'd helped Fabian use the threat of the faes' death as a bargaining tool.

"You all may have denied me, but I'd never do the same to you. The safety of the fae will always be important to me. And that of the queen, the most important. Search for the queen. She is in grave danger here with them," Elizabeth said, frowning at us. She pointed at Wendy. "This one barters with demons, against the rules of her coven. Turned her back on their natural practices. She's a dark practitioner. Her coven has been made aware of this, and of her involvement with Erin. I do believe she's made a pact with a demon for the queen's body. He only needs the body." She waved a dismissive hand in my direction. "I suspect this one will take the magic."

This looked bad. Terrible. *Fuck.*

"Can we search your apartment?" Very few STF laws mirrored the human laws, but this was one. Unlawful searches weren't permitted, but denying a request reeked of guilt.

"I want my coven Elder," Wendy said.

"Your Elder was contacted before we arrived," provided one of the witches with the STF before his eyes cast downward. "She has declined involvement."

Wendy sucked in a ragged breath. She would be without a coven and would not be afforded the same courtesies.

Neri grumbled a sound of contempt and pushed his way past me and Wendy, followed by his guards. "I don't have to abide by these ridiculous rules. If Adalia is here, I will grant you permission to plead for your lives."

They dispersed, going through the rooms with precision despite Madison's objections. Her eyes were emotive, showing the various scenarios that ran through her mind and how each would affect me, her career, and the balance of the supernatural community. When her gaze finally moved in my direction, I held it and shook my head slightly, hoping to get my message across: *Don't ruin your career and your standing with Neri for me.*

"Do we have your permission to search?" Madison asked again.

Defeat had placed a sour look on Wendy's face and there were no traces of the woman I'd interacted with before. "I don't care," she managed in a low hoarse voice.

Madison and her team started their search behind the guards, and the house filled with noise and chaos. Neri returned with Adalia in his arms and an explosion of curses and threats of violence.

"What is wrong with her?" he demanded, gently placing Adalia's motionless body on the sofa.

"I don't know," Wendy answered in a small voice, draining all the animosity and anger out of me. I couldn't kick her while she was down, and we were in this together, linked in a setup that preyed on our history.

"It's a spell to siphon her magic to be used by someone else," Elizabeth offered, navigating around everyone. "May I?" Still showing a faux reverence she didn't possess for the fae, she requested permission to touch Adalia.

She invoked a spell which revealed the marking that had been displayed earlier. "The person siphoning her magic will have the same. Erin, I need your arm."

I extended my arm without hesitation, confident I'd prove my innocence. After invoking the spell, a frigid breeze twined around my wrist revealing an identical mark. It was a familiar tinge that I recalled feeling at Fabian's touch. The bashful look he'd given was a misdirect. It was never about imploring understanding but setting a trap in the event I rejected him. Elizabeth had no idea that this treacherous plan was a result of me declining his offer to sever ties with her. Literally.

"I think I can undo it. May I try?" Of course she could undo it because she was the architect of the spell.

Elizabeth lowered herself to the floor and made a production of asking for various ingredients. Between what Wendy possessed in her home and what the mage and witches had, she had her supplies. Moments later the invocation of the spell caused golden embers to unravel from Adalia's body as if she was being unbound. The sigils pulled from my arm and joined the marking from Adalia's, winding around each other and disappearing. She stirred but didn't wake. Her breathing increased noticeably, and her wan appearance improved, giving hints of her arresting beauty and vibrance.

"I had nothing to do—" Wendy's defense was cut off by Neri lunging at her, pinning her against the wall and pressing a knife to her throat. A rivulet of blood streamed down her neck from the tip pressing into her skin.

"Were you going to give my queen to a demon?" he growled.

"No. Not at all. I give you my word."

"Your word means nothing," he hissed. He drew the blade back to cause more damage when a shifter moved quickly to grab his arm. "Let go of me, wolf." The venom placed on the *wolf* was wise replacement of whatever vile thing he wanted to call him.

"Neri, if you kill her, you, too, will be arrested. With her Elder no longer involved and her no longer possessing coven affiliation, this cannot be a matter between the coven and court," Madison reminded him. It didn't look as if Neri cared and there was no thought or computations in his eyes. Just wrath. It wouldn't be satisfied with just her death. Mine would be the cost as well. I suspected Madison would also receive some form of punishment and shunning by association.

"Kill her. Kill me next and you'll end up at the Stygian. No way around it and all this would be for nothing. You save your queen only to not be with her," I said.

His eyes snapped in my direction. It didn't matter because our death was priority number one.

"Stop it," Adalia demanded, sitting up. She looked at her attire of a nightgown, then around the room trying to make sense of it, and had a moment of recognition when she saw Elizabeth. I noticed Elizabeth's hands had cuffed around Adalia's arms. I didn't trust her having contact with her in any way.

"Elizabeth, I have questions," Madison said, beckoning her.

Irritation flitted over her expression and with great effort she managed to usher it away. "Of course."

Neri had released Wendy who was gently rubbing her neck and grappling with the turn of events.

"How did you come to be involved in this?" Madison asked.

"You know who I am." Not the half elf/fae nemesis but

the Woman in Black, which was the attire she'd returned to as if aware her role would be part of the investigation. "People come to me when they need help. I don't think you realize how much people fear Erin. She can cause death. She's killed before." She directed her attention to me. "I hope she receives adequate punishment for her actions this time."

"Continue," Madison probed in redirection. "Can you give me the names of the people who sought protection from Erin?"

"I pride myself on being discreet. With the crowd gathering outside and the publicity this will garner, I'm quite sure they will come forward." Of course, with urging from her.

"You have to understand, I'll need those names for verification," Madison said in an attempt to plant a seed of doubt. "I don't have to tell you that when things are sensationalized, as this will be, there will be false claims. I'll need your participation—for the good of the investigation."

Elizabeth's saccharine smile would have been disarming if not for the menace behind it. "Of course." But she didn't offer any names and it was apparent she had no intention of doing so.

"To siphon magic from Adalia, Ms. Jensen would have to possess magic to perform the spell. How did she achieve such a feat without the ability to use magic?" Madison challenged.

Elizabeth shrugged. "Perhaps that is something you should ask her. But you saw the same thing Neri did. She was bound to Adalia, siphoning her magic. Her resourcefulness is astounding. Surely you are aware of this."

"I demand arrests now," Neri said.

I wanted to point out that it was inevitable that Wendy and I were going to be arrested and it had nothing to do with his *mantrum* and bloviated demands.

With a regretful look Madison nodded to the officers. This wasn't her department, and her involvement was only because she was fae and under Neri's request. She'd been promoted out of the investigations department and now headed her own. This was a high-profile case. She would have to adhere strictly to the rules and would have to hand it over to the head of investigations or major crimes. Abduction and magical murder were major crimes.

Damn. I was screwed.

Wendy was placed in iridium handcuffs. Two witches stood next to me, their brows raised in question toward Madison.

"If she was siphoning magic from Adelia, then she shouldn't have magic now," Madison said. A look passed between us. "It is best that we err on the side of caution. Iridium cuffs."

Elizabeth clenched her jaw but couldn't say or do anything to urge them to use Palladium, which based on all accounts in books were used against an extinct group of beings. Why would she suggest such information out of the blue?

She received a well-deserved smirk from me as I was read my rights and hauled away. If necessary, at least I could escape. It was plan D or somewhere along the lines. Living as a fugitive wasn't something I wanted to do.

A crowd of people had gathered, gawking at me for the second time in my life. Neri glared at me as they ushered me toward the car, and Fabian emerged from the throng with a cynical pleasure plastered over his face. I resisted the officer nudging me to get in the car and locked eyes with Neri.

"I didn't do this, but I will find out who did. And I will make them pay." I vowed it to Neri but it was intended for Fabian. My words meant nothing to Neri, who remained unconvinced of my or Wendy's innocence. His revenge was placed on hold until he knew the consequences I'd suffer.

Wendy's impassive look didn't speak of a person who was innocent but one who no longer cared what happened. Fear had to have driven that into her. If we were found guilty, we'd go to the Stygian, a supernatural prison often reserved for those whose crimes could not be pleaded and reduced with the backing of their sect, or who had been denounced by their sect and no longer had their support. In many cases they felt you were irredeemable and wanted nothing more to do with you. Made you the sacrificial lamb for PR or to soothe irate human groups who were upset by a behavior, and proof that supernaturals were held accountable for their crimes. The mages had never claimed me even when the rest of the world thought I was a death mage. Gods and elves were an unknown. I was alone in this. So was Wendy.

I will kill you. The quiet promise showed on my face. Fabian saw it and probably felt my pulsating anger, although it wasn't enough to remove his smirk of satisfaction as I sat in the patrol car. He locked eyes with me as the car started to drive away. I couldn't make out all the words he spoke, but I knew two of them. "Beg" and "Mercy."

Someone would beg for mercy, but it wouldn't be me.

CHAPTER 13

The handcuffs had been traded for an iridium manacle around my arm as I sat across from the lead detective of MMC, Major Magical Crimes, a shifter who could easily detect lies or at the very least discern slight changes in my vitals. He looked to be in his mid-late forties, which wasn't any true indicator of his age. Shifters aged slowly and never really showed their age. Light creases in his fawn-colored skin. Nearly seven feet tall and bulky. Despite the smooth fit of his suit, he seemed like he'd prefer to be in anything else. I knew little of him other than he was a bear shifter, something that couldn't be missed. Bear shifters were rare, tended not to join the Wolf or Lion packs. When the number of a species were small, like Ursidae and Equidae, individuals could be in an ancillary group but often chose not to join. They were sought by the STF because they had no affiliation with a pack.

"This is a courtesy, not an obligation," he reminded Madison when she took a seat next to him. It was more than a courtesy: Madison came in to inform me that my attorney was on the way. I had remained silent until her arrival. Implication stirred in the shifter's voice. The accusations and distrust of the department were starting to have a beleaguering effect. Madison's wary demeanor made it difficult to focus on the shifter interrogating me and not try to comfort her about the situation.

My attention moved to the manacle on my arm. As the shifter fired off the same questions he'd been asking me for the last ten minutes, I answered. He flicked a look in Madison's direction, aware that she was the reason for my compliance. I was careful with my answers.

His deep frown to my responses quickly disappeared, offering nothing readable. He studied me for a few minutes after my third or fourth assertion that I'd been set up. Relaxing back in his chair, his fingers clasped behind his head, sharp caramel-colored eyes homed in on me. "How were you framed, Erin?"

I had no idea and most of the time while I waited in the cell, I'd tried to work it out. Had they used the plant spell? Had Elizabeth been in contact with Adalia and performed the spell on her and days later Fabian on me? How long had they been working on setting me up like this? I wanted answers, too, and I couldn't get them while in jail.

The unanswered questions turned in my head as I debated whether to expose the existence of elves, my relationship with them, and Fabian and Elizabeth's dedication to destroying me. If anything, it would cast reasonable doubt and an alternative suspect.

"I don't know," I admitted. "But I need to find out."

"You plan to play detective?"

"I'll have to if you don't," I shot back and immediately regretted it when he looked at me like I was a fish and he was ready to shift to his grizzly.

"This will be further investigated," Madison said, earning a sneer from the shifter.

"Of course it will be further investigated, but the evidence we have doesn't seem to be in your favor. That doesn't matter to you, does it? You live by a different set of rules." His words sharpened to a searing edge. His lips pressed into a tight line as he gave me an appraising look. "I've received several calls from Asher." That didn't work to my advantage at all. "Do you feel that his unfounded entitlement extends to you?"

"Redirect. Her relationship with the pack doesn't have any bearing on why she's here," Madison said.

His low rumble pierced the silence. "I don't feel any sense of entitlement," I said. "I do want justice. Don't you want the right person to be found?"

"Ah," he mumbled. "Of course, we don't have the right person, do we?"

"You don't perform spells so you're not aware of what some practitioners are capable of," I said.

He nodded slowly. "Yes, but I've interviewed"—he made a show of looking down at his notepad—"Elizabeth and she seems to believe you borrowed magic to perform the spell. Have you come in contact with Adalia recently?"

"No."

He looked down at his notes again and frowned as if my response contradicted his information. The questioning continued until Van, the shifters' attorney, arrived and stopped all further questioning and told me how inadvisable it was to say anything.

Van stayed in step with me as we made our way to his car after my bail hearing. "Your bail's higher than anything I've had to secure for any of my clients. I guess innocent until proven guilty means nothing to them."

The high bail was undoubtedly motivated by the past incident and the influence Neri carried. I was so focused on how indebted I was to the pack, it startled me when Van's hand pressed into my back and guided me toward officers standing outside. They kept a suspicious eye on us as he pulled out his phone and made a call.

"The driver will meet us here," he told me. Then I followed his finger as he pointed at the two frowning fae standing in the direction we'd come from.

This was going to be my life until I proved I wasn't involved with Adalia's abduction. If they believed the story of me siphoning her magic to deliver her to a demon—they'd want revenge.

I met their cold stare. If they expected me to cower, they were wrong.

"Don't challenge them," Van whispered. Human, most of his dealings were with shifters. It was never a good idea to hold the gaze of a shifter, but with fae, it was a show of resoluteness. Honesty.

"They won't take it as a challenge. I'm not guilty."

"Or they'll see it as you being comfortable in your crime. The only thing that will help this situation is actual proof," Van said, jerking his head toward the car that had driven up.

My door swung open before I could get my keys. Heading into my apartment, I stepped over the large wolf resting at my door. "Hi, Daniel," I greeted him.

"Madison filled me in on most of it," Cory told me, stepping aside to let me and the wolf in. "She's trying to prove it was Elizabeth."

"And Fabian," I added, supplying my suspicions about his part in it.

Daniel trotted past with the small bag in his mouth that appeared diminutive next to the huge creature. He scurried off to the bathroom, taking heed of the scolding I'd given him the previous day about changing in the living room and exposing his giblets to everyone. When he emerged in a wrinkled t-shirt and sweats, he was wearing a sympathetic smile.

"You just can't catch a break, can you?" he said.

"It looks that way," I admitted. But when fate refused to give me one, I decided to make it.

"I need to talk to Asher," I told them, looking around for the tote of magical objects we'd removed from Mephisto's collection.

Asher hadn't responded to the two text messages I'd left or my calls, but Daniel had an idea where he could be found. He drove us to a large ranch-style home where one of the cars I'd seen Asher drive was parked in front.

Doors opening before I could announce my arrival with a knock was something I'd never get used to, no matter how many times it happened. In the house, Asher greeted us with a rigid smile and a heavy sigh I was positive was a result of dealing with the home's new occupant. Ms. Harp was seated in a comfortable leather recliner, watching a court show I wasn't familiar with, sipping from a cup that I knew was more parts Kahlua than coffee, and putting a lot of effort into ignoring Dr. Marisol Reyes, a member from another pack working with the Northwest to determine why Ms. Harp responded to the full moon the way she did.

"Are any of these one of the objects Elizabeth used during the spell?" I handed him the tote, splitting my attention between Asher going through the bag and Ms. Harp who seemed especially interested in me as a way to ignore Dr. Reyes.

"I wish I could go home," she told me.

"This is your home," Asher grumbled back.

"I'm being held captive," she complained. Looking around the room, I saw modern rustic décor. Cozy rug, textured cognac-colored sofa that complemented the oyster-colored leather recliner. Built-in bookcases filled with books from the classics to popular fiction. Weathered, unvarnished woods were warm additions. Stone fireplace in the corner added to the relaxing atmosphere. I ran my hands over one of the soft blankets thrown over the sofa. A lot of attention to comfort had been taken in decorating Ms. Harp's new home, down to the oversized television that took up most of the wall in front of the chair, where I suspected Ms. Harp preferred sitting. A table next to the chair held her mug of coffee, which was definitely more Kahlua than coffee, a Kindle, and several books were nearby on an easily reachable shelf.

I'm sure the same level of care and comfort had been extended to the other rooms. The kitchen was tidy. White oak cabinetry, wood beams, expensive appliances, and unique light fixtures left me with the impression that the kitchen was more for style and appearance. Hints of eucalyptus fragranced the air.

Asher sorted through the objects while I made my way toward Ms. Harp.

"Poor captive. Life must be so hard," I teased. She started to make a face, but it fell into something serious. Sitting upright, she met my eyes and studied me for a long time in silence.

"What's wrong, Erin?" The concern and sincerity stunned me. My answer didn't come easily.

"Nothing, it's being handled."

My response was met with a frown, her gaze trailing to Asher reviewing the object from the tote. She remained unconvinced but reached for my hand and touched it. "Where's your friend?" Ms. Harp wasn't a fan of Mephisto although she accepted his presence in my life. She'd warned me against him, but it seemed that was guided by her position as founder, president, and vice president of Team Asher.

"He's go—was taken away from me." It might have just been semantics, but it meant so much to me. He didn't leave on his own volition; he was forced away. She caught the hitch in my voice and offered me a sympathetic smile.

"I have no doubt that you will get him back." I never realized Ms. Harp was the cheerleader I needed. "This look. I don't like it."

I grinned. "I have a look?"

"Yep. I don't like it. Annoying you in this state takes the fun out of it. I don't like it."

"Ah, I see you've attended the Asher school of *I need you safe and happy because it pleases me*," I teased.

"It wasn't any of these," Asher said, interrupting our conversation. Before I could stand, Ms. Harp took my hand and gave it an encouraging squeeze to assuage the disappointment I couldn't keep off my face.

"Without knowing the name of the object, I can't search for it from other sources," I admitted with an exasperated sigh. I sent a picture to Madison, asking if she had any idea what it could be. She responded that she didn't but would consult the others on her team. Asher kept viewing the drawing, a pencil in hand, adding more detail that didn't help with identifying it.

"What's next?" Cory asked, once Asher had moved away to speak with Dr. Reyes, who was kneeling next to Ms. Harp and having a sharp whispered discussion. Asher joined the conversation, his expression displaying the intense shrewdness of a hostage negotiator. Ms. Harp's face was set in its usual defiance. I was positive things weren't going to go his way.

"I'll need to figure out a workaround," I said, scrolling through the notes of the spell that I'd put on my phone, the murmured conversation between the shifters and Ms. Harp's responses a distraction I couldn't quite make out. The words were indecipherable, but if the tone was any indicator, they weren't going to come to an agreement. Occasionally Ms. Harp would raise her voice enough for me to understand the discussion seemed to be about her actively shifting.

"Shifters," I whispered to myself.

"What?" Cory asked. I told him to hold off and called for

Asher. After a quick evaluating look, he gathered it was a discussion that needed privacy and led me through the house to a small office where he waited patiently for me to speak.

"I want to give you the elven magic," I rushed out in a stream of excitement.

Cory and Asher shared a concerned look.

"The object Elizabeth used to give shifters outside the Veil magical immunity simply allowed you and Sherrie the ability to use her magic to affect the same animal family with immunity. It's irrelevant in this situation. You don't need to use the magic. So, operate as a vessel to store the elven magic and store it. Shifters can't use magic. No one would suspect that it's a person storing the magic."

Asher stroked the hairs of the light shadow of beard forming on his jaw, his brow raised and uncertainty in his stance and posture. I didn't blame him.

"You're sure this will work?"

"Magic never has a hundred percent certainty. But I'm sure enough," I admitted.

"What's *sure enough*?" Asher asked after sharing another look with Cory, clearly looking for changes in him.

"What's the worst that could happen if it fails?" I asked. "Nothing. Either it's unsuccessful and the elves keep their magic, or it's successful and I get my father, clear my name with the fae, and serve Elizabeth and Fabian with the justice they deserve."

"Okay," Asher said.

I blinked at how quickly he agreed. Perhaps it was the desperation in my voice that was the reason for his speedy response. Nevertheless, I was grateful for it.

CHAPTER 14

We didn't have the luxury of time and the element of surprise was my most useful weapon. We gathered a mile from the parameters of the Havenage. The members of the pack split evenly between human and shifter form and were accompanied by the peculiar hyperactive fox who'd shown up at my home previously.

"He's a great scout. No one really questions a fox traipsing around, and we can hear his bark," Asher offered in answer to my raised brow. As with all shifters, the fox was larger than its natural counterpart but looked out of place surrounded by massive wolves.

"Once you can see the Havenage, find my father, please. I'll go after Elizabeth and—"

"I have Fabian," Cory interjected. He'd never liked Fabian and all Fabian's preceding actions had only reinforced the disdain.

Asher sent the fox away to scout. Moving closer to Asher to perform the spell, I could feel the weight of Dr. Reyes's disapproval. Her interaction with Asher and the pack led me to believe her stay wasn't going to be just temporary, especially after he requested her presence during the spell. I couldn't imagine a situation where she would be needed but Asher had. It was a reminder of how ancillary positions in the pack had special privileges. An Alpha will always accept suggestion and council but has the final say.

As I prepared to perform the spell, Dr. Reyes inched in to place the silver bracelet around Asher's wrist to keep him from healing once I administered the cut. She stayed close to him, offering me a tight smile. "If anything goes wrong, I want to be able to remove it quickly so he can change."

I nodded, nicked his finger with the knife and then mine. Holding his hand, I recited a slight variation of the spell Elizabeth had used to give the shifters magical immunity and allowed Sherrie and Asher partial use of her magic. Now it would allow a shifter to be a conduit for mine. My eyes watered and my body tensed as magic peeled from me. After moments of no noticeable changes or effects, Asher's grip on my hand tightened like a vice. His eyes widened with distress.

"Asher," I called him. Unable to respond, he collapsed to the ground. Cold, predatory wolf eyes sharpened. The horrid, distressing sounds their bodies made to give way to their animal half pierced the air. Typically, they changed so quickly that it often went unnoticed, but watching it happen in slow motion looked painful.

"Reverse whatever you did," Dr. Reyes demanded, lowering herself next to Asher as he writhed on the ground in the midst of his change and attempted to shove her away. His features folded into a pained grimace, and I couldn't determine if he was trying to ward off or speed up his change. Dr. Reyes avoided his frenetic shoves as she tried to unclasp the brace. Cory snatched her back just as Asher exploded into his wolf, sending the brace flying from his body; I leaped back just in time not to be injured by the massive body before me. The wolf collapsed on the ground panting, his eyes squeezed tightly shut.

"Reverse it," Dr. Reyes demanded again. I eased slowly toward him, my voice level and soft, explaining what I needed to do. I continued to give quiet reassurance as I pierced the animal's paw and reversed the spell. Once the final word of the invocation was recited, his wolf form melted and a naked, noticeably fatigued Asher lay on the ground.

It took a few minutes before he gathered the strength to stand. Cory used magic to quickly clothe him before I could. The pack in animal form eased into a half circle around me and Cory; the ones in human form formed a barrier between me and Asher. All eyes turned to me. Aggressive eyes. Vengeful eyes. Holding up my hands, I took several steps back, avoiding stumbling over the wolves.

Asher blinked several times, the confused anger draining from his eyes and leaving a look of concern. The pack occasionally looked back at him, trying to ascertain his level of distress. There was some because they were responding to it while protecting him, their Alpha, from a potential threat.

I didn't miss Cory's pained expression at Alex who stood in front of him, blocking him from Asher as well. Relationships aside, they saw me as a threat. It was difficult not to find some level of offence in it, but Cory looked devastated. It heightened when Alex remained stoic.

"Are you okay?" Dr. Reyes's soothing voice asked. Her position prior to Asher changing left her feet away from him and blocked by the wall of shifters.

"I'm fine." His rough raspy voice proved otherwise. He edged his way past the protective bodies, offering me a tight smile. A sheen of sweat remained along his brow and his breathing hadn't returned to normal. I'd never seen him look distressed before. Dr. Reyes was allowed closer to him. Her fingers brushed his. Moments later, I was surprised when his fingers extended and loosely twined around hers. His look of distress faded. His breathing quickly returned to normal and he stood taller, the Asher I was familiar with reasserting himself. The response didn't go unnoticed by Cory, either. His brows inched together as he tossed Alex an inquiring look. One that went unanswered. Alex's expression remained ascetic, his posture protective, and his eyes held a predacious intensity I wasn't used to seeing on him.

"You weren't able to change back, were you?" Dr. Reyes asked, positioning herself in front of him, their fingers still loosely connected and her back to me, a clear indicator she wanted to block me from their conversation.

"No." There wasn't any inflection or emotion in his voice, but I could imagine how frightening it was for him, of all people, not to have control of his wolf.

"I'm so—"

He held up a hand to stop me. "No apologies needed. I agreed, knowing there could be risks. I shoulder the consequences." A sentiment that only he shared but the others had the courtesy not to voice, although it continued to show in their expression.

Asher's head snapped to the right and eventually the fox came into view, transitioning to a man about five eight, lean, features as sharp and vulpine as his fox, and disheveled burnished auburn hair. His dark brown eyes were alight with confusion.

"What happened? The ward started to fall. I could see a housing subdivision and people and then it snapped back up."

If he saw it, then the residents of the Havenage did as well.

I no longer had the element of surprise.

"We had to stop the spell," I told him. The fox shifter looked at the tense wall of people who still maintained a protective closeness to Asher. Then to Dr. Reyes's position near Asher, whose lips were pulled into a rigid line.

"What's next, Erin?" Asher asked before giving a signal to

the shifters who reluctantly moved from their position. His question made me want Mephisto at my side. At least I would have magic, another resource who knew of protective objects, and I'd have a chance against the elves with their magic. And him. I wanted him and the reassurance he gave me. *My demigoddess.* His voice resounded in my head, making me miss him for more than the alliance and assistance he provided. It was him. I missed him.

"Regroup. I need to try to find the object you described or something complementary. That may be the only option I have."

Asher hesitated as if he expected me to change my mind. It didn't seem decisive because it wasn't. But it was the wisest decision.

"I'm sure," I said.

He dismissed everyone. The ones in shifter form changed and piled into the SUVs they'd come in, and he left with Dr. Reyes in his car.

"You okay?" I asked Cory, who stood next to me, staring at the vehicles driving away. The look of abject confusion and betrayal lingered on his face. He and Alex only had the opportunity to give each other a brusque departure wave before he'd gotten into the Navigator.

He frowned. "They're very ostentatious, aren't they?" he said finally.

"Shifters tend to like to make a statement that they've arrived," I noted, taking in the black car, darkened windows, tires that I assumed were puncture proof. The doors seemed to be heavier than typical ones for that model, presumably reinforced.

"Dating a shifter has a lot of advantages. They are intense—even with their affections, protection, and love," I said.

He nodded, but he looked grim and I was desperate to see a dimple appear. For it to be an authentic smile and show that his mood had lifted. But I didn't think it would be anytime soon.

"I just experienced the disadvantage of it," he whispered, turning to head for the car. I rushed to it and got into the passenger side. If Cory couldn't work out to redirect his emotions, driving was the second-best thing for him.

He was silent as he drove toward my apartment, giving me time to problem solve. Madison hadn't responded to my earlier text. I hoped it meant she was still searching. The STF also had a selection of magical objects, task forces, and departments that I didn't have. Although she might have wanted to give it priority, it was doubtful that it was. Bogged down with doing damage control of a sister linked to a murder—that I was never cleared of now that we knew the truth. It was Nolan. Now I was the prime suspect in the abduction of the fae queen, which was most definitely the work of Fabian and Elizabeth.

Cory's silence might have been companionable, but his etched glower wasn't.

"He was protecting Asher," I said. "I know it's hard not to be offended and not take it personally. At that point you were a faceless threat. You'd do the same for me."

"I would. My brain understands that. It's my emotions that have the difficulty. In the abstract, pack dynamics doesn't seem so definitive, but in reality it is. Protect the pack at all costs." He gave a wry smile. It was the very reason I could never be with Asher. In the abstract it seemed possible, but I'd seen how it worked on many levels and it could never have worked for me. It seemed Cory was contemplating whether it would work for him.

Madison responding that she hadn't been able to find a name for the object or find anything that looked close to it reduced me to pacing through my apartment, Cory tracking my movements from one end to the other, occasionally perusing the papers and spell books on the table.

"Ms. Harp is the answer," I said, stopping abruptly. Before he could question me, I started rambling. "The spell worked. The ward was starting to fail. Reversing the spell because of its effect on Asher was the only reason it failed. Magic doesn't work on her the same. She can't shift." I opened my door, phone in hand ready to call Asher, when Cory stopped me.

"Should you think on this longer?"

"What's different? Cory, I would never put Ms. Harp's life in danger. She can't change into an animal form. I don't have a lot of options nor the luxury of time. If I can't clear my name Neri is going to try to kill me. I know you saw the fae watching us as we came in."

He nodded thoughtfully. I'd be watched constantly. I'd never be sure if they were looking for a vulnerable moment or just plotting. Clearing my name and taking the elves' magic was of equal importance. Nodding again, he released my hand. His fingers scrubbed over his jaw, and he gave a shaky nervous breath.

"I guess she can't be more human," he offered in a light, airy voice. I figured there was more to it. Ms. Harp was a friend of the pack and would be protected as such. Any issues that arose with her would trickle down to Alex and possibly place another strain on Alex and Cory.

I placed a reassuring hand over his. "I'm more confident using her than I was with Asher. Her being such an anomaly will work to our advantage. I would never ever harm her."

"I know you wouldn't."

CHAPTER 15

"No, find another way." Asher was leaving no room for debate. Cold, intense eyes pierced through the video call.

"I understand—"

"No, you don't. I couldn't change back, Erin. I didn't have control of my wolf," he barked out. The anger and frustration that he'd controlled flooded his voice. He sighed. "I've *never* not had control. Even with the animancer fae, I was able to control my wolf."

His tone had lost some of the heat, but it was as tight and strained.

"She doesn't change," he pointed out. "What if it forces her into changing?"

"Worst case scenario and that happens. How is that a bad thing? You and Dr. Reyes said that her changing might be what would keep her from suffering the bad side effects from not changing. You'd be there to hasten the change and help her through it."

He noticeably inhaled and blew it out slowly, his expression becoming considering. Could this solve my problem and his?

"The decision must be hers. But it must be made with fully informed consent. She must know everything, Erin."

Okay.

Ms. Harp took in the information as I relayed it to her, from me finding my father, magic being returned to me, the discovery of who I was, up to me being set up for the abduction of the fae queen. She asked pertinent questions and displayed more sympathy, and I was surprised to see her eyes glistening several times. Despite wanting her to agree, I didn't want it to be out of sympathy.

"I'd like your help but do it because you feel confident in the process and not because you feel sorry for me," I ended. "I'll figure out something else if you decide against it."

"Do not go into sales because you're terrible at it." She looked at Asher. "Who ends a pitch like that?" She scoffed her derision.

Her face twisted in consideration as she rocked back and forth in her chair. I knew why Asher was there, even Sherrie, the Alpha of the Lion shifters. Ms. Harp was a cat shifter and if anything were to go wrong it would be imperative that Sherrie was there. It was Dr. Reyes's presence, just inches from Asher at all times, that I wondered about.

Despite the initial antagonistic relationship she and Ms. Harp had, Dr. Reyes appeared as protective of her as Asher was.

"Could I die?" Ms. Harp asked the question I was sure everyone was thinking.

"Magic has its risks. Your safety and life are my priority if you agree. I'll stop at any unusual signs of distress."

Her expression left nothing to read as we waited for an answer. "Are you going to be transferring to this pack?" she asked Dr. Reyes.

She blinked several times at the question. "I'm not sure what that has to do with this situation?" Her eyes darted to Asher before returning to Ms. Harp's inquiring expression.

"It doesn't. You abruptly stopped the conversation when you heard me approaching and I want to know the answer. So, if you give us the answer to the question, I can answer theirs."

Cory snorted a laugh that he quickly cut off. *Ms. Harp is going to be Ms. Harp.* There's no way around it. "Erin will need an answer. Her issue is more pressing than the one you're addressing," Dr. Reyes tossed back, shooting her a sharp, wolflike look. A rare reminder that she probably viewed herself as a predator first, a physician second.

Ms. Harp took several more minutes of consideration and was about to speak when Asher spoke up first. "I have offered Erin the assistance of the pack. I did not offer her you. I have my doubts about this," he admitted with an apologetic frown. "I don't think you should take the risk."

"Really? I had no idea that's how you felt since you did such a great job hiding it," Ms. Harp mocked. "I want to help. For no other reason than—" She grimaced. "Luck can only be on your side so often, Erin. I'm very familiar with Neri and his antics. He'll kill you before you have to worry about the elves. I don't want you to die," she admitted.

"Thank you."

"What's your concern?" Sherrie asked Asher.

"Her changing and it being painful. Or her inability to return to human form if she does change." A haunted look passed over his face. I had underestimated how traumatic not having control of his wolf was.

Ms. Harp stared at me, pondering the new information before turning her attention to Sherrie.

"Let's see if I can change."

Her response left Asher and Dr. Reyes's mouths partially agape and speechless.

"Just like that? You've always shut off all discussions of changing whenever it was brought up."

"We've discussed it enough. I didn't want to look into changing, just to do it. Things are different now."

I mouthed a thank you, fully aware that she was accepting the risk on my behalf. She skewered me with a glare and brushed it away. Asher closed the distance between them and whispered something to her. She followed him into the room we'd used previously for the discussion. They returned minutes later. I was unable to gather anything from his expression.

"Can you attempt to shift her? She's never shifted before, and this should be treated as one stuck in transition."

"Asher." Sherrie, seeing past the emotionless landscape, offered him a reassuring smile. "I will care for her because she's mine," reminding him that Ms. Harp was technically a cat shifter and if it wasn't for his rapport with Ms. Harp, he'd have no involvement with her. Asher hadn't revealed the type of shifter Ms. Harp was, and their interaction piqued my interest.

At my inquiring look, Asher gave me a slight smile. "Lion," he offered. It explained Sherrie's behavior. Alphas were protective of their own, but Ms. Harp being a lion shifter like her heightened Sherrie's instinct to shield her from harm.

"You never wanted to shift into your form?" I asked, taken aback by such a denial. Sherrie enjoyed her animal form and the shock that it invoked seeing a lion traipsing down the block. It was the reason I understood the protests, apprehensions, and issues humans had with shifters.

"Never had a desire."

It wasn't about helping herself. Ms. Harp was doing it for me. Again, my look of appreciation was met with a scathing glower. I jerked my eyes away from her.

"Her change needs to be coaxed now. It's better to be

prepared than faced with it when magic is involved." All eyes turned to me and Cory, the interlopers, who would not be privy to this intimate moment between shifters. Dr. Reyes nodded in understanding and departed. When we made no efforts to leave, we were unceremoniously invited to do so.

"We can't even be in the house?" Cory grumbled as we made our way to the car. "Like I said, shifters are ostentatious."

"Not ostentatious. Changing for the first time is a very complex moment. During the process of changing—if Ms. Harp can with Sherrie's help—they'll be in a very vulnerable state. It shouldn't be shared with outsiders. I'm quite surprised Asher was allowed," Alex clarified as he approached us from the car parked next to mine.

Cory and I came to an abrupt stop at the reminder of shifters' preternatural hearing. "I was told you were here and thought we should talk," he explained in response to Cory's inquiring expression. Alex ran his fingers through his hair and had a difficult time holding eye contact with Cory. When he directed Cory to his car, I had to force myself not to tag along. Alex's uncharacteristic nervousness had me wondering if this was about to be a break-up or a reconciliation, and all I wanted to do was protect my friend.

I pressed my lips together, tamping down my words. *Don't break my friend's heart.*

Cory's discussion with Alex while they sat in the car next to mine looked heavy. I shot furtive glances in their direction and made poor attempts to read lips that seemed to barely move. Forced to rely on their nonverbal communication for hints of what was happening. Alex's kiss on Cory's cheek: Was it to soothe a blistering remark, an apology, or a goodbye? Cory stroking Alex's hair could mean a number of things: His type A personality couldn't continue the conversation with Alex's hair a shambolic mess? Was it understanding? Acceptance of a break-up?

I was unraveling and reviewing my spells on my phone, scrolling through pictures of the many objects I'd retrieved over the years in case I'd missed anything that resembled Asher's pic. Which led me to ruminating over the second uncertainty. Ms. Harp. Were they able to change her? If so, how would this affect the spell? Her anomaly made her the best candidate for it. If Sherrie could coax her into shifting, then she could coax her out of it.

Asher's appearance at the front door beckoning me relieved some of the tension. After a quick look at Alex and Cory where they too had seen Asher but were continuing their conversation, I made my way to the house where I was met with vacant looks.

"She can't be changed," Asher disclosed. Disappointment and conflict settled in the warmth of his voice. Her not changing would serve my spell well, but she'd continue to suffer during the full moon.

"When do you want to do the spell?" Sherrie asked.

"Today." We'd already lost the initial element of surprise, but perhaps a second attack on the same day would be unexpected. It wouldn't allow time for safeguards.

With a nod, he and Sherrie started making phone calls and sending texts. Ms. Harp returned to drinking her "coffee."

While we waited for the plans, Cory returned with Alex close—very close—behind. His lingering hand on Cory's back offered me the reassurance that I needed. It must not have made it to my face because I received a message from Cory. *We're fine. More than fine. Talk later.*

CHAPTER 16

In the same formation as earlier but with double the people and the addition of the cat shifters, I was grateful for the army. I reiterated my request that everyone be kept alive, including Elizabeth and Fabian. The directive not to hurt children didn't need to be given. Shifters were more protective of cubs, a reference they used generally. Human cubs, witch cubs, mage cubs. A descriptor that wasn't shed until the late teens.

Positioned far enough from the ward that the repulsion spell was barely noticeable, Sherrie stood on one side of Ms. Harp and tension-filled Asher on the other. Gifted at masking his emotions, Asher appeared unable to do so now. It didn't go unnoticed by the pack or Sherrie. Periodically, Dr. Reyes's finger grazed along his hand when she wasn't offering him a comforting smile. When she leaned over to whisper something to him, Ms. Harp abandoned paying attention to my instructions.

"Are you staying or not?" she demanded, making a flush of color creep over the bridge of Dr. Reyes's nose and her cheeks. An uncomfortable silence fell with the question lingering and unanswered.

Dr. Reyes's clear discomfort prompted me to push the silver bracelet Asher had worn during the spell in Ms. Harp's direction. "I know you can't change, and you haven't shown signs of sharing their advanced healing, but we should err on the side of caution. I need the cut open the entire spell."

As I performed the spell, everyone watched Ms. Harp while she kept narrowed eyes on Asher and Dr. Reyes, demonstrating little interest in the invocations. Magic pulled from me; the undeniable loss felt like a shadow. Ms. Harp's hands gripped mine tighter as the illumination spread over her body. Asher sucked in a breath and held it. Sherrie watched with intense scrutiny, and I could feel the collective weight of the shifters' attention on me. The illumination gave way to a silver patina. Eventually it commenced to a bout of push and pull. Ms. Harp's diminutive frame absorbed and repelled it. No longer in control of how the spell behaved, I joined the others in rapt interest. I felt the absence of the elven magic. I'd mourn the loss of it later. Time crept by as the silver patina surrendered into Ms. Harp. She slumped, losing her balance. Asher took hold of her before she could hit the ground. Dr. Reyes was next to him, checking her. From what I could determine she seemed fine but fatigued, which was quickly confirmed by Dr. Reyes along with the shifters turning to the sound of the fox bark in notification.

At Asher's instruction, a shifter took Ms. Harp to a car and left with her while we made our way to the revealed new world. The Havenage was fully open to us. Our entrance was met with a small cadre of armed, confused elves. Hard eyes homed in on the shifters. A bullet from the direction of the home whizzed past one of the cat shifters who dropped to the ground, avoiding being hit. The bullet got a wolf in the leg. It let out a sharp sound and stumbled midstride, falling to the ground. Alex shifted from wolf form to human to tend to the fallen animal, while Asher surveyed the area. He darted toward where the bullets were coming from. The sounds of fighting, screams, and curses rang through the air. Cutting through all the noise was the elven child who had been unimpressed by my round human ears. Pasha's small voice calling for his parents pierced the area. It stopped me mid-pace in my search for Elizabeth. I turned in his direction but before I could get to him, Asher had made a detour, calling out for someone to stop the shooter.

He scooped the small boy up. "He's fine," Asher called over his shoulder. Asher asked him something and Pasha pointed to a house. Asher sprinted in that direction as I held my breath, waiting until they'd made it safely. Then I returned to running toward the house where Nolan and I had been housed. The spray of bullets suddenly stopped. A twinge of pain went through me when I considered how they were stopped. Shaking my head to clear it of the thoughts and hauling toward the house, out of my periphery I saw Sherrie twisting and barely missing a sword-wielding elf, one I hadn't seen during my visit. The elf moved with expert precision as he slashed at Sherrie, who managed to parry and move, warding off any connection. She dropped down, swiped his leg, and managed to grab the discarded sword, disable the elf, and warn him off moving as she placed the blade of the weapon at his neck.

I spun around to more guns firing, and one of the shifters collapsing to the ground. Another shifter in human form heaved the massive creature over his shoulder and raced him to safety.

Asher returned from the house where Pasha had directed him. "Go," Asher urged me. I had expected violence and that the elves would protect themselves, but I hadn't expected this level of efficiency. The magically inclined always deferred to magic for their protection, which often left them vulnerable when they had to defend themselves without it. These elves didn't seem to have those limitations.

The strike of something hard against my shoulder sent me off course and a shooting pain through my arm. I dodged the second blow from the baton Sanaa wielded, her expression tight with determination and eyes blazing with anger. Panting, she advanced into another strike that I evaded by lobbing a sphere of magic into her chest. Rage giving her persistence, I had to hit her with several more, each one increasingly larger. An unyielding volley of thrashes left her flat on the ground. She dragged her upper body up, but the fight had gone out of her, leaving behind reluctant acquiescence. Her eyes fluttered with virulent anger. Any compassion or understanding that I'd garnered in the past had disappeared. I was as horrible as Elizabeth had made me out to be.

"So much talent and magic and you use it against us?" The disappointment and pity that laced her words cut deeper than I thought it would.

"I didn't have a choice," I attempted to explain, but she rejected it with a wave of her hand.

"To punish us all for the sins of Fabian and Elizabeth shows your lack of discernment and mercy. You and Malific will always choose cruelty. For the likes of your kind, there is no other way." Giving in to the desolation and failure, she fell back. Although she wasn't fighting me anymore, she had delivered a powerful final blow. Guilt and shame overtook revenge and retribution. Her words stung in a way that I never imagined. Even as I pushed Elizabeth and Fabian's acts to the forefront to justify things, the truth remained: I might not suffer any casualties of this war—but the elves did. Their magic.

I shook off the feelings. If the elves were to exist, I'd soothe them by punishing the ones who led me to such extreme measures. Seeing them would reignite the flames and chase away what I was feeling. Running toward the house with renewed determination, I burst through the door.

I found Nolan and Elizabeth standing in the living room. Her hand shot out to perform magic. Nothing happened. As realization of her being magicless took form, her mouth parted. A small smile crept over my lips. I'm sure as the others lost their magic and the ward fell around the Havenage, she'd taken some comfort in still having her fae magic. And that would have been the case if I hadn't made a small modification to the spell, using the hair I'd snatched from her head. It wasn't the elven magic that Ms. Harp had trouble fully absorbing, it was hers.

It took longer for Elizabeth's magic to be taken, which must have given her a false sense of hope and access to it while the others realized theirs was gone.

Emotions coursed over her face in a wave. Anger and confusion blazed in her expression. "What did you do!?"

If there was any doubt, I wanted to remove it. "Your hair." When I modified the spell, I hadn't been able to test it. Whether it would be successful was pure speculation—an educated decision. But I had nothing to lose. Even if she'd kept her fae magic, she would be significantly weaker than before. I preened at the horror that my magical capabilities and potential brought to her face.

Elizabeth's body vibrated with anger. Turning her ire to Nolan she hissed, "This ultimately falls on you. You did this to us!" The implicit understanding that accompanied their sibling affections was washed away by Elizabeth's rage. In a swift sweeping movement, she ripped a knife from the sheath at her leg and lunged at Nolan. I hit her with a sphere of magic, sending her crashing into the floor several feet away. Nolan was quick to snatch up the lost knife. Holding it with deadly consideration, he looked down at his sister.

"I accept the responsibility of Erin's actions." He lowered himself to the ground, the knife still in hand. "Everything you and Fabian have done. Your treatment of her. Keeping me here against my will—*for my protection*." He scoffed. "You can't believe you aren't deserving of this retribution from her. Loss of your magic is such a small penalty for what you truly deserve." His eyes flicked to the knife, his voice tremulous as he spoke. "She's served her justice. Dear sister, what retribution have you earned from me?" She swallowed the answer as she held his gaze. "You were about to kill me," he said, his pain so heavy and deep it forced a painful scowl on his face. The hurt had removed the compassion from him. His unfamiliar hard, cold demeanor was unsettling.

"Nolan," I whispered, but he behaved as if he hadn't heard me.

"Elizabeth, what do you deserve?" Emotion had drained from his voice, leaving it paper thin.

"Better. We all deserve better than to be punished by Malific's daughter. We all deserve better than for Erin to exist. And I deserve a better brother." Her words cut more than the knife. Before he could retaliate with an actual cut, I took hold of his hand and took the knife from him and put it in my pocket. Grabbing Elizabeth's arm, I wrenched her to standing.

She punched me. I responded in kind, hard enough to jerk her head back. Grabbing her by the throat, I backed her into the nearest wall where I secured her. Sparks of magic that flickered from my fingers drew her eyes. Denying me the show of fear, a fleeting look of it moved over her expression.

Elizabeth struggled to breathe as my hold grew tighter. The magic I'd summoned commanded her attention.

"I still have magic. As you pointed out, I am Malific's daughter. Don't force me to end your life in a manner that would disgust even the likes of her," I ground out inches from her face.

The threat didn't land because she knew she was needed to clear my name with Neri. "Once your involvement is known, I assure you he'd revel in me killing you torturously. You're coming with me to clear my name."

Removing my hand from her throat, I grabbed her arm and pulled her toward the door. Digging her heels in, her fist shot out to punch me. I caught her fist and smashed my forehead into her nose. It was hard but not enough to break it. Her eyes watered. While she was distracted by the pain, a hip toss landed her on her back. I rolled her over and retrieved the zip-ties I'd brought with me. Once secured, I hauled her to standing. I prepared for her to collapse and become dead weight, forcing me to carry her, but to my surprise, she moved with me. Nolan stayed close behind, his brows drawn together in confusion; I knew she hadn't disclosed what she'd done to me. On our walk to the entrance, I told him about Fabian and Elizabeth setting me up for Adalia's abduction. He no longer had disgust or surprise left in him and met the story with a wry smile. Nothing I could say would ease his emotions, so I held my empty platitudes.

CHAPTER 17

More elves than I remembered from my visit were corralled at the entrance of the subdivision. Some of them zip-tied, some seated on the ground with desolate looks of defeat. The only people not accounted for were Pasha and his family.

"They're in the house. I didn't want him to see this," Asher said. There were significantly fewer shifters. My heart raced.

"No need to worry, Erin. A few were injured—nothing significant but I wanted them to leave and get treatment. Two of them were hit with silver bullets." He glared at one of the men zip-tied on the ground. It was only then that I noticed the points of some of their ears. No magic, no glamor. There were more half-caste now, who didn't have pointed ears. The full elven ears were revealed on the ones whose hair didn't cover them. Arius was bound in his imp form with an iridium brace that was too large to enclose his wrist so was secured with a zip-tie to his leg where his pants had been torn away to place it directly against his skin.

"Got to him before he could change. If I hadn't, things would have ended differently."

"Can he change?" I was still convinced that a great deal of his magical ability was linked to Elizabeth. Although nothing he'd done supported it, I remained curious whether he was affected by the spell. Ignoring Arius's glare that promised unspeakable harm if released, I surveyed the captive elves.

"Fabian?"

"We can't find him anywhere," Cory provided.

"I tried to track him from the scent from his home and it ended." Annoyance made Asher's voice tight. Fabian made sure he couldn't be tracked. I was surprised at the part of me that believed he'd stay with the others. It only confirmed that he was the disloyal reprobate I suspected all along. His pronouncement in support of misdeeds and bad behavior being for the good of the collective was complete BS.

"What do you want us to do with them?" Asher asked. It was a question he'd asked prior to us entering the Havenage, which I hadn't had a concrete plan for then. Faced with the situation, I still didn't have an answer. Locking them away seemed so cruel now that they were magicless. But anger and thirst for vengeance was worn heavily on many of their faces, defeat on a few. Would they act on it?

Sweeping a long look over the captives, I didn't see a threat despite their anger. "Leave them." I pointed to Arius. "Will you keep him until I can establish his current abilities?" The others were magicless, and I didn't believe they held the same blind loyalty to Elizabeth as they had for Fabian. But Arius did. Leaving him behind would ensure he'd either seek revenge or attempt to rescue Elizabeth. Or both. It was safer that he remained in our custody.

"You plan to leave us like this? Magicless?" Sanaa challenged.

I nodded. She glared.

"Find Fabian and I'll reconsider it," I said in concession. I had Elizabeth, and with Fabian, the heads and the most problematic ones were gone. They'd be too worried about reorganizing and regrouping to worry about me.

She scoffed and looked at Nolan at my side. The elves

teemed with the guilt they had assigned to him, their scrutinizing eyes tracking his movement. If it weren't for him, I
wouldn't exist and Malific wouldn't have ever been freed.
With their magic stripped from them, he'd be ostracized. If
his mournful disposition was any indicator, he knew it, too. I
hated this for him—for us.

"Fabian deserted you all! The people whose protection he
claimed was of utmost importance and yet he left you
behind. How can you remain loyal to him?"

Sanaa scowled. "He's the one most likely to discover a
way to return our magic. Magic that *you* stole. I'm glad he
escaped."

I'd balked before at their cultish language. Now I was
questioning whether there was more to it. Or maybe it was a
result of their us against the world mentality.

"I don't want to make this any worse than it is. This is
how it is going to be. At least for now. Consider leaving you
here like this an act of empathy. But if you attack me, I won't
treat you with any kindness."

"This is kindness?" Sanaa sneered. It was hard determining if this new surly disposition was her true personality
or a result of being rendered magicless.

"It's the only kindness I can extend. Bring me Fabian, I
will return your magic. Attack me and I will take your life."
With that directive, I pulled Elizabeth out of the Havenage
toward my car.

"You'll have a few shifters at your house," Asher informed
me as they followed me out of the Havenage. One of the wolf
shifters had Arius hoisted with one hand. I started to decline
but it was a good idea. I thanked him and had to call out my
gratitude to Sherrie's back. She was getting in her car, shrugging off the aftermath and any associated issues. She was a
reluctant ally and wasn't that invested in what happened
next.

"I'd like to go with you," Nolan pressed after I instructed

him to go with Asher. He may have had a change of heart regarding his sister, but I believed it would be short lived. Elizabeth had attempted to kill him and whatever would transpire with the fae and her, I didn't want to subject him to more cruelty and darkness. Elizabeth and Nolan exchanged a look. His started out a skewering glare that transitioned to sadness. I was positive it would morph into remorse eventually. His thirst for revenge against Malific had put him in a precarious situation and he'd become the source of blame and ridicule from the elves. Reluctantly, he went with Asher and I shoved Elizabeth into the back seat of the car.

Elizabeth's death stare bored into the back of my head. It could be felt even if I hadn't been able to see it from the rearview mirror. In her magicless state she seemed diminutive, but her indignant anger remained as vast as her self-assurance. Knowing the catalyst of my issues with the fae was in my custody was satisfying, but I wanted Fabian. He had proven to be the most cunning and dangerous. His loyalties questionable. Sanaa's words replayed in my head. *He's the one most likely to discover a way to return our magic.*

Was that what he was doing now? It was likely. He'd discovered a way to override my other spell. My only comfort was that no one who would willingly help him had magic. I drove faster to the royals' home, my thoughts split between Fabian, clearing my name, and the anticipation of seeing Mephisto. The latter was taking up the vast majority of my thoughts. Staying on the task at hand was a challenge. With the elven magic gone, so was the spell that closed the Veil.

The Veil is open.

"You are your mother's daughter," Elizabeth hissed, breaking into my thoughts. I'd prepared to be berated the entire drive. Captured and en route to face the consequences of her actions, I expected her to behave like a cornered rabid animal. She couldn't physically lash out, so she'd do it with words.

The background noise of the scenic drive consisted of Elizabeth telling me how she should have denied Nolan and never helped him. Anger warped all semblance of logic as she blathered on about wishing she'd killed me the moment she saw me, seemingly forgetting my death at Ian's hand was the reason Malific had been released from the Omni ward. Killing me as an infant would have hastened her release. Elizabeth seemed to be most aggrieved by my escape from the demon realm. Her rageful words became nothing more than blithe confessions and explanations as to why Wendy had been pulled into this situation. She had to pay for her part in helping release me.

"I should have started recording her the moment she started ranting," Cory whispered from the passenger seat. "Accountability has taken her over the edge."

Grunting at his assessment, I knew it was deeper than that. It was more than just accountability. She was magicless. Having her magic removed by the person she hated the most must have been too much to handle. I'd bested her in the worst way.

The gate to the royals' home opened slowly and as the car rolled up the driveway, guards watched us with their weapons at the ready. I'd left Neri's curiosity unsated when I called him and simply told him that I had the person who'd abducted Adalia and would be there in fifteen minutes.

I realized ignoring his calls would heighten his curiosity and add fuel to his anger. That's what I wanted. I planned to take advantage of his fiery rage and have him do what was needed. Killing Elizabeth.

Faced with the actual prospect of accountability, Eliza-beth did what I had expected her to do at the Havenage. She went limp. Still feeling the energy suck from the spells I performed earlier, the dead weight made it impossible for me to get her out of the car. I was only able to snap the iron bracelet around her and required Cory's assistance to transport her into the house. He pulled her out of the car, draped her over his shoulder, and carried her into the royals' estate. Greeted by guards who had no intention of letting me in, I knew one move too quick or a failure to comply could end with an arrow in my back. Not from the sentry at the door but the ones hidden around the estate that they probably assumed I hadn't noticed. Security had increased since my last visit—no one was getting in or out of the home without their knowledge. I wondered how much they invested in wards. Their ignorance of elven magic would always leave them vulnerable, and Elizabeth had exceptional abilities. She had gotten around their protective wards and Wynded Adalia away. I wasn't sure about the extent of what else she'd done, but I'd find out. I was confident that Elizabeth was cunning and skilled enough to circumvent even wards that prevented Wynding. If she couldn't, Fabian could. They were the power couple no one needed.

I was greeted by Neri's stony expression when Cory stood Elizabeth in the room where we were escorted. I shoved an uncooperative Elizabeth toward him.

"If you want to assassinate anyone for Adalia's abduction and magic siphoning, this is your culprit."

His uncertain frown converged into disgust. "Erin." His sneer expressed his disbelief better than his words could. "I am to believe *she* is behind this. Your accuser? The one who saved my Adalia and directed us to you?"

"Yes. If you don't believe me, ask her."

"Speak," he demanded of Elizabeth.

Indignation lifted her chin high as she looked him in the eye. "I revealed to you that which is true. As you can see"—she showed her bound arms—"I have been brought here against my will. Erin's desperation to live a reckless and lawless life with impunity has also made me a victim of it."

It wasn't shocking that she was skilled at effortless lying. Neri believed her. Adalia stood on the opposite side of the room, her elegant grace revealing none of her thoughts. Her expression was a blank landscape as she watched everything unfold.

"Incline her to truth," I suggested. "If she has nothing to hide, she'll agree to a truth spell."

Neri's frown deepened at the suggestion of a spell he was incapable of performing.

"I can do it," Cory offered.

Neri dragged his eyes over Cory as he waved Adalia to him. As soon as she was within reach, his fingers linked with hers, seeming in desperate need of contact with her. His dedication and love for his spouse would have evoked warm and fuzzies in me, but since it was the source of his ire and attempts on my life, it was as dangerous as a weapon.

"Magic can be manipulated, and you'd do anything to protect your friend. Will I get actual truth or Erin's truth?" Neri challenged.

"The truth," Cory promised.

Neri looked unconvinced. If this situation was to end today, I needed Neri to leave this situation without a hint of doubt.

"Would you trust her word under the compulsion of a vampire?" I rushed out. It was the purest form of truth-seeking that didn't require casting a spell. Neri could direct the questions and the answers would be pulled out of Elizabeth. Elizabeth lobbed a scornful glare at me.

Keeping my eyes fixed on the royals, I awaited a response, refusing to let my attention drift in Cory's direction but fully aware he was treating me to an admonishing wide-eyed look. Neri wouldn't just request any vampire, but *the* vampire. Landon.

Neri agreed with a slight nod of his head. Moments later, with his arm around Adalia's waist, he disappeared through a door in the far right of the room after letting us know he needed to speak with Landon. Elizabeth dropped onto the sofa, examining her bound hands. Once the source of great power, now they were simply hands. In the royals' absence she spent the time silently glowering at me when she wasn't looking around the room, presumably searching for an escape route. With the level of security, and without magic or preternatural speed and strength, escape was impossible.

CHAPTER 18

Fear slithered around my spine. We'd been waiting for over half an hour. The constant intrusion of the security moving in and out of the room had me speculating whether Neri had decided against finding the truth and taken the nuclear route of destroying all likely suspects. His history hadn't left me confident that it wasn't a plausible option. I was confident of my survival of any of his attempts, although it would come at a cost of making me a public enemy. All the good PR in the world wouldn't help me.

My concerns were squashed when Landon walked into the room in a flourish of effortless grace, flanked by Elon and Dallas. His entrance cued Neri and Adalia's return.

Landon's lips trembled at the effort to offer me a smile. "Erin," he purred, advancing toward me, his voice void of the animosity I was sure he felt. "What a surprise to see you here," he gritted out, finally attaining the smile he'd been desperately working on since entering the room.

I'd bet my left pinky toe that my presence wasn't a surprise, but I played along. Offering him a faint smile, I greeted him with an enthusiastic firm handshake. Using my hand as leverage, he pulled me closer and leaned into me.

"If you are ever stripped of all your worldly possessions, I know you'll always maintain your audacity," he hissed in a rough whisper. Aware of Neri's attention, Landon stepped away. "May I have a word with Erin?" he asked.

"It is best that we proceed. They've waited too long for answers already," I said.

"A moment please." He bared his teeth then turned on his heels and headed to the hallway in a dramatic display of speed and agility. Cory started to join me but I raised a hand to stop him.

The second I was in the hallway with the door closed behind me, Landon devoured the space between us within a heartbeat.

"You have your nerves," he pushed through clenched teeth. His lips furled back to show his fangs.

"I'm not the one who called you here. It was Neri."

"Am I to believe you had no hand in it?"

"They don't want magic that can be manipulated to be involved. Vampire compulsion for answers was the only option."

"Do not think for one moment I don't see this for what it is. A request for another favor. More debts. The wanton audacity." Thundercloud-dark eyes blazed, apparently at my *audacity*. His movements driven by his overwrought emotions were animated. It would have been a source of amusement until he furled back his lips and presented his weapons. I was reminded of the danger. Armed with a knife sheath at my hip and magic that would require quick reactions left me feeling safe but fully aware that I'd have to use both before he could use his most adept weapons—his fangs and preternatural speed and strength.

He pulled himself taller, squaring his shoulders and allowing all emotions to fall from his face. Cold, calculating stoicism. My audacity had lost its shock and whatever charm he found in it in the past. It was an unsightly blemish that he seemed unable to look at.

"You renege on our agreement, ignore my insistence that you honor it—"

"You mean the threat you left at my door?"

He responded with a glare. "The roses? Hardly a threat. Just a simple nudge to honor your agreement. One that you've ignored. Now, you wish for more favors from me to clear your name?" He ran his fingers through his hair, long legs eating up the length of the hall as he paced. Stopping periodically to look at me, his mouth opened and closed, appearing unable to find the words to express his incredulous disdain. Or contemplating how fast he could kill me.

"I promised you something better than two progenies and I plan to honor that. But if my name isn't cleared with the fae, I'm not going to live long enough to fulfill even that. I can't make things right between us if I'm not here."

He stopped, huffed something under his breath, and shoulder checked me as he headed back to the room. Stopping just shy of entering it, he leaned down and whispered, "You *will* honor our initial agreement. There will be no further discussion or negotiation."

When we returned to the room, Landon's cool disposition with me put Neri at ease, removing the wary skepticism he'd initially had.

Elizabeth managed to maintain a modicum of confidence while I removed her binding. The assurance dropped briefly at Landon nearing her. Whatever scheme had given her such certainty vanished as Landon extended his open hands to her. To my surprise, she took them without hesitation as if she didn't have anything to hide. Elizabeth gave Neri and Adalia an over the shoulder look before focusing on Landon, following his direction as he eased her into compulsion.

Her eyes widened and became glassy. Breathing steadily, she kept her awareness on him and awaited his questions.

"Adalia went missing five days ago. Had you seen her prior to that?" Landon asked.

"Yes, of course," she responded.

"Where?"

"At Kelsey's."

"Tell me about your interaction," he urged.

"There's nothing to tell. I saw the fae queen and greeted her as all have."

"Did you touch her?"

"I greeted her. Of course."

Landon's head tilted as he watched Elizabeth, her breathing heavier than previously. I couldn't determine if she was attempting to fight the compulsion or struggling to recall the events. The only way to fight a compulsion was not to decline to answer. She had to answer.

"Yes, I touched her. I greeted her by touching her hand."

Fuck, she was being careful with her words. If the right thing wasn't asked, she'd never admit it. "That's not what he asked. Did you do a spell on Adalia when you touched her hand to greet her?" I blurted.

Landon and Neri glared at me. Adalia turned her nose up at my rudeness. *Screw propriety, I'm trying to get a confession.*

Elizabeth exhibited more slow, pronounced breathing, but she didn't respond. I urged Landon to repeat the question. After a glower of displeasure at me he asked the question.

"Yes, I did a protection spell. We must protect the queen."

I hurried next to Landon. "That's not the right question."

"What exactly is the right question?" he snapped. I whispered it in his ear, not wanting to give Elizabeth a second to come up with a duplicitous answer that managed to answer the question truthfully while absolving her.

"Was the protection spell to protect the queen or to protect a spell you'd placed on her?" he asked.

Elizabeth swallowed. "Yes, I did a protection spell. We must protect the queen," she repeated.

"Was any other spell done to me?" Adalia's sharp voice demanded. Elizabeth startled at the anger in her voice. Her cold, ominous tone appeared to stun Neri. Witnessing the collected and elegant veneer drop from the level-headed heart of the couple shocked everyone. Her eyes swept over the room, taking in our response. Ushering a placid smile, she requested that Landon ask the question.

When he did, Elizabeth struggled, her body trembled, her jaw clenched as she fought back her response. Not answering was a tacit admission. Either way, I was no longer a suspect.

Neri wanted a confession. Fury marked every step he took as he approached Elizabeth. "You will answer the question," he demanded.

The faux veneration she'd displayed earlier vanished. Her eyes became the cold and unyielding ones I'd dealt with before. She reverted to the one who had negotiated bad faith deals with people who had come to her for assistance, brokered a deal with Malific to protect all the elves but me, sent me to the demon realm, and punished the demon who helped her because I escaped. She wasn't a shrinking violet but a savage rival.

"I don't have to answer a damn thing and I refuse to." Her sharp eyes challenged Neri's. That wasn't what I cared about; it was the calculations behind them that I'd seen so many times before.

The silence was thick with tension. The only person remotely entertained was Landon, who was suppressing his amusement into a tight smile.

"Would you please answer the question?" Landon asked, dark delight making his voice a feathery whisper.

Elizabeth glared at him, clearly not enjoying being the source of his entertainment. "I placed the spell on Adalia but I had no intention of harming her." Elizabeth's breathing became slow and measured. "I made the promise to never hurt Erin, but she's dangerous and has been protected with the help of Madison and the wolf shifters' Alpha. You were my only path to making sure she is stopped." Warmth crept into Elizabeth's eyes as she directed them to Adalia.

Neri's face flushed and twisted into a scowl. Rage permeated off him in waves. He looked to the door and nodded once. An arrow whizzed past me and was just inches from being lodged in Elizabeth's throat when Landon plucked it from the air, examining it with a smirk.

"Well, that's uncalled for. Neri, be angry if you must, but will you deny yourself learning the truth?"

"What more do I need to know? She put Adalia's life at risk. I don't care about the reason. Nothing she supplies will justify it. The queen is never to be used as pawn. *Never.*"

"Understandable, but for the safety of the fae and others, wouldn't you like to know how someone so powerful would be reduced to such measures?" Landon's eyes cast aspersion in my direction.

Adalia stepped closer to Neri, placing a comforting hand on his side. "Ask her," she directed Landon quietly.

Landon took time forming his questions. "Why do you think Erin is dangerous to the fae?"

"Erin is a menace to everyone. Caution should be exercised at all times when dealing with her. I have sound knowledge that she and Mephisto were involved in a spell that would have killed off all the fae," she offered. It wasn't a lie. Part of her response could be considered an opinion but the other was true, but the way she told it was manipulative. The mention of Mephisto's name heightened my longing for him. I would have liked him at my side at that moment.

I met her challenging eyes. "She's right, but don't leave out the part where *you* were the person involved in creating the spell that put the faes' lives in jeopardy." I moved closer. Face to face with her. I looked at Neri and Adalia. "She wanted to force my hand to do her bidding, and when I didn't, she used a spell that would kill all fae to do it. It's no secret that Madison will do anything to protect me, and I'm sure you know I'd do the same. If it affects Madison, it affects me. She's fae. So fae problems are my problems. That is my oath because I will protect Madison by all means, and by association, the fae."

Elizabeth's face blanched at my admission but the computations continued. She didn't have the luxury of planning and had to counter with a response quickly to make me appear to be their enemy. That was the only thing saving her. A person who has little to lose tends to be the most reckless. "I needed her to do my bidding because of her elven magic."

An audible gasp came from both Neri and Adalia. "They're extinct," Neri countered.

"They're not. Just hidden. Erin seems to be the only one who wants to possess their power since she removed their magic and mine." She exposed the iron link on her wrist.

I had the attention of the room. A culmination of admiration, fear, and envy. I knew behind the emotions was the speculation of whether it was good to have me as an ally or gone for good. I had taken magic from an entire race of people.

"I don't need this," Elizabeth continued. "She put them on me to deceive you. To hide what she'd done."

Elizabeth might see the end was near and was reckless, but I wasn't. I had every intention of walking out of the estate with my name cleared and in good standing with the royals.

"I did it so you can't hurt anyone any longer. Including the fae. I took the elves' magic because they've enabled her reckless behavior while living in the shadows." I turned to face Neri and Adalia, my voice reverent and considering. "I am an ally of the fae because I will always protect my sister. I sacrificed my own for her. Let me be candid. You all are alive because I'll do anything to protect Madison." I hoped they understood the underlying meaning as well. Not to mess with Madison.

A slow smile moved over Adalia's face and warmth filled her expression. She nodded her head in understanding. Her soft elegance was overtaken by the seraphic look she gave me, Cory, and Landon. "It is appreciated. We are happy for someone as remarkable as you to have our best interest." She offered us all a gracious bow. "Thank you, until we meet again."

Her dismissal came with three uniformed fae entering the room with crossbows in hand. At their appearance, Landon graciously accepted his invitation to leave and slipped out of the room within a heartbeat. Cory took a moment to understand what was about to happen. Once it came to him, his mouth dropped open. As he positioned his hand to perform offensive magic, I gave him a magical shove strong enough to move him out of the line of the fae. Hauling toward him, I grabbed his arm and pulled him out of the room. I looked over my shoulder at Adalia who had positioned herself in front of Elizabeth. Whatever she said was precise and short. Then she moved out of the way.

When the first arrow was released, Elizabeth dropped to her knees with an agonized wail. Seconds later, there was another gurgle of sound. I knew exactly where the other arrow had gone. There was no way she'd survive that.

"Are you kidding me, Erin! You're not going to do something about it?"

"And you won't either," I said, grabbing his arm and pulling him out of the royals' home.

He whipped around. "They're going to kill her."

"I'm sure she's already dead."

Color drained from his face as he shoved his fingers through his hair. He took several long slow breaths that did nothing to give him the clarity and calm he was seeking. "I know you said you'd…you would…" He took another breath. "I knew you said you planned to kill her. I just thought, in the end you wouldn't."

"Why? She almost killed Nolan in the house." The new information made him suck in a sharp breath that shuddered upon release.

"There would always be something with Elizabeth. Even without magic she would have made my life a living hell. Now she can't. My hands are clean of her murder."

"You didn't stop a murder. Your hands are not clean of it," he refuted. I'd shoulder his disappointment because Elizabeth's death was a pathway to peace and me giving the elves their magic back.

But Cory's judgment hurt and despite my efforts to hide it, I couldn't. After moments of rigid silence standing in the driveway, Cory positioned himself in front of me and offered a wan smile. "When the anger and frustration is gone, will you be okay with this, E?"

I nodded. "I'll probably be more okay with it than I am today. The only regret I may have would be my face not being the last one she ever saw."

He gave my arm a decisive squeeze, turned around, and marched back into the house. Moments later, I set off after him but was forced to stop abruptly at the sight of him being escorted out by two of the crossbow-wielding guards. A deep frown was embedded on Cory's face as they roughly shoved him in my direction.

"Go away," one of them demanded. "Neri and Adalia request that you only return if invited."

I had a distinct feeling neither of us should be anxiously awaiting an invitation.

CHAPTER 19

"What the hell was that, Cory?" I asked once we were in the car, buckling our seatbelts.

Slowly shaking his head, he said, "Trauma. Undeniable trauma."

Probably from seeing the result of Elizabeth's body being pierced by who knows how many arrows.

"After the incident in the Blose Chasm, there was a part of me that didn't believe Malific was dead. I kept expecting her to return. I'm confident she's truly dead, but I would have liked for one of us to have seen the body. I felt uneasy relying on the deceptive duo for that information. I needed to make sure Elizabeth was dead, so you could have that peace of mind without question," Cory divulged in a rough whisper.

I nodded my understanding. Elizabeth didn't have magic; she was still wearing the iron bracelet. If by some chance her fae magic was still present, she couldn't use it. I heard the death-spiraling sound she made with the second arrow. I knew without question, Elizabeth was dead.

"I need to find Fabian."

"Do you have a plan to do so?"

I shook my head, slowing my driving speed, my eyes still

going over the scenic view until I couldn't resist any longer. I stopped the car, hopped out, and ran toward the forest, with Cory close behind.

Whispering the spell to reveal the Veil, I smiled at the alternative world that revealed itself to me.

"It's open, isn't it?" Cory asked, disappointment making its way into his words. Unable to see the Veil would continue to be a source of bitterness for him.

Combating the urge to go in and search for Mephisto, I whispered, "Yes." I could hear the longing in my words and knew Cory wouldn't miss it, either.

"Seems like you should go home where Mephisto could return to you rather than hanging out in the woods like a weirdo. But I'm a solutions guy and I'm just spit-balling ideas here."

He flashed a grin at my glaring response. Pulling me into a hug, he whispered, "You did it." Pride twined over each word. Pressing his forehead to mine, he repeated it as if he couldn't believe it. Part of me didn't, either. I wouldn't feel the success until I'd seen Mephisto.

"Erin, go home," Cory urged, nudging me in the direction of the car when he saw my resistance to leave. "He'll come."

We had to navigate a hallway of shifters. I directed all but two to go home, which resulted in derisive snorts. Being condescended to by wolves was never a good feeling. I could go several lifetimes without experiencing it again. Having hoped that Mephisto would be at my apartment when I arrived, my disappointment couldn't be hidden. Cory kept a concerned eye on me as he packed his things to return home.

"It's only been a couple of hours," he reminded me, showing an optimism that I no longer shared. Mine was dwindling by the minute.

I considered waiting for Mephisto to arrive, but I still had pressing matters to deal with. I needed to check on Ms. Harp and get my father. Guilt rose in me at the thought of seeing Nolan. It wasn't just getting him from Asher's, but the task of telling him his sister was dead. I wasn't looking forward to that.

With my waning confidence that Mephisto knew about the Veil being reopened, I decided that if he hadn't returned by the evening, I'd search for him. An adventure I wasn't looking forward to since he'd directed me the first time to where I assumed he resided. I'd figure out a way to navigate it myself. I needed to see him.

All thoughts of Mephisto were interrupted by Madison's incessant texts. They were more persistent than I was used to. Most of them asking me to explain the clusterfuck that had led to her being *summoned* by the royals. Not invited, *summoned.* She made sure I recognized the distinction and the perils that one of them held.

There were too many clusters to discuss, and I couldn't explain in a simple text. Pulling over a few blocks from Asher's home, I called her. Madison's responses were terse. She sounded distracted and I figured she was trying to deal with the issues of Adalia's abduction and managing a summons by the royals. We arranged to meet at my apartment later.

She seemed most concerned with the summons than the clusters of fucks and cornucopia of crap that had occurred over the past twenty-four hours.

You'll be fine, I thought. With everything going on, I had undeniable confidence that after her summons, she'd discover she was in favor with the royals.

Efforts to remain expressionless as I entered Asher's home failed. My appearance was met with a grimace and sympathetic sigh. Did I reek of death? Was my heart beating too fast, my breathing too slow, or did he sense a mournful disposition?

Nolan caught Asher's expression, which served as segue to what I needed to tell him. Tracking my every step, he exhaled a ragged breath and before I could take a seat next to him, sorrow faded the light in his eyes. He whispered, "Not here."

He turned away from me and stood, mustering a weighted half smile for Asher as he headed out the house with slow, measured steps as if each one took something from him. Not knowing if he just needed time, or time away from me, I used the time to get an update on Ms. Harp.

"She's not any less surly," Asher provided, splitting his attention between me and the door where Nolan had exited.

"Were you hoping for that?" I teased.

He shrugged, withdrawing his attention from the door to focus on me. He answered my question with a scrutinizing look. "It would be nice to go at least twenty-four hours not being challenged by a septuagenarian who's more Kahlua than person," he blew out. The etches of worry that he'd displayed prior and during the spell were completely gone, replaced by concern and sympathy. I couldn't determine if it was extended to me or Nolan. Perhaps both.

His expression relaxed. "Did things go as poorly as the scents coming off you?"

"Stop smelling me. Everyone thinks it's weird!" I snapped.

Looking over my shoulder to make sure Nolan wasn't in earshot, I gave him the abridged version of the situation with the royals, including the hope that the charges against me would be dropped and his bail money returned.

He waved away the bail as inconsequential, but I couldn't have another debt hanging over me.

"I need to go."

"You don't sound like you want to," Asher said.

"I'm not sure I do. This is the hard part," I admitted, bold with my satisfaction in my aunt's death, who'd hated me and made it a priority to show it by making my life miserable. It was a deserved death. But I wasn't as courageous about telling a brother his sister had been killed. Despite all that she'd done, including nearly killing him, I wasn't wholly convinced his sibling bond and love for her had severed. Details of her death were going to unleash a pain that might be unbearable for him. I sobbed at the thought. I hated every moment of despair I felt that was solely directed at Nolan, but Elizabeth was entwined in the feeling. Asher pulled me into his arms and I buried my face in his chest.

"This sucks," I choked out. "She deserved to die and there shouldn't be any remorse for it."

"Yes." A succinct response not intended to console me. I knew that in Asher's mind, Elizabeth's death was inevitable. If the orchestrated attacks she'd made on me had been directed to his pack, she would have been seen as a clear and present danger and handled as such without a shred of remorse or any extensive deliberation.

"There's still this part of me that feels like I did this to him," I admitted.

The low growl that reverberated in his chest differed. "*She* did this to him. The arrogance of her believing that her behavior and actions would not warrant extreme retaliation falls on her. It was a failure on her part and no one else. Understand?" He moved me away so he could look me in the eyes. I blinked away the tears.

"Do you understand?" he repeated.

"I've understood that from the moment I walked through your door. Doesn't make causing Nolan hurt any easier. I like him." *I like my father.* Another indictment of the web of complexity that detailed our relationship.

Asher nodded his understanding and I pulled from his hold to retrieve my phone. This time it was a notification of a missed call from Madison. She'd have to wait.

With a heaviness I couldn't offload, I put some distance between me and Asher.

"Arius?"

"We had to secure him in a cage at one of our houses. He's feral and dangerous with that knife of his. He got three of us with it. It's on us, we underestimated that imp. He's braced. Although his magic doesn't affect us, he can use it against objects. It was a pain dealing with that. At this time, there isn't any reasoning with him. You'll need to figure out your plans for him. He's a potential problem. Elimination would be best."

That's where the divide between shifters and others lay. Most times I agreed with Asher. Understood his sheer goal to protect his pack. At times, I didn't agree with his preemptive strikes and how he bordered on extreme cruelty to make a point.

He gave me a considering look. "I don't think you'll have to worry about the elves' retaliation, but he is a concern."

"Let him stay where he is until I figure out what to do with him. I'm focusing on finding Fabian."

"I have my wolves looking for him but all we have is scent. He was proficient at masking his scent at the Havenage. I'm not sure we'll have any luck."

"I appreciate the help. Thank you for everything," I said, milling around at the door.

Asher gave me a look then darted his eyes past the door several times, urging me to stop procrastinating.

I nodded, exited to my car where Nolan was standing on the passenger side. I opened the door and he got in with the look of a person who wasn't ready to hear any bad news. I drove nearly ten minutes, following his directions to his home.

I took a deep breath and exhaled, ending the solemn silence.

"About today—"

He placed a gentle, entreating hand over mine. "Can we just drive to the house?" he requested in a thin, tight voice. I wanted the reprieve as much as he did. From the sorrow that enveloped his words, as I suspected earlier, he already knew. Would he want details? I didn't want to give specifics of Elizabeth's final moments, but I refused to have half truths or lies between us.

Nolan's home was a modest one-story building. One wall was taken up by built-in bookshelves, filled with books. Some shelves just books of magic, the others a range from nonfiction to history to botany. I could see his love for plants throughout his home where they hung from the corners and sat on side tables. The small and intimate living room reminded me of nature with its hues of brown, tan, and green. Scents from magic performed and ingredients lingered in the room. It was more noticeable now that the scent of elven magic no longer clung to him.

He directed me to the cloud sofa which I sank into and sighed as I rested back. Our silence so heavily weighted and somber it needed to be broken. I turned my head to look at him where he'd rested back on the sofa just inches from me. A tableau of sorrow and pain that could be etched into something that would make onlookers weep. I was on the verge of doing it myself. But anger kept the tears at bay. This victory should be sweet, and I hated that it wasn't.

Blowing out a slow breath, I opened my mouth to tell him when he spoke.

"She's dead."

I nodded.

He made a sound that landed somewhere between a sob and sigh, blinking several times until the tears finally fell.

"I'm sorry," I whispered.

"No apologies, please. If anything, I owe you more than I can give. Foolish actions led to this point and blind love for her made things worse." He grunted. "It wasn't blind. I saw what she was becoming and the vendetta she had against you. I just thought she'd eventually see the error in it. That I could convince her to stop. I failed and you were left to handle a situation of my making. For that, I am sorry. Don't feel sorry for her death. Feel sorry for her misguided ways."

He mistook my apology for regret for her death. I had none. I waited for questions that never came. She was dead and that seemed to be all he wanted to know.

Our heads resting near each other, we stayed in that position. His hand continued resting over mine, and occasionally a deep sigh from one of us pierced the silence. In that moment, it felt like we were engaged in an unspoken conversation and agreeing to a pact. It was comforting and peaceful and what I needed.

The solace ended with Nolan standing and retrieving a water can and spray bottle. He went to the plants, speaking words of encouragement while watering them and giving them food. After the third plant he said with resolution, "They won't turn Fabian over to you."

He confirmed something I had suspected.

"Even the threat of permanent magic loss won't convince them," he added.

And once they got word of Elizabeth's death, they'd be even less inclined to do so, adopting the same view of me as she had.

"I don't want them magicless. It puts them at risk. But Fabian is a danger to me and others. He has to be apprehended." Apprehended sounded better than put down like a rabid animal.

"I agree. He is quite deceptive in his practices. I was fooled by him. Although I do believe he wants to protect the elves and keep them from being vulnerable again. He suffers from power lust, which often overshadows any good intentions." Nolan frowned before giving a plant in the corner a spritz of water.

"He doesn't have magic, so that should make it easier to find him." I sounded surer than I felt. He'd managed hiding from the shifters.

"Not necessarily. Lack of magic didn't take away his ability or his desire for power. It just limits him. Do you have the address of the place he kept outside of the Havenage?"

I didn't have it, so Nolan went to work giving me all the information he had on Fabian. And the information of every half-caste that had been in contact with him and people he could recall Fabian mentioning. Nolan's unassuming nature meant he was often viewed as innocuous, but he paid attention and had a wealth of information. There was power in that.

"I will return the elves' magic but not until I have Fabian. I don't want you to be without magic."

Nolan twisted his mouth in consideration. "You took away Elizabeth's fae magic when you removed it from the elves. When you return it, can the same be done?"

"You want me to give you her magic? I'm not sure I can."

He shook his head empathically. An undeniable refute. "No. Return their magic but not mine."

I sputtered out a "What?" Had there ever been a time in the history of magic someone requested for their magic to be taken away? Grasping for some understanding—nothing came.

"Nolan, when I return their magic, it will be on the condition that they have representation among the supernaturals. Which means they must have a head. I think it should be you."

"I'm half elf and human. They would never consider me as their leader, and I shouldn't be. And you designating me as the head after—" He swallowed the words about Elizabeth's death. "Whatever is to be Fabian's fate will leave any trust they have in me in tatters. They wouldn't trust that I'd be a good leader. I'd be deposed immediately."

He found a smile under all the sorrow that cloaked him and marked his movement and expression.

"Let them pick who they trust to lead them. You be the shadow that guides. Even if you don't want to be part of the community, don't completely abandon them."

The silent comfort that we shared earlier was dwindling into something tenebrous.

"And you?" My voice thinned with the questioning.

"You said you wanted normal—or your normal. I do, too."

"I want my normal with magic, my friends, and people not trying to hurt me or kill me every other day. Your normal seems like you're giving up. If I don't return your magic, you'll age like a human and have no other way to protect yourself."

His wry smile was unsettling. "Humans manage to wake up and live this way every day. I think I can manage it."

No matter how well he took Elizabeth's death, he was dealing with grief and making decisions based on it. I'd take most of what he said with that in mind. I walked over to him and hugged him, his hands at his sides, the water can in one and the spray bottle in the other.

"The reason I exist is complicated and dark and I realize you feel some guilt about it. Mistakes were made. Don't feel any guilt about my existence. I'm happy to be here."

Holding the cumbersome containers, he still managed to give me a hug. I felt the appreciation in it and hoped it would nudge him toward changing his mind. I wasn't sure I could manipulate returning the magic to exclude him and had no intention of looking into it.

Staying longer than I planned, nothing could be said to obviate Nolan's compounded emotions. Time would be the only thing.

CHAPTER 20

By the time I made it home, I felt the drain that using strong magic, dealing with Neri and Landon, and the threat of death and imprisonment had placed on me. Several times during the drive home, I couldn't help but stop at a weald and reveal the Veil, depleting the remainder of my energy and my morale as I waited at the edge of it for Mephisto to appear. Going through it to search right now wasn't possible. I hadn't forgotten that it was the home of the most powerful and ruthless supernaturals, either, and I wasn't in a condition to stave off any attacks.

Fatigued, I mulled over the fact that I was in possession of just parts of my magic and that Ms. Harp had the rest. The shifter who didn't change in possession of elven magic. Would she tell Asher if she wasn't doing okay? I knew she was being cared for and checked constantly, but I needed to hear from her that she was doing fine.

Ms. Harp answered my call immediately. "Yes."

"You doing okay?" I asked.

The long pause was worrisome. "Ms. Harp?" I eased out, concern heavy in my words and difficult to miss.

"No," she said, sending a rush of panic through me and the darkest of scenarios flooding my mind.

"What's wrong?"

"Everyone's bothering me," she spat out. Her voice dropped to a whisper. "Dr. Reyes won't go away. She just sits and watches me. Then she probes and prods me seemingly every hour."

"What does the probing and prodding entail?" The queen of drama was at it again. I was willing to bet it consisted of assessment of vitals, questions about her well-being, and to slow down on the *coffee*, which was alcohol and a few drops of coffee.

"And Asher called to tell me he's stopping by. I hope it's to take Dr. Reyes home," she grumbled. A diversion tactic. My question wasn't going to get answered.

"I'm fine and I can't do spells. That's what they were worried about." That had been a matter of concern as well.

"How did you determine you can't do spells?"

She kept her voice low to the point I had to strain to hear. I suspected Dr. Reyes was near and even if she wasn't, her preternatural hearing would deny Ms. Harp the privacy she wanted.

"Dr. Reyes had me try some. Nothing happened. I couldn't even do spells from a beginner's book. She also asked Sherrie to make another attempt to shift me. Nothing."

Failure and inability had never brought me so much relief. She was still Ms. Harp, who was finished speaking with me and ready for some privacy.

"If anything changes, will you let me know?" I asked.

"Of course. And if I don't, Asher will." Ms. Harp ended the call seconds after rushing out a goodbye. It had to be a difficult transition from living alone to the suffocating and intrusive position of "friend of the pack," but knowing what I did about the shifter who didn't change, I was glad she had them.

The news about Ms. Harp relaxed the tension that I

hadn't realized was coiled among the other tensions. At my apartment, to my surprise, I didn't have to navigate around a hallway of wolves. The door swung open the moment I was in reach of it by a beleaguered-looking Madison and a wary Cory. Their gazes swept over me, and Madison attempted to pass off a grimace as a smile.

"Your phone's dead," she sighed out, leaving a wide breadth for me to enter. Which explained Cory's return. His landscape of worry switched to a reprimanding glare. My steps felt heavy, and if I didn't have visitors, I'd face plant onto the sofa.

"I guess you don't feel like talking," Madison surmised.

"I can talk." That's about all I could do at that moment. "The elves are without magic, the Veil is open, Fabian is missing, I've cleared my name of the crime against Adalia, Elizabeth's dead, Landon is being a total and complete ass—and is definitely going to be a problem for me."

Cory breathed a sigh of relief at my acknowledgment that Landon was a problem.

"When I return the elves' magic, Nolan wants me to exclude him so he can live a human existence, and just fucking die," I continued in an emotionless stream of words while I rested my head back on the sofa. Cory and Madison's silence was heavy in the room while the ubiquitous awareness of the situations we made, avoided, and possibly worsened lingered.

Madison studied me with a grim understanding. "It's only been a couple of hours, he'll come," she said. She made an attempt at a smile that didn't quite reach her eyes. I wanted to be encouraged by it but wondered if Mephisto didn't know. Was he in the Veil, working on a way to escape? Did the broken spell shatter in an elaborate way signifying that it was gone? Nothing spectacular happened on our side, so maybe it was the same there. He probably didn't know.

Madison's questions about Nolan were a welcomed

distraction. "You know that decision is based on his grief," Madison pointed out.

"I know, but it doesn't make the situation better," I admitted with a sigh. With a grim smile, I asked, my voice perkier than I felt, "And how was your day, dear sister?"

She whooshed out a breath that made her lips rumble. Hauling off to the kitchen she grabbed one of the bottles of wine that I'd designated for special occasions only, took out three glasses, and emptied the bottle into the three. Cory joined her in the kitchen. Grabbing one glass, he took a large gulp, leaving just a little more than half in it. Madison's pull wasn't as massive but equally impressive in consumption. She continued to take sips before bringing the third glass to me.

"I knew about Elizabeth." She made a sour face. "They didn't bother hiding the evidence when they summoned me." The dark cast that roved over her face told me she had been tasked with handling the situation and the annoyance she had to feel about them feeling so entitled they made no effort to hide the crime. Adding to the problem was probably the conflict of her duties as an agent and a fae. I didn't envy her position.

"What are you going to do?"

"It's been handled," she acknowledged. Her look of self-condemnation squashed the questions that rose in me.

"Wendy?"

"She's been released but she still has no coven affiliation. Adalia has made it clear that she wants to move past her abduction and would not cooperate with a trial. No coopera-tion—no case." Madison gave a weak shrug and took another sip from her glass. She grimaced into the glass, likely contemplating the mounting complexities of magical poli-tics, bureaucracy, and our existence being known by humans and the scrutiny that accompanied it.

"The royals offered me a job with them. It's triple what I make with the STF. But it seems like one of those keep your enemies close type of situations. What happened between you and them?"

I relayed everything that transpired in the conversation. That I would always be an ally of the fae because of her.

"They appear to have very little interest in me and a great deal in your lineage as an elf and 'whatever other fiendish' breed you're mixed with. They appear to believe you're part demon."

"I take it you did nothing to change that assumption?" Cory speculated, splitting his attention between her and the kitchen in the direction of more wine. It had been a bad day for us both, and I suspected he was minutes from taking liberties with my snacks as well. Before I could make the suggestion for food, he'd returned to the kitchen.

"It's best that they don't know for sure. I think the mystery will protect you more than the truth. Now they're aware that elves aren't extinct, and that you have the power to remove magic from races of supernaturals—"

"Just elves," I corrected.

"The close relatives of fae," she countered. "Your affiliation with Wendy isn't disproving their assumptions." She groaned. "Her dalliances with demon magic aren't as secret as she believed. Just overlooked. But it won't be for long."

Cory returned from the kitchen with a refilled glass of wine, crackers, and a bag of chips. Placing the wine and crackers on the table, his face folded into a guilty frown. "I'm going to have to do a cleanse tomorrow, add more cardio tomorrow, or something."

"Or you can do none of those things and just enjoy the delights like us norms."

He flashed a smile and waved his hands over his body. From experience, I knew we were moments from getting glimpses of the results of his workouts and low-carb lifestyle. I was eternally grateful for the knock at the door that interrupted us from fake fawn of abs, pecs, and fit body parts he'd put on display.

I opened the door to Mephisto's lips spread into a welcoming smile.

CHAPTER 21

Without any care for the audience, I gasped his name and launched into his arms. He lifted me to him, and my legs curled around him. The room seemed to consist of just the two of us. Everything I felt poured into my kiss. Commanding, ravenous, and fervent. His tongue ran over mine as it explored my mouth. One hand moved from its position on my ass and ran under my shirt, kneading at my skin, warmth spreading over me. Pulling away, I buried my head in his neck and breathed his scent in before kissing him again. Softer, more subdued, but just as hungry. Brushing away strands of his hair from his face, I took in every curve and line of his face before kissing him again. His fingers curled into me as if he was willing himself to be closer to me. When I pulled away, he ran his tongue seductively along my bottom lip, coaxing for more. I wanted desperately to oblige.

The desperation and sadness that I'd been holding fled from me in a shaky breath. Mephisto ran a soothing hand over my back. His lips pressed lightly to my cheek, corner of my mouth, before covering mine with another kiss.

"We should at least have to pay a subscription for content like this," Cory griped. "Although, to be honest, it's not worth more than three bucks ninety-nine. Still, don't just be giving this content away for free."

We pulled away with the intention of responding to Cory, but we couldn't seem to tear our eyes from each other.

"What did you do?" The accusation in his voice implied he knew that it wasn't a simple spell that released them, but satisfaction lingered in it.

Mephisto inching farther from the door cued Clay to peek his head in. He took a look at me in Mephisto's arms and his lips pulled into a tight, disapproving smile. It trailed past us to Madison, where it widened, and he quickly moved toward her. Madison being a person ever aware of her surroundings, I knew she would never display a greeting like Mephisto's and mine, but I wasn't anticipating the tight smile and short hug ending with Clay giving her arm an affectionate squeeze. His hands kept a loose grip on her fingers as they stood side by side.

Cory's brows inched together in confusion. "What the fuck is that?" he bellowed. I quickly bit back my laugh. "These two gave us an Only Fans scene and you two hug like you're what? Cousins? You don't have to paw at each other like animals in heat." He cast a derisive look at Mephisto's hands that hadn't moved from under my shirt, and at my legs still wrapped around his waist. "Maybe fifty percent less than that. Grab something hard or soft on each other, I don't care, but more than whatever the hell that was."

I scrambled out of Mephisto's hold and erupted into a laugh cough. "Cory," I derided.

"What?! We saw how distraught she was when he left. We know they had many rounds of mattress time." Madison and I cringed at that. He persisted. "Wall time. Probably in the car. Who knows? We've caught them half naked playing Scrabble." He air-quoted Scrabble. "Why are they behaving like this? Fine. Everyone turn around so they can give each other a proper greeting." Then he directed his instruction to

Clay and Madison. "Make sure to touch some place inappro-priately."

No one moved. Madison's expression moved from cringe to the bright glow over her nose that appeared whenever she was embarrassed. She looked like she wanted the floor to swallow her. Clay looked amused by Cory's antics.

"I'm quite happy to see Madison." He leaned down to her, turned to block anyone from reading his lips, and whispered something that revived that glow over her nose and made it migrate to her cheeks. Her teeth gripped her lips. Then he pressed a soft kiss to her lips then temple.

Cory's lips curled into a smile that made its way to his eyes. "Better but still needs improvement. Should we leave?"

"No one needs to leave." I shot a chastising look at Cory on Madison's behalf. She decided on death glares. Cory ignored them both, hauling himself to the sofa and plopping down on it before returning to his chips.

Mephisto stood close. Ever aware of the intensity and heat of his gaze on my face, I turned to face him. He cradled my face in his hands, his thumb running languidly along my cheeks. "My demigoddess," he whispered. His body melting into mine, the hug and the weight of his muscled physique was heavy against me.

I felt his reluctance as he pulled away. Curiosity drowned out everything else for the moment. I reveled in the closeness of him, his peculiar magic that threaded around me and the enigmatic pull it had on me. It had changed; something in it tugged at my awareness. Mephisto, a man who always displayed masterful control of his emotions, appeared to be directing a great deal of effort in tamping them down. He gave in again, pulling me into another hug.

"I've missed you," he whispered against my cheek.

"Me too."

He inhaled a deep breath, and some semblance of his veneer had been restored by the time he released it.

"How did you do it?" Curiosity wove its way through his rich voice. His fingers threaded through mine. The small space allowed between us was devoured again.

"I took the elves' magic."

"What?" Clay was the first to respond. Surprise and hints of doubt in his question. He moved away from Madison to me. Anticipating a night of questioning, I took a seat on the couch next to Cory and Clay and Mephisto stood close, their intrigue palpable.

Recounting it all with two gods leaning into me, clinging to my every word, was more euphoric than I'd imagined. Whatever misgivings or apprehensions Clay had about me had slaked away. Engrossed, his mouth was a small O throughout, snapping closed when I got to the discovery of Benton's information.

Mephisto and I held each other's gaze for a long time, with so many unspoken words between us.

"Are you hurt by that?" he whispered. Was I? The information helped me, but did it override the feeling of having been observed like a specimen under a microscope?

"I don't know how to feel about it," I admitted.

"I believe you're the only one of your kind. It was more than just curiosity for Benton and us. We needed to understand your abilities and limitations to help you."

He inched closer and knelt in front of me, worry painted over his expression, searching for something.

"I understand why it was done, so it's difficult to be angry," I said, which was true. "The thought of being the only one isn't difficult."

The collective understanding eased the tension in the room. It didn't change the fact: I was the only child of a despotic Arch-deity and an elf. I should get a shirt.

My hand covered his in reassurance. "The information helped me. In the end that's what matters."

Clayton's hand stroked over his jaw as he processed the

information. "You removed the elves' magic," he mused with a tone that hinted at appreciation. "I doubt anyone can deny your lineage and its endless capabilities." Despite his compliment, there was a note of reservation, perhaps caution.

His comment wasn't meant as an insult, but it unsettled me. A poignant reminder that my magic mirrored Malific's and my capabilities with magic a reflection of Elizabeth. They both had done more harm than good with it. I didn't want that to be the case with me.

"I plan to return it."

Clay and Mephisto offered a half smile, a look passing between them an indication of their silent communication. Whatever exchange occurred, Clay maintained a look of reservation. Being Malific's daughter would come with wariness, concern, and constant speculation over whether I'd become her. I wouldn't.

"Then finding Fabian needs to be of utmost priority," Mephisto surmised. "Giving them magic now would give him the advantage. I guarantee he's working on a way to undo what you did. Sanaa was right. Of those capable of such a task, it would be he or Elizabeth." A cool dismissal of Elizabeth swept over the words and was congruous with how we all felt. There would be no mourning for her but a relief that half of the problem was gone.

Several hours were spent trying to determine the best course of action. The primary goal was to obtain any objects that could be used to return the magic.

Cory had lingered, questioning Madison about her plans for the rest of the night. Based on the looks she and Clay had been giving each other most of the day, we all knew. But Cory had developed an unhealthy fixation on them.

"Well, if you don't have plans, let's go to dinner," he suggested to Madison before taunting Clay with a smirk.

"We've spent enough time with each other," she shot back, skewering him with a playful glare.

"I don't think we spend enough time together. I want to hear more about your day, in great detail. Unless you have other plans?"

"Why are you like this?"

"Like what? Irresistibly adorable?"

"I can guarantee that's not it. At all," she shot back, heading out the door without further discussion, Clay close behind and Cory beaming, prouder than anyone should be for displaying such puerile behavior.

"They were fun," Cory said, giving us a wave.

"Leave them alone. Accept they're weird about their situation-ship. Stop harassing my sister," I demanded.

He pulled me into a quick hug. "I will. It's just so fun. Did you see that look? She was definitely considering abusing her power as an agent and doing menacing things to me."

"Yet you persisted."

Shrugging, he treated me to another dimpled grin. "Sometimes I'm just a jackass."

"Don't be proud of that," I told him as I playfully nudged him out the door.

The door closed and Mephisto pulled me into a long kiss, warm lips coaxing a moan from me. His tongue lightly caressed mine as his hand splayed over my back, kneading at my skin. He pulled away and studied me for a long time, dark eyes scrutinizing me with intent. Overjoyed by his return, the events remained with me. I wouldn't mourn Elizabeth's death; she was deserving of her ending. Stripping the elves of their magic was a necessary evil, but I couldn't ignore malevolence. Clay's words lingered in my thoughts.

"Do you mind if I have a glass of wine?" he proposed. I knew it was an excuse to give me some needed space to decompress from the day.

I shook my head. "I'm going to shower."

He offered to join me later. I was looking forward to it.

CHAPTER 22

I was on the second lather, the steam filling the bathroom and the relaxing scent of my eucalyptus bodywash enveloping me when the curtains inched back. Mephisto stepped in behind me, the heat from his body adding to the warmth of the room. Pushing away damp hair, he pressed kisses to the nape of my neck and ear before slipping around me. Lathering the sponge with bodywash, I ran it slowly, meticulously over his chest, abs, the crest of his hips. I let my hand slip down to stroke him, keeping eye contact as he hardened in my hand.

His breaths became shallow and rough. Mephisto's tongue slid across his lips before he gathered my hands and held them above my head with one hand. His eyes darkened as his other hand trailed over me and rested on my breast. Fervent lips covered mine, his thumb stroking lazily over my nipple that hardened with his touch. Languid and slow, his hand skated my body, cupping the swell of my breast before teasing with his tongue, coaxing a moan from me before continuing the journey to my stomach. A shiver passed through me as his nails grazed over my skin before slipping between my legs. His fingers teasing, gliding, and stroking as

I panted against his lips. With a devilish grin, he delivered light nips to my bottom lip, releasing my hands from his hold. Wrapping my arms around him, my fingers curled into his back, begging for more. The heat of his body suffused around me as his fingers continued rhythmically stroking my engorged nub as I writhed against him, wanting more.

"You brushed over all your dealings with Landon today. Am I to believe your issues with him are resolved?"

"What?" I rasped out in a shaky breath.

My nails grazed over his water-slick back. I inhaled a breath and blew it out. It was difficult to focus on his words when I wanted to feel him inside me.

Licking my lips, I said in a throaty, inviting voice, "I think the Landon situation can wait. I'll deal with it later." Mephisto reared back but kept his teasing fingers in place, my body craving more while his other hand rested at my waist. I was aware of the firmness of his touch and his effortless seduction. He could devour me with a look.

Resisting my kiss, his brow inched up. Leaning forward, his tongue teased my bottom lip while masterful fingers delivered more inviting strokes. Soft moans escaped between low entreats for more. I pulled him to me, slipping my fingers between us and taking him into my hand. Stroking him, trying to lure him to me. Hating him for his restraint when I was craving to feel him.

"I?" His warm breath wisped against my lips. Lifting me, he guided my legs to curl around his waist. He taunted me, pressing his cock against me. I moved my hips closer to him.

"This isn't fair," I ground out against his lips.

"Now I'm the one fighting dirty," he said, pressing light kisses to my cheek, throat, and bottom lip.

I attempted a kiss and he turned his head slightly.

"I?" he repeated, dark mischief sparking in his eyes, taunting me with a promise of pleasure as he slowly gyrated his hips against me.

I swallowed. "*We* will deal with Landon later," I conceded. His lips covered mine in a ravenous kiss, and I gasped as he entered me. Feeling the strain of his size, eventually my body gave in to the delicious fullness. Pliant in response to his deep strokes and hot, commanding kisses. His name melting onto his lips, my fingers digging into the muscles of his back, meeting his voracious thrusts as he brought me to climax several times before seeking his own. It wasn't until he pulled away to turn off the water that the cool splashes pulled me out of the aftershock of my orgasms. I shuddered at the chill of the cooling room, and Mephisto enveloped me in his arms. Secured against him, I was carried to the bed where he deposited me, moving enough to allow his eyes to trail over every inch of my body. Departing to grab towels, he reappeared quickly and dried us off. Not fast enough to prevent the sheets becoming slightly damped.

He rolled me to my side, his palm pressed against my face. "I missed you," he whispered. It was different than before. Anguish and sorrow hung on his words. I draped my hand over his waist and kissed his chest.

"I missed you, too." I'd never seen his eyes look haunted and hollow before. "Did you feel some consolation being home after all these years?"

Getting home had been what he'd dedicated fifty years to. His business, connections, and questionable dealings were all done to achieve one goal: break the spell that kept them trapped here.

He offered an absent shrug. "Life went on without us. New Huntsmen recruited. Our legacy remained, but it was different. Resuming life as if nothing was wrong was difficult. I was trapped again, but this time without you. None of us liked it. Our time wasn't used getting acclimated but searching for a way to return, to walk freely between the two worlds. To see you at will," he admitted quietly. "Same task, just from a different side of the Veil. I should have known you'd find a way before we did. My resourceful demigoddess." He kissed the top of my head.

It wasn't the demigoddess who succeeded. It was the elven magic—or rather the removal of it.

"And elf," I whispered.

His brows drew together, probing for an explanation of the addendum I'd never felt the need to offer before.

"I want that part of my magic back," I admitted. "I thought losing it would be easy. After all, I've lived this long without it. With Malific passing and gaining access to all my magic, it was the first time I felt complete." It explained the violently panicked responses magic wielders showed when they were braced and their magic inhibited.

Pulling me closer, he cradled my hand into his neck. "Is that what you were holding back today? You breezed over the situation with Landon. That was intentional"—he inched me back and nipped my lip in chastisement—"but I felt like you were holding something else back. Was that it? Are you embarrassed for feeling that way?"

I shook my head. "Nolan." The burden of grief returned as I told Mephisto about my discussion with Nolan.

Mephisto searched my face for my plans, but I was so conflicted I doubted it would offer any. "I suppose I could take it away the same way I did it with Elizabeth, but I don't want to."

"Then don't. I suspect he will change his mind, when the sorrow eases. He'll realize the pleasure of having his magic and being with his daughter."

"I hope you're right."

"I am." He held me tighter. "May I get a promise from you?"

"Depends on what it is?" I teased.

"It should be simple. Don't keep things from me. I can tell by the way your body feels against mine that it was something you needed to discuss. Disclose everything you need to, if only to unburden yourself."

"Maybe I'm relaxed because of the orgasms?" I teased again.

A low rumble vibrated in his chest. "I'm sure that helped." There was a smile in his words. "But I know the difference. Believe me. I know you." His hand indolently slinked over my curves. "Just talk to me. Always. My instinct will be to try to fix it, but if you only want me to listen, I will. I want to be the person you feel comfortable talking to because you need to get it off your chest. Okay?"

"I promise. Don't study me like you were. It helped me with my goals, but it felt intrusive."

"It was never meant to be. You're a bigger anomaly than you care to believe. It wasn't to make you feel like a specimen under a microscope but to better help you navigate things. As far as Benton observing and making notes, that's him. I wish I could order him to stop but, well, you've seen how he is."

"So I'm not the only one!" I beamed.

"No, you are the only one when it comes to his interaction with you. You seem to bring out his more cantankerous nature," he provided, kissing me and rolling me onto my back. "I quite enjoy that about you," he whispered against my ear.

He settled between my legs, his fingers sliding between them, and groaning at my response to him. "I believe you're due for more relaxation," he said, his voice rough with need.

CHAPTER 23

I awoke to an empty bed and the smell of food wafting into the room. My stomach let me know that I'd had an exhausting day that ended with a long night of sex with Mephisto and making up for our time apart. Showered, dressed, and my hair styled in something that was passable as a braid, I stopped midstride at the sight of the guests in my living room. Simeon, Kai, and Clay. Mephisto was in the kitchen, his back to me, preparing something on the stove. I smelled steak and saw a plate of pastries, croissants, and bagels on the counter. He was dressed in different clothing than the day before. The tote next to the sofa storing the magical objects I'd borrowed from him was gone. And he was preparing steak that I didn't have and there were pastries and bagels, I assumed he had gone home and run errands while I slept deep nearly until noon.

Used to eyes that always held a hint of speculation and apprehensive concern, I wasn't prepared for them to look appreciative and curious.

"Thank you, Erin," Kai offered, breaking the moody silence. Simeon and Clayton offered nods of agreement.

"You would have found a way," I said, quickly making my

way to the plates and grabbing a croissant. Devouring it to settle my growling stomach, I returned my attention to the Huntsmen. Happy to see them, I knew it was inevitable they would be close to Mephisto, no matter where he was. They seemed to feel comforted by each other's presence. I didn't know if the ease in Mephisto was because his restriction between this world and the Veil had been lifted or whether it was the return of his brothers. I wouldn't do well in the Veil, knowing Madison and Cory were here, and we hadn't spent centuries together.

"We searched for Fabian last night, but in vain. We have very little to go by," Simeon admitted.

That's what they were doing. I felt bad they were continuing the search to end this while Mephisto and I... Well, we definitely weren't searching for Fabian.

Clayton dropped a notebook on the table and pulled out a bag, several objects, pictures, and an athame. "Benton put this together."

I perked up at the mention of the druid and savant of snark. "Is he here?" I asked.

Clayton nodded. "He's at M's, in his library where he's been since our return. Doesn't seem like he can rest until it's guaranteed that we won't be locked out of the Veil again."

Kai inhaled a sharp breath, a dark cast moving over his features and settling in a frown. "No," he whispered to the question that wasn't asked. I knew what he meant. He couldn't be restricted again, and I knew the others would move mountains to make sure he wasn't. Their attention moved to Kai, the etch of worry that always showed with him resurfacing.

"It won't happen again," Mephisto assured him. A promise that I knew he'd do everything to enforce.

"These are the spells, objects, and possibilities that can be used to undo your spell on the elves," Clayton said.

Mephisto placed a plate near me, and I started to eat

while he examined the objects and spells on the table. "Do we have all of them?"

Clay nodded. "All except two, but we have an idea who has them. We'll have possession of them soon." He lifted a hexagonal, milky-colored, fragile-looking object. He handled it with care. "It's a Redono. From our knowledge there's one more out there. I have no idea who has it but, in our favor, it requires a great deal of magic to use. Before any spells can be used to undo Erin's, the source holding the magic will need to be obtained."

"The source is well protected." I was confident of that. "Asher would never allow anything to happen to Ms. Harp." The mention of Asher's name made Mephisto clench his jaw.

Leaning in, I examined the pages and pages of spells that Benton had come up with; most of them used dark magic requiring sacrifices of life and blood. Desperation made people do dangerous and unethical things. Fabian was amoral and he'd dismiss any danger if it guaranteed the return of his magic.

"These spells could be done without Ms. Harp. If he figures out she's holding the magic, just as I broke the spell he cast on the Veil by removing elven magic, the same can be done by—" I couldn't say it, but it immediately made me lose my appetite. It could be done by killing the source. Nausea moved through me.

"She's technically a shifter. If they can get rid of shifters the spell could be overridden," Mephisto pointed out.

Denying that Fabian would do such a thing stuck in my throat because, of the many things Fabian would do, he'd consider that the least nefarious. He'd easily sacrifice the lives of the shifters in return for the elves' magic.

"Can you all find the missing objects?" I asked the Huntsmen, searching the room for my phone. "I'll contact Cory and see if I can compile a list of magic wielders that practice dark magic." With my phone in hand, I started to call Cory.

"Not just dark magic, demon magic," Simeon said, looking over the spells. These would be beyond the capabilities of a witch or mage. Demon magic would be the most powerful next to ours. If allowed out of their realm, demons could be the allies Fabian needed.

We couldn't let that happen.

Twenty-four hours after the Huntsmen had been sent out for the two remaining objects, we'd obtained the list of witches who'd possibly practiced in dark arts and dealt with demons. I was able to recruit the shifters to monitor them. Kai was tasked with surveillance of Wendy.

As my thoughts went to Wendy's face when she was informed that her coven had disavowed her and how the avaricious, arrogant, and morally ambiguous witch I'd dealt with in the past had devolved into a helpless, desolate woman whom I pitied, I couldn't imagine her helping Fabian. It was Mephisto's assertion that the loss of her coven would make her more dangerous and prone to allying with him. I remained unconvinced. Covens were important to witches, and I believed she'd be more concerned with finding favor with them in hopes of being allowed back. The chance of that was slim, but it occurred often enough to spring hope.

Feeling like I was standing on a razor's edge, I had done everything in my means, yet it wasn't over. I wanted it over. Fabian found and this ended. Magic returned to the elves and Ms. Harp and the shifters removed from any potential harm. A feeling Mephisto shared. Fabian's demise was his priority.

There wasn't anything deistic about the god before me. Something primal and raw lurked behind the tense eyes that tracked every step I made as I approached him in his office. Having returned to his characteristic clothing, his charcoal suit complemented with a steel-gray shirt without a tie, he leaned against his desk.

"Where does a magicless elf with a vendetta and power-lust go?" he mused, pulling me to him and resting my back against his chest. He pressed his face into my hair and inhaled, his arm firmly around my waist. I'd missed him; his constant need to be connected in some form or another showed I wasn't alone in that feeling.

"I've been thinking about that. I don't think he would return to the Havenage."

"No, he's looking for a way to break your spell, which will be impossible without magic." Pulling away, I turned to face him. His hand dropped down, inching to mine, and his familiar warmth suffused over me.

"None of the contacts Nolan gave me have seen him. I had him check since he knew of them, but no one claimed to have seen him." Mephisto became distracted, his eyes screwed tightly together in concentration before snatching up his phone. "Kai, what were you trying to say to me?" Kai was monitoring Wendy and their silent communication wasn't effective when they were far away.

Mephisto's eyes locked with mine.

"Wendy," I asked, with the reluctance and disappointment of a sibling or parent. Hoping I was wrong, I wouldn't bet anything I cared about against it. Without a coven, desperate and aligned with someone with a wealth of knowledge. I cursed under my breath and was right behind Mephisto as he headed toward the garage.

"She may go into this thinking she has an ally, but she's going to be the victim," Mephisto said. Victim was rather strong. She was going to be the casualty of her own making. I would bet something I cared about that she was going to summon the demon believing she would help Fabian get his magic back and be rewarded well for it. I was certain she was about to be sacrificed to the demon. She'd dealt with demons so much that she'd built a physical bond. It would be easier for her to serve as the host. All Fabian had to do was kill her. I hoped she forced him into an oath of protection before working with him, but it was doubtful. Fabian was cunning and would find a way to skirt one anyway with wordplay. His specialty.

We arrived at Wendy's home to find the door forced open, Fabian held against the wall by Kai as he writhed and spewed his words of hate, and a demon looking lasciviously at Wendy sprawled on the floor, drained of color, a syringe next to her. Mephisto got to her first, his hand pressed to her neck searching for a pulse.

"What's in the syringe?" Kai asked as Fabian gurgled out words. Kai loosened his grip and asked again only for Fabian to scoff as a response. Before exploiting any movement afforded to him, he glared at me. Hate filled his eyes. Mephisto smelled the syringe, took another look at Wendy, and took out his phone to call the ambulance.

Her pulse was so faint, I feared she wasn't going to make it. Over my shoulder I made sure the demon circle was intact, because the moment she slipped out of life, the demon would gain the ability to use her body.

"Fabian can't get away. If he does, he'll break the circle," I told Kai, who looked like he was ready to make any movement by Fabian impossible. Seeing Kai's expression, I said, "We need him alive." *For now.*

I started a round of CPR but Wendy didn't respond. Whatever poison had been used needed an antidote, not me compressing her chest to get her heart to pump. Once my arm fatigued, Mephisto took over. I gave the syringe a whiff.

"What is this?" I demanded of Fabian.

A light curve lifted Fabian's lip. "If I told you, do you think you can save her before the body is used?"

He was so smug in his confidence I couldn't help but be suspicious. *The body is used.* Were we not at the scene of the crime, or was this the scene of a set-up? It was Wendy's body he wanted, but this may not be the demon who'd get it. She'd interacted with so many demons. I recalled her face sprawled all through the demon realm when I was trapped there. Stupid, stupid woman.

"Is there another demon?"

As if he'd give me the truth. Overly confident, he did it with a smile. "No. That demon is going to use her body."

How? There was no way we were breaking the circle.

The demon would use a trigger spell that would remove the circle, similar to what was used to imprison the Huntsmen in the Veil. Mephisto sneered at Fabian, I guessed coming to the same conclusion. Why the hell would Wendy agree to such a thing? Of course, she would be believing she wouldn't be the one subjected to it.

Panic made me irrational. And creative. Spells ran through my mind. With the three of us in the room, the demon escaping could be killed. It was whatever spell he had the ability to perform that I was concerned about. Had Fabian figured out it was Ms. Harp holding the magic? Could the demon do a spell that could hurt or kill shifters? I wasn't about to provide the opportunity to find out.

"If she dies, can she be brought back?" I whispered to Mephisto, who was concentrating on keeping his compressions from being so strong that they would do more harm than good.

He shook his head. "This isn't a magical death. She'll need

an antidote for the poison. Let's switch. I need to look at the circle."

While I continued the rounds of CPR, Mephisto walked around the demon circle, the occupant of it more concerned with Wendy clinging on to life than the powerfully magical god circling him. Crouching, Mephisto examined it closer.

"I see it," he said. Unable to stop applying chest compression, I nodded.

"Tell me how to disable it," Mephisto demanded of Fabian. Gurgling choked sounds came from Fabian's direction. "He can't speak, Kai. Fabian, goodwill may work in your favor," he urged.

Kai loosened his hold only enough for Fabian to spew a curt challenge. "I doubt that it will. Figure it out."

"Your death can't come fast enough. And believe me, it will come," Mephisto ground out through clenched teeth. Foreboding silence filled the air apart from the sounds of my compressions and Mephisto's careful, measured steps as he moved around the circle. There was something familiar about the silence. Communication between Kai and Mephisto.

"Thank you," Mephisto said. More weighted quiet before Mephisto's dark chuckle filled it. "No, Kai, I believe that pleasure should be left to Erin."

A hard knock against the wall, a grunt of pain from Fabian was followed by Mephisto shooting Kai a warning look.

Mephisto's hands made rote movements in the air as he whispered a spell. Out of my periphery I saw burnished gold floating through the air and the demon spouting angrily about betrayal and revenge before he was gone.

Wendy's heartrate was weakening by the moment when Kai, moving with that annoying imperceptible movement, hauled Fabian to another room. Mephisto went to the door, hearing just snatches of the comments they made, the door opened, and the EMT entered. While they took over, I gave them the abridged and heavily edited version what had happened. One of them took note of the markings on the floor from the demon circle.

"What is that?" he asked, although I got the impression he knew what it was.

"A spell," I simply said, ignoring his narrowed accusatory look at my response. I'd have to let Madison know that a spin would need to be put on Wendy's condition because there would be the humans' version floating on social media and the news. Probably something along the lines of "Vigilante prevents witch opening the gates of hell" or something similarly sensationalized. Hoping that I wasn't recognized, I provided the attending police officer with the same information I gave the EMT. That I had a meeting scheduled with Wendy and when she didn't answer, we broke down the door and found her in this state. We knew we'd be questioned, but since it was a witch involved it would be handed over to the Supernatural Task Force. Skepticism marked the officers' questioning as they performed a sweep of the room. Mephisto gave my arm a quick squeeze before I could challenge them. They wouldn't find Kai or Fabian in Wendy's home.

Once the police and EMT left I made one call to Cory for him to contact Wendy's coven to let them know she was in the hospital. Despite being disavowed, they wouldn't abandon her in this state, alone. And another call to Madison.

CHAPTER 25

Fabian looked resigned, crouched in the middle of the living room in Mephisto's home.

"As you requested, he wasn't hurt," Kai had said with barely suppressed hostility as he tossed Fabian at our feet. His deceptively cherubic features hardened into something cold and ruthless and he looked upon Fabian with contempt. One that I understood. Despite how innocuous Fabian looked at that moment, he'd proven capable of unspeakable cruelty.

Fabian had been left unrestrained. I looked at Kai, who appeared to be waiting in anticipation for Fabian to attempt an escape. He made no effort to do so. Standing, he locked eyes with me. Cool arrogance and traces of irritation wafted from him as he straightened to his full height.

He sneered; an acceptance of a fate that seemed inevitable. When I removed the distance between us, a frown replaced his sneer.

"It is only fitting that it is Malific's daughter who ends it for me," he whispered. He lunged at me, but a reflexive defense of magic slammed into his chest, sending him skidding across the room. Before he could respond or come to stand, Mephisto had snatched him up and held him midair by his throat. Mephisto's jaw was clenched and he panted from the effort to restrain himself. All the color drained from Fabian's face as Mephisto's grip grew tighter. Pale and gasping for every breath.

"Mephisto," I whispered. That did nothing to rein in his anger.

It was several beats before he found the composure to lower Fabian to the ground. "Do you know what you've done? How much chaos you've unleashed? For what? A bitter rivalry between the gods and the elves that only you were involved in. Only for this to be your fate."

Fabian scoffed. "*A bitter rivalry that only I was involved in.* Gods and elves can't exist together. Is this not proof?"

"This is of your own making," I snapped in response, hating him taking the first shot and playing victim when faced with the consequences.

The expression fell from his face, leaving an indecipherable canvas. "I did what was necessary for the collective. You are quite skilled, beyond what I expected, but has your full potential been realized? A truce through a blood oath will ensure our legacy and save our people. If you kill me, you will never have a place among the elves, even if you return their magic. I am your path to them." He looked briefly at Kai who was barely containing his anger, then to Mephisto who seemed to be only controlling his for Kai's sake. "They will protect each other and their own. If ever they must choose between their own and you, what do you think will be the result?"

"I don't know, but will it be worse than sending me to the demon realm, manipulating me to use magic against a demon, making him human and killing him in front of me, threatening to kill my sister, or setting me up to be murdered by the fae?"

"I understand how you see those as acts of cruelty, but

you are now more knowledgeable and skilled because of that. Your mastery of magic and spell manipulation is a result of our doing. You may not have approved of our tactics, but they made you what you are. Don't repay my misdirected assistance with death."

Blinking several times, I could only look at him wide-eyed, my mouth gaping at his response. *And the gaslighting begins.*

Snapped my mouth shut at the absurdity of the spin he was putting on his actions. He continued with his spiel, but I zoned out, giving him the courtesy of last words that would not change the outcome. His defense of his actions became more desperate at my approach. None of it expressed remorse and he knew it. Even in his desperation, his intentions were blatant and unyielding. A hollow defeat came over his expression when Mephisto handed me a knife and I recalled Fabian taunting me that I'd beg for mercy. He would never extend mercy to me if the roles were reversed and I had none to give.

"Are you finished?" I asked, gripping his arm and piercing his hand, holding contact with him as the flicker of hope dimmed from his face, ushering in defiance.

"I'm the only one who considered you as our own. They will never accept you, forgive you, or allow this to go without retaliation," he pushed out through gritted teeth.

"Their acceptance means nothing. Any retaliation will be met in kind. I don't care about their forgiveness. I *won't* forgive myself if I let you live."

The depths of his eyes changed as anguish and fear crept in. It only served as a reminder of everything he and Elizabeth had put me through. An inexplicable lust for wrath surged in me and I didn't want to give him the peaceful death that the *Venenum* would give. Without magic in his body, it was essentially a death spell. Efficient in its execution, it would cause me discomfort as well as it ran through my body.

Locking eyes with him, I could see no sign of the smug man who'd wanted me to beg for mercy.

"I should have listened to Elizabeth and killed you when I had the chance," he said after showing me a moment of bleakness. "The elves deserve better than you." There was so much vitriol in his words, I wasn't sure if it came from a place of desperation and the need to inflict as much emotional pain possible or, with death imminent, he'd decided to tell his truth.

Piercing my own finger, I whispered the *Venenum* spell. His body convulsed and seized, fighting for a life he didn't deserve. Panting, his lips moved feverishly, still not used to not having magic at his whim. He continued to will magic that he no longer possessed and clawed at my hand to no avail as I maintained my hold.

Fabian clung to a life that was quickly leaving. "We would protect you. Don't do this. We are one and the same," he managed in a hollow voice that took his remaining strength to deliver.

The spark of life in his eyes faded. Hard and fast breaths diminished to light gasps before there was nothing. His eyes closed and he slumped to the ground. Dead.

Mephisto frowned. "He deserved worse."

"Perhaps, but I couldn't give worse," I admitted. Even now, despite knowing he had earned his fate, there was a grave, sooty feeling that lingered in me. I turned to look away. Mephisto knelt next to Fabian's body. Whispered a spell, and Fabian's body combusted into dust that was reminiscent of a vampire's true death.

The occupants of the Havenage tried to remain expressionless as they gathered around me. Death glares slipped through and glowers with the promise they'd never forgive me were shot in my direction. I ignored it all. Accepted it for the anger it was.

Still debated whether arriving alone was brave and exhibited good faith intentions or naïve and would prove to be a bad decision. The elves didn't have magic, but if they were thinking about hurting or killing me, me being the only one able to return their magic guaranteed some level of safety. That was the argument I used with Mephisto and Cory, who both wanted to come. Madison understood the importance of my symbolic gesture of meeting them alone and the need for that approach.

Sanaa seemed to have ascended to be their tacit leader. Frowning, she broke from the group. "Are you here to deliver the news of Fabian and Elizabeth's deaths?"

They'd probably heard of Elizabeth's death, but Fabian's had only occurred hours ago. It was unlikely they knew.

"I've come to let you know your magic will be returned to you tomorrow."

"So, they are dead," she speculated.

I nodded.

She closed her eyes, took a small breath, and when she opened them, they were glassy. She'd probably assumed, but hearing confirmation of their deaths was different. A few more days, I was sure word of Fabian's death would have made it to them. I couldn't let more time pass because I missed my elven magic as much as they probably missed theirs. It had formed a symbiotic mesh with the Arch-deity magic in a way that made its absence notable. I'd recognized it even more when I performed the *Venenum* spell. Having both magics made me feel whole.

"What conditions must we adhere to for the return of our magic?" A shrewd sneer transmuted Sanaa's typically kind features. Used to her being economic with words, I wasn't expecting such an interrogation.

"Peace. I don't want to be at continuous war with the elves or have to worry about retaliation. Know that the response to Elizabeth and Fabian was just." I raised my voice for them all to hear. "But I take no joy in it. I will unleash all that I have if you come for me. Just leave me alone."

"We ask the same of you. You've turned your back on us, it is only just that we do the same."

Prior awareness of their feelings about this dulled the edge of hurt it caused. The sting remained. Cory had his coven, Madison the fae, Mephisto had the Hunstmen, and I'd remain without any affiliations. A fact I had to bitterly accept.

"And Nolan. He is not welcome, either."

Another punch that I knew was coming but hurt, nonetheless. I felt the hurt of the rejection on his behalf. It would compound his desire to live a human existence.

I nodded. "Anonymity is no longer an option. Decide who your representative will be, who would be considered an elf in the eyes of the collective, and you must become a registered denizen. It will offer more structure, a voice with the laws, and protection. Anonymity has its advantages, but it does put you at a greater disadvantage."

Sanaa looked over her shoulder to the elves surrounding her before turning to me. "That is fair and compliance is noted."

Waiting for more, it became apparent that was the closest I'd get to a thank-you or an acknowledgment that I wasn't the monster they believed me to be. As I backed away to leave, she simply added a nod, ending further discussion.

No, there wouldn't be any affiliation with the elves. Nolan and I were outcasts.

CHAPTER 26

It had only been a few days since Elizabeth's death, and I had no idea what to expect from my visit with Nolan. He greeted me at his home with the empty gaze of someone battling with sorrow. Nothing I'd say would change that. He needed to grieve in his way and the time he needed. I was still thinking about his defeated expression when I admitted that I could probably keep his magic but wouldn't.

"I guess I took away your choice, now you're taking away mine."

It broke my heart.

"You bound my magic to protect me, and I'm denying your request for the same reason," I countered, leaving no room for argument. "You're a source of information when it comes to elven magic, and I have much to learn. And I want to learn it from my father."

The smile brightened his eyes and his words. "You've proven to be quite adept. I don't think you need my help."

"Nolan, you're not implying that a person should stop learning?"

His smile broadened. "Of course not. I'm sure you can teach me as well."

Hours later, I could still feel the warmth of Nolan's embrace when I told him about the invite for dinner with the family. The family who raised me. It didn't remove the anguish that lingered in his eyes, but it eased him some. It felt like I had taken the community from him and I desperately wanted to replace it with another. My family were surprisingly enthusiastic about meeting him, my mother reiterating the same sentiments I had. "The reason you exist is dark and flawed but it doesn't change how happy we are that you do. It's because of him. We would love to meet him."

Relaying my mother's words to Nolan eased the worry etched in his brow, replacing it with an eager smile.

"Don't be too excited," I told him. "There's a suitcase of board games and once they open it, there is no escape."

"I look forward to being captured by your family and encouraged to play the board games."

"Remember that when you're three hours into a game they purchased at a game convention," I teased, giving him a hug. The warmth that I felt when he returned it left me encouraged that he'd be okay. I needed him to be.

Arius's hollowed hate had festered, which was expected from the haughty little imp. My presence had become the proclamation of Fabian and Elizabeth's deaths, touting the information as efficiently as a town crier or placard. Arius received me with a knowing look of contempt, his eyes slipping from Asher, moving to Mephisto who had accompanied me, then down to my double-edged karambit.

Giving us the illusion of privacy, Asher slipped into the corner of the sparsely decorated basement that had just enough warmth and furniture to keep it from feeling like a dungeon. A large inexpensive rug was laid over dark vinyl plank. A utilitarian sectional took up a substantial area. A bookcase held a few books and magazines. The most impressive thing in the room was the cage used for shifters who'd lost control, and now a snooty imp who even behind bars maintained his air of self-importance, looking over his glasses and down his nose at me.

"Are you proud of your hand in their deaths? Has your brutality been satiated?" he lamented.

Pulling up a chair, I sat in front of the cage. "Yes, I am satisfied with their well-deserved deaths and will be with yours, if necessary."

His mouth parted, shocked by my curt response. Snapping it closed he snorted derisively. "Malific would be proud of her creation."

"Elizabeth and Fabian should be proud as well. They had a hand in what I needed to become to deal with them. Will you be proud of the actions you took that will lead to your death? I want to release you and allow you to live a full life, but I understand you were close to Elizabeth." He rolled his eyes as if "close" was too mundane and simplistic a word to describe their relationship. "You may wish to avenge her, but I'm going to make a good faith request that you don't."

"If I don't agree?"

"I'm going to kill you now and save myself the trouble of doing it later."

He looked horrified by the impropriety and directness. I didn't want anything to be lost in florid words and vagueness.

"Will you agree not to seek revenge against me or mine on Elizabeth's behalf?"

What the actual hell? Does he really have to think about it? Refuse or die, those are the options. And he needs to dwell on it.

It was my turn to be taken aback by a response, or rather the lack of one. Time ticked by and after several moments I stood, my weapons at my side. With a sigh, I said, "Open the door—"

"I agree," Arius rushed out, his lips furled back.

Nodding, I turned to leave with Mephisto at my side. I started up the stairs, but he remained at the bottom.

"Arius, I've come to understand that Erin is the softer of the two of us. She extends diplomacy and goodwill to those who have voiced their wish to do her harm. I do not possess such qualities. I will not mince words here. If any harm comes to her and it can be traced back to you, I will exact *my* revenge. And I can assure you I will not extend you the kindness of it being a swift or painless death. Wherever destiny may take you now, I ask that you first return to the Havenage to deliver this message to them as well. Make sure they understand the terrors that Malific inflicted will seem quite gentle compared to what I have in store for them if they do not abide by this. I am asking you to deliver this message because I fear that if I get a hint of their intention not to adhere to this simple request, I'd react poorly." The steely low voice sent a shiver through me despite not being the recipient of the message.

With a slight blanch in his coloring, the imp nodded. "Your message has been received."

"I hope it has."

Once we were upstairs, I pulled Mephisto aside. "The threat of murdering people in the most vicious manner possible after discussions with people can't be our thing," I said.

A foreboding dark smirk lifted the corners of his lips. "Of course it can." He extended his hand to me and I took it, linking our fingers. "I don't think this can be considered a threat. But a promise." He stopped and turned me to face him. "It is that, Erin. To you as well. I know you don't want to become anything like Malific. And you live with the perpetual fear of becoming heartless and pitiless. You respond with exceptional caution to prevent yourself giving in to violence and power lust. It is who you are now, but that caution has become a cudgel." He pressed his hand to my cheek. "I don't share those concerns for me. And I will act on threats against you without hesitation."

I started to speak but he swallowed the words with a soft kiss.

"Don't plead for compassion for those who dared not to show you any," he whispered against my lips with a hint of finality.

I nodded after a few moments of consideration. Sensing the concerns I left unspoken, he pressed his forehead to mine. "I won't be cruel without cause. But I refuse to allow your life to be endangered for things that are beyond your control. I won't." It was more than just a statement but an oath.

"I'm glad you're back," I said.

"Me, too."

Waiting the three days after Arius's release from the pack's house had the elves on edge, and I'd received calls and a visit from Sanaa. Perhaps it was petty, but I wanted to drive in the point and give the impression I was fine without my elven magic. A lie that just kept on giving. Entering Ms. Harp's residence, I saw Asher seated on the sofa, but it was Dr. Reyes who answered the door. It didn't surprise me that whenever Asher was there, she always seemed to be there, too.

With the comfortable confidence that shifters seemed to share, she smiled. "I'm here in case I'm needed. Sherrie is on her way," she offered in explanation. I knew that Sherrie would be involved. Asher didn't take chances and wanted to be prepared for any mishaps.

Ms. Harp was making a concerted effort to ignore us as she sipped from her cup and watched TV.

"Evelyn."

She dragged her eyes from a court show I wasn't familiar with to Mephisto at the door.

"You're back," she said in a tone of indifference. A fact.

She'd moved from anti-Mephisto to *meh*, where I believed it would firmly stay.

Mephisto made no attempt to change it. "Yes." He offered a smile that seemed to melt some of her coolness. "It is my understanding that you had a big part in that. Thank you."

Drawing her attention back to me, I said, "I want to thank you, too. I owe you a great debt."

She shrugged it off and looked at me with questioning eyes. "Were you able to achieve what was needed? *Everything?*"

"Yes."

"Are you safe?" The heavy concern in her voice made me want to hug her, fully aware she wouldn't have any of it.

Completely safe? Could anyone ever believe that to be true? My situation with Landon still needed to be dealt with. And when the elves finally revealed themselves to the public, the upheaval at the discovery of a race previously believed to be extinct could put the elves' safety at risk. Humans would have to deal with and reconcile with new magic in the world. I maintained solace in the knowledge the elves wouldn't claim me as theirs, so I would probably evade most of the fallout.

With the resolution of my debt with Landon, I anticipated a simpler life without the threat of people related to me trying to hurt or kill me. After performing a cursory survey of the room, I leaned in.

"I know you feel like a captive living here."

She gave me an exaggerated "Mmhmm," as she took a sip from her cup, the strong scent of Kahlua wafting from it.

"I can break you out of here," I suggested.

Taking another appreciative drink, she said, "No, it's a burden I must learn to live with," and added a theatrical sigh. *And the award goes to...*

The intense scrutiny of Asher, Sherrie, and Dr. Reyes was a reminder of how others viewed the mercurial nature of magic. It was understandable as I performed the spell, unable to hide the difficulty I had pulling the magic from Ms. Harp. It required me to repeat the spell after the first one left her in a stiffened state, an illuminated ring forming around us. I grappled with it, pulling it from her, invoking the spell again to rein it in and pull it to me. It left us both panting and leaning against the sofa. Ms. Harp appeared as if her legs were going to give out and Asher quickly helped her onto the sofa, a harsh look of disapproval directed at me.

It took several minutes for Ms. Harp's wan disposition to change to something that allowed the shifters and me to relax. After Dr. Reyes's examination of her, she advised with a pensive smile that chilled her warm eyes that visitors needed to leave. I suspected the next invitation to leave wouldn't be offered as kindly.

"Stay out of trouble. I don't want to do this again," Ms. Harp directed through shallow breaths as she rested back on the sofa, her eyes fluttering to stay open. I didn't want her to.

Asher stopped me on the way out the door with Mephisto. Looking over his shoulder at Ms. Harp, who had fallen asleep, her pallid coloring slowly recovering, I knew what he was going to say. Often able to hide his emotions, he now wore them prolifically over the etches of his frowning expression.

"Erin, if needed, my pack is available." His scowl deepened. "She isn't. I don't care what the situation is, okay?" Sherrie punctuated his statement with a glare that was cosigned by Dr. Reyes. The looks softened when they returned to Ms. Harp.

I nodded, although it was a moot point because I'd never ask. Grateful for her assistance, I'd never put her at risk again.

CHAPTER 28

I'd expected Mephisto to split his time between the Veil and here, but in the seven days since his return, he'd settled business as usual, returning calls and speaking with people as if he'd not resumed another life in the Veil. Did he plan to actively live in both? I hated to admit it, but it was unsettling he planned to maintain his business on this side of the Veil. I didn't want to share his time when he was here. It might have been selfish but there wasn't a point in being dishonest with myself. I didn't want to share Mephisto with the world when he wouldn't be here a hundred percent of the time.

At the door of his office, I tried not to read too much into the text he'd left to meet him in his office when I awoke. It was disconcerting when he addressed me as the Raven. A signifier that the other Huntsmen used that linked me to Malific. I didn't like that reminder.

"My raven," he whispered, standing from his seat at his desk. The new endearment made me pause, studying him with skepticism. I'd gone from his demigoddess to raven. Was the reminder of my origin for me or for him? I couldn't determine it from the meditative look on his face as he leaned forward. Mirror images of one another in an attempt to understand the other's thoughts.

"You see the raven as a creature of death whereas others marvel at it for its ability to survive and thrive in a wide range of habitats. Ravens are one of the few birds that exist in the Veil. You constantly show yourself to be the epitome of that, my demigoddess."

"Why was Malific known as the raven?"

He offered a small smile at my rebuttal. "You can have two ravens. One can be known as being portentous to death, the other for its ability to thrive and survive. But if you don't like it, then—" He waved it away with a hand movement, moving from his desk to kiss me. Resting his hands at my hips, his eyes slowly traced over the lines of my face. Then his hands roamed over my back, hips, and butt. Occasionally he'd lean forward, run soft, languid kisses over my cheeks, jaw, and neck. His idle acts colored by his deep thoughts and a stoic expression that revealed nothing.

"What are you thinking about?" I asked after a long stretch of silence that started to become uncomfortable. His hands slipped from my waist, clasping my hand before leading me to the sofa where he stretched out and positioned me with my back against his chest. He wrapped his arms around me in a snug hug.

"You and my life in the Veil." His failure to elaborate simultaneously piqued my curiosity and made me reluctant to ask questions. "I dedicated so much time to trying to get back to the Veil, to my old life. It meant a lot to me, and I felt like this side of the Veil was too small for me. I had a bigger purpose. Then I was locked out of it. I wanted— No, needed to see you. I thought my discontentment was because of that. Now it's available to me." He sighed. "I can freely walk between the two and I remain here."

My heart sank at the time and caution he took with his words. "I know you don't like being raven," he whispered, "but it's quite apropos." This was the worst break-up ever. I chewed on my lip. "It signifies the death of an old life. One I can't have anymore."

"But?" It hung in the air, unspoken and I wanted to know. Needed to know his doubts.

He leaned forward, resting his elbows, and exhaled a long breath. "You are so very Erin. A woman who would burn a bridge and plunge into treacherous waters just to prove you'd survive." He chuckled.

"You think I'm reckless?"

"Not at all. You're determined. I'm lured and afraid of it."

Untangling from his hold, I turned to look at him. "Afraid?"

Giving me a half smile, dark amusement and reticence played in his eyes. "Are we a good match if I'm the type of man who'd stand right beside you and want to inflict unspeakable wrath on anyone who forced you into standing on a burning bridge?"

"You don't think we're good for each other for that reason?"

"I don't know if we are, but every part of my being wants us to be together. I wasn't being hyperbolic when I said you are my weakness." His smile fell. It was the first time I'd seen that particular expression. A culmination of a lot of emotions. Confusion, concern—no, fear? No, not fear. There was concern and apprehension in it?

Turning, I planted a kiss on his neck, then another on his lips. "I'll be as gentle with your heart as I know you'll be with mine," I promised softly. Taking his hand, I led him to his bedroom where I slowly removed his shirt, the warmth of his body against my fingertips and his unique magic holding me compelled. A light smile feathered over his lips before they drifted over my face. Briefly, he closed his eyes as if he was trying to imprint them to memory. A transient look of sorrow moved over his features so quickly, it would have been missed if I hadn't been watching him so intently.

"What's wrong?"

"Nothing. In fact, this is…" He exhaled a breath. He kissed me gently. "Right," he whispered against my lips. Slipping my shirt off, his hand splayed over the valley of my back before cupping around me. With unnerving and enviable quick movements, he placed me on the bed, his arms caging me. Devouring me with his kisses, deep and hungry. He pulled away, his eyes lingering for just a moment as warm wisps of breath swept over my skin as he traveled over my ear, the hollow of my neck, the swell of my breasts. Cupping them, he laved slow, sensual circles over my nipples until they hardened, pulling a shudder from me and a low whine.

He let out a dark chuckle and continued to tease me with his touch, continuing his painfully slow migration over my body. Gentle nips, tantalizing kisses, and warm licks followed that path. Inching down my body, he pulled away to peel off my leggings and underwear, delivering erotic kisses as his fingers strummed over my delicate engorged nub, coaxing an orgasm from me. The warmth of his breath sending a shiver through me. His erotic teasing and taunts to my body had me whispering his name as his tongue and lips left trails of warmth and he navigated the length of my body.

Settling his body deep between my legs, he kissed me again. Gentle presses against my lips. I trailed my nails over his skin. I widened my legs to accommodate him and pulled him closer to me.

"We can't stay like this, can we?" he whispered.

"I don't see why not. I'll find less trouble here," I said, stroking his cock and guiding him into me. "Maybe not." Our movements a slow wind as I widened for him, wrapping my legs around him and pulling him deeper into me. Ensorcelled by his heat, our thrusts coming harder. Torrents of hot plea-sure in each movement of our hips. Pleasure building in me, our motion becoming more frenetic and uncontrolled. I fisted his hair and pulled him into a ravenous kiss as we climaxed together.

Facing each other in silence, Mephisto's eyes were intense in thought, his face pondering.

"Instead of thinking so intently about it, why don't you tell me what's on your mind?" I suggested, rubbing his furrowed brow.

"Landon," he said. He secured his arm around me when I attempted to roll to my back and escape the topic. "Erin, it's not a problem that will go away by ignoring it."

"I know, but I don't have a solution, yet. I'm certain the debt can be negotiated. It's just a matter of finding something that appeals to him more than having progeny," I said.

He made a sound that was a combination of a hum and a growl. "I believe I can end this situation with Landon. Should I?"

I gave his question a moment of consideration. Longer than I expected. I wanted the Landon problem over, but Mephisto's sharp look of anger and frustration hinted at how it would be taken care of. I was doubtful it wasn't violently.

"I appreciate it—"

"Don't appreciate the help, accept it, Erin. You are not alone." Cradling my face, he gave me a beleaguered look of resignation and huffed a breath. "You want to satisfy the debt?"

Nodding, I said, "I agreed to it in exchange for him saving Dr. Sumner's life. Repaying it with violence—or true death—is wrong. I may not be the one to give him the children he wants, but I don't want him to walk away aggrieved. His help deserves better."

He stroked my hair, then kissed my forehead. "You are not Malific's daughter," he whispered with a satisfied smile. "Undeniably Erin."

"Yeah, so I need to find an Erin solution." I returned the smile.

For several moments he was silent, a grimace appearing and disappearing several times. "I think I may have one," he said eventually. "Understand that what you offer him for preventing him creating dangerous vampires that you don't want in this world may have just as devastating consequences."

"Perhaps, but at least I'd be dealing with a known."

He nodded, accepting that this was a damned if I do or don't situation. I had been in a lot of them lately. It was just one more added to the list.

CHAPTER 29

Twenty-four hours later, Benton greeted me at his office door with a hesitant look that made me even more cautious of whatever solution Mephisto had managed. Mephisto had his fingers clasped behind his head, cool assessing eyes easing over the object on the desk. Benton shook his head and frowned at it.

"I'm against this," he said.

"It has been noted," Mephisto said. "The others have voiced their concerns as well. I've dealt with Landon enough times to be confident in assuring you that your worries are unfounded."

He unlocked the black case and moved it on the desk toward me. Opening it, I removed the object that was blanched spiraled wood forged into a single point. Brandished letters and sigils were laced over it and a strong scent of sage and oak wafted from it. I studied it, waiting for either Mephisto or Benton to provide more information about the object remarkable enough to be exchanged for the two progenies with elf/god lineage Landon wanted. I watched Mephisto as he moved to a corner of the shelf, his finger slipping to the side and with a slide of his hand, a small compartment opened.

"These are from a collection of objects I hope you never need," he said in a low grave voice although apparently, I needed them now. "This serves no other purpose than pure destruction." He pointed to some of the writing on it. "It's an Obscuro Mors."

"Dark death," I said, reading the brandished words near the point.

"It's more than just that. It's an eclipse of death."

"Okay?"

"He will know what it is because from my understanding, he's been in search of this for a very long time. The person who sired Landon is the reason he desires it so much."

The word "eclipse" turned over and over in my mind and its relation to magic and vampires. "Total death." A complete death.

I wished he'd tell me instead of being amused at me putting the pieces together. When it came to me, I sucked in a sharp breath. "It kills a sired line, doesn't it?"

Mephisto nodded. "Having progeny will be no good to him if you have the ability to destroy the entire line by killing just one vampire in it," he said.

Cursing under my breath, I understood Benton's reticence. "What other objects of doom are in your possession?" A forced smile warmed the words although it didn't ease my concern. Mephisto was dangerous. Not just as a broker of great magical power and exceptional knowledge but also because he'd spent over fifty years acquiring magical objects in an effort to find his way home. He came from the Veil where his survival hinged on him being the most ruthless and dangerous. I understood this and being with him meant I had to accept all of him. Having him in my life worked to my advantage, but it didn't stop me being unsettled by all I knew of him.

"I like knowing I have a means to control a situation when it becomes exceptionally dire," he said cryptically.

"Witches, mages, fae, and shifters?" I asked.

His face didn't reveal anything. "I've just recently acquired access to these objects, and it will never be my go-to option," he assured me. "This is about you and your deal with Landon. I'm giving you a way to end it on your terms."

Locking the Obscuro Mors back in the box, I thanked him for it. He was right; I was trading one bad consequence for another. Without a lot of options, this was the best of the ones I had.

The colorful floral gift bag in which I'd placed the *Stake of Doom* or Lineage Stake, which had a less ominous sound, had put a smirk on Mephisto's face even as Elon directed us to Landon, who was perched on the throne-like chair that had unsurprisingly become his favorite. Relaxed back into it, his obsidian dark eyes tracked our every step toward him before moving to the gift bag. His smile widened.

"Ah, you've come bearing gifts. Is it a response to mine?" he asked, a cool timbre in his tone as he clasped his fingers over his stomach. I hadn't even considered the symbolic gesture of my gift bag to the threat left at my door.

"No." Why did my voice sound so small? I was giving him the gift of a lifetime. It was the dark cast of menace that he held. Viper ready to strike. Shrewd knowledge and thirst. Those couldn't be denied. Without debate, I preferred the Landon who hadn't ascended to power. I missed the theatrical levity of his personality.

"You've been looking for this." I handed him the bag. Taking it, he pulled the box out and opened it. Studying the stake, he put a great deal of effort into remaining emotionless, but the excitement showed in his eyes.

"I do believe we've discussed this acquisition quite often, and you gave me the distinct impression you had no knowledge of it." Cool eyes drifted from Mephisto to me and back to the Obscuro Mors. They slowly roved over it, taking in its intricate carvings as if trying to commit it to memory.

"Would you have preferred I told you I didn't want you to have it?" Mephisto asked.

"You've had it all this time?" Landon's brow arched.

Mephisto nodded.

"Now you've changed your mind?" Landon's attention returned to the stake.

"Not at all. I still don't want you to have it, but the situation demands that I make this concession."

With a slow nod he chewed on the response. "Why am I now deserving of such an exceptional gift and concession?" he asked with a brittle edge.

"It's not a gift. It's to satisfy my debt to you," I said.

Landon's lips curled into a smirk. "Ah. But this is not what I requested."

"Perhaps not," Mephisto offered. "But it is also what you've wanted for some time. Now you have it. Accept it as repayment. Erin's debt to you is cleared. You wouldn't want this object to get into the wrong hands. You've acquired a substantial number of enemies. It would be quite a devastating turn of events if Erin were to help you create your progeny only to have them, and you, die at the hand of one of your enemies who possessed the stake. Now it's yours. You have full control of your life and complete death."

Cruel amusement flitted in Landon's eyes. "Well, this sounds like a threat rather than a repayment of a debt," he said.

"It's not." I sighed into my response. Landon was fucking exhausting. I wanted to throat punch him, tell him to take the payment, flip him off, and saunter out of his house.

Dallas casually walking past the door and Elon in the vicinity reminded me I needed to play nice.

"You know what I am," I continued. "And what me helping you create vampires could mean for the world. We have a responsibility to protect the system and maintain our tenuous relationship with humans. The people you'd like to be your sired aren't going to be responsible with new gifts. They'll be a danger and be far more work than either of us want." I was trying to appeal to the humanity of someone who didn't seem to have any. I searched his eyes for some understanding, sympathy, assumption of responsibility.

He cast a look at the stake. "The decision seems to have been made for me."

"If you still want progeny, I will help you, but they won't be created with me."

"Do you think I'd have a problem finding someone to help me create a vampire?" He preened, his brand of arrogance shining through.

"No."

"Since you don't have problems with such things, you and Erin shouldn't need to have any more dealings," Mephisto said, inching closer to me. Landon noticed.

"You two have united to form quite the power couple," he quipped, leaning back in the chair and examining the stake again.

"I suppose the progeny I desired is no longer in the plans." He dismissed us with a wave of his hand. "I'm quite disheartened." He twisted his body to the side, away from us, putting an end to the conversation. A powerful person essentially pouting and doing the child's version of "I'm mad at you and refuse to talk to you! Leave me alone."

"I do appreciate the gift—it will serve me well," he said eventually, easing the concern that had settled in me. Landon was often unreasonable but power would always prevail. He could sire vampires with mage, fae, or witches and have exceptional progenies and now, thanks to us, he had a tool that gave him an advantage no one else had. I wasn't happy with the trade, but it was a necessary evil. I had to live with that decision.

CHAPTER 30

Mephisto leaned down and kissed the corner of my upturned lip. "You're still smiling," he whispered as the man in the pristine uniform of gunmetal vest and black slacks guided us to the back of the luxe cigar lounge. It was an increasing occurrence that I was quickly getting used to. Three days since I'd given Landon the Obscuro Mors, he'd been quiet, and I hadn't heard word of him making threats to destroy other vampires. Taking it as a sign he'd accepted the alternative payment. Earlier, Madison and I had dinner with our family and Nolan. It was more pleasant than I'd predicted, the only obstacle was Nolan stiffening in our mother's overzealous hugs during their meeting. My father was cordial but noticeably restrained at the beginning of the meal. By the end of it he'd warmed enough that Nolan's cautious glances in his direction had stopped.

His comfort with them still brought a smile to my face each time I thought of it. The satisfied expression that lit his eyes had lifted another burden off me. Although he'd become a casualty of the suitcase of board games, he didn't see it for the battle loss Madison and I knew it was. Our plans with Mephisto and Clay allowed us to escape the night of board games and tedious explanations of games they'd discovered at a game convention.

Mephisto and I were escorted through the lounge that didn't just hint at exclusivity but wailed at it. Navy-colored walls, heavy shades covering the windows, and muted soft lights made the oversized space appear warm and intimate. A built-in bookcase filled with leatherbound books took up one wall. In front of it, leather chairs, luxe task lights, and a small table between. I was willing to bet that if I neared it with the explicit intent of reading the collectors' editions books, I'd be shooed away.

Clay and Madison had arrived earlier and were waiting for us on a curved sofa near the back of the lounge. My strapless apricot-colored midi dress was a contrast to Madison's slim-fitted cream-colored pantsuit with complementing corset with lace overlay. Mephisto didn't deviate from his typical style, wearing a gunmetal suit. Clayton's slacks and shirt's shade of blue was an intentional effort to harmonize with Madison's outfit.

She mouthed for me to take a picture, then lifted her martini glass to Clayton's lips before pulling him into a kiss. I took another picture.

"Send it to Cory and tell him if he ever comes by my house uninvited again, I'll make him regret it."

"Not to be that person—" I started slowly, the words sliced off by Madison's arched brow.

"He's only like this because you two were being weirdly secretive. It piqued his inner sleuth," I teased.

"Aw. That's a sweet way of saying he's nosey, overbearing, and intrusive."

"But in his defense—"

"There's no defense," Madison shot back.

"He's invested," I offered. She waved away my sympathetic smile. Her annoyance had placed a light glow over the bridge of her nose, while Clay suppressed a laugh at her response. He wasn't bothered by Cory's antics. I suspected he'd wanted more clarification as well.

I sent the picture and a text with a sarcastic "Are you happy?"

Cory responded. "Finally! Tell them to stop being weird about their relationship."

Relaying Madison's message about how she planned to handle his next unprompted visit caused him to shoot off a text to her. After a series of exchanges, Madison's lips were curled into a devious smile.

"Maddy?" I inquired with suspicion. I wasn't treated to that look often, but it always accompanied a level of pettiness that wasn't typical for her.

"I just informed him that all those reels and videos of him working out—that no one asked for—would feature guest appearance." She beamed. "And I'll spoil the ending to every movie until I grow bored. He folded."

I would have loved to witness the exchange in person, but Cory had declined our invitation to join us. With the tension and issues in his relationship with Alex exposed, they seemed to be working diligently through it. Cory admitted that the relationship had changed. I hoped their efforts would lead to a better understanding and ability to navigate the complexities of dating a shifter, although experience and cynicism made me anticipate the beginning of the end. I hoped I was wrong.

"Will Simeon and Kai be joining us?" I asked. Mephisto hadn't discussed the Veil often and had only returned there once in the past three days. Clayton and Simeon hadn't returned at all. Kai returned daily but never stayed longer than half a day.

"Simeon has Pearl, and Kai is in the Veil. He plans to return in the morning."

I'd seen Simeon in passing. He was making up lost time

with the domesticated snow leopard he'd grown overly fond of.

"Would it be so bad if the world learned of gods?" I asked, dividing my attention between Clay and Mephisto. Worry always crept into their eyes whenever Kai was discussed because his life was the most restricted. The Veil was the only place he could fly, something he needed to do. He was clipped here, and the forced constraint wore heavily on him.

"I don't know. The government, other sects, and humans' response to the elves revealing themselves will give us some idea," Clay provided. "Our magic immunity would not be well received, nor the measures needed to render us defenseless. And Kai's ability complicates things even more. You don't have bird shifters on this side of the Veil. He has magic, he's extremely strong, and he's fast. Imagine how people would respond to someone having that level of command from the air?"

Mephisto and Clay's cool discord permeated the space as worry eclipsed their expressions. I dropped the topic. They would never expose their existence if it would compromise Kai's safety or well-being. Further discussion was moot.

The unresolved issue was the timeframe of the elves revealing themselves. My exclusion from their community meant I didn't have a say in it. Anonymity gave them power and they'd delay it as much as they could.

"I'll give them three months. That's enough time to have established a leader and a course of action regarding their reveal. Anything longer is just a delay tactic. I don't trust them enough to give them the benefit of the doubt," Madison told me, reading the concern in my expression.

Although we made an attempt to keep the conversation light, it kept circling back to discussions of preventing the Veil being closed again, speculation about how people would respond to the elves' existence, and ways to mollify humans about the elves' magical abilities. It all led to the conclusion that the level of panic and worry that would ensue with the discovery of gods meant it was best to never disclose their existence. The primary goal was to make sure the Veil could never be closed. Mephisto and Clay either missed or ignored the shift in Madison's expression in response to that decision. We disagreed about it. Madison didn't believe the Veil should be closed but wanted the ability to do so if needed. I couldn't determine if she'd allow Mephisto and Clay's imprisonment for the greater good.

Minutes of studying her didn't give me any clarification. Pulling my attention from her weak, conflicted half smile, I directed my attention to my wine glass. That discussion was for a later time.

Left unsaid by both Clay and Mephisto were their plans to resume their duties in the Veil. They appeared to be more part of this world than the Veil. I wondered when they'd come to the same conclusion and if they did, would it change things?

Mephisto's fingers linked with mine as we approached my apartment. "Madison wants to keep a means of closing the Veil, doesn't she?" he asked.

Stopping abruptly, I pressed my lips together, unable to provide an answer that wouldn't betray Madison's trust. I opened my mouth several times to speak but nothing came.

Pressing a light kiss to my forehead he said, "You two may not communicate the way I do with the Huntsmen, but you do have a means of communication. I don't understand the nuances of it, but it clearly exists. There was an exchange between you two and I gathered that was the gist of it. Am I wrong?"

Fumbling over some words, nothing coherent came out.

He went on. "I understand her reasoning behind it, and I agree. There should be a way of closing it and of keeping it closed. I feel quite comfortable with you and Madison being the stewards of it. Even to your detriment and discomfort, you two do what's best for all that would be affected. Qualities required of anyone who would have to make such a decision."

It was a job I didn't want but knew it would be needed. Would I make the right choice? He had more faith in my ability than I had right then. The past weeks had stifled my willingness for abnegation and self-sacrifice.

There was a box outside my door. Ripping it open revealed the stake of doom. Landon hadn't returned it to the lockbox it had been in previously. Attached to the stake was a concise note.

I've ensured that this will never be used against me. You will honor your debt.

Trying to swallow, but the lump in my throat wouldn't move. Shallow gulps of air replaced regular breathing and it was only a matter of time before I would pass out.

"Erin?" Mephisto probed, cradling my face. But words wouldn't come so I simply handed him the note.

"Landon," he spewed his name with the venom of a curse. Raw anger wrapped around the words. "He's going to sire someone you care about to ensure you'd never use the Obscuro Mors against him or let it fall into the wrong hands," he said, confirming what I suspected. He let the note drop from his hand before taking hold of mine.

Forcing deeper breaths, I took out my phone to call Landon. The sense of foreboding made my words a raspy whisper.

"What have you done?"

"What was necessary. Now it is up to you. Do you want your human to live as a vampire or die?" he asked.

My human: Dr. Sumner.

Tears blurred my vision. Mephisto's thumb swept away the ones that coursed down my face.

"Come to his home, if you want him to live," Landon instructed.

Not giving him the courtesy of an acknowledgment, I ended the call. Mephisto slipped my phone from my hand, preventing me from hurling it into the side of the building, the need to destroy something unbearable.

Mephisto took hold of my arm as I started to rush to the car. "What are you planning to do?"

"Save Dr. Sumner," I bit back. It felt like trying to tow a boulder as I struggled to pull from him.

"Erin?"

"What!" I snapped, my tears in free fall.

"How are you going to save him?"

I glared at him.

"The only options are to make him into the type of vampire you railed against creating, or letting him have a human death," he provided when his first question went unanswered.

Holding it together became a task I failed. Gulping and wiping away tears, I sobbed. "He doesn't want to be a vampire," I told him, my voice so tremulous, I wasn't sure he understood what I said.

Mephisto pulled me into a tight hug. "Erin," he eased out in a calm, soothing voice. "He doesn't want to be a vampire and you don't want to create one. You know what has to be done."

I hugged him harder.

"I'm so sorry, Erin."

No platitudes or consoling words could change the inevitable. Dr. Sumner was going to die.

"I don't want him to die."

Pulling from me, Mephisto cradled my face in his hands. "He's already dead. If you don't feed him, he'll die. If you do, he becomes a vampire. His human life is gone."

Grasping at a reality of a world without Dr. Sumner made me desperate. The tenets I held no longer seemed important. "He should be a vampire. He wouldn't abuse his power. I know he wouldn't. I'd monitor him and—"

"He'd be a vampire. No longer be the Dr. Sumner you know. You wouldn't be able to reason with him because his loyalty would be to the one who sired him. A shallow vestige of the man you knew would be all that existed. He told you he didn't want to be a vampire, so honor his request. He deserves that."

"He'd never be Landon's. He's mine!" I ground out, pulling from him. Sorrow had driven me far from reason, making it impossible to see any parts of it. "He's mine," I whispered.

"He is," Mephisto offered quietly. "He'd want to say goodbye to you properly. Will you do that?"

Beats of time went by while I wept, slowly falling into the acceptance of what needed to be done. The right thing for Dr. Sumner, for everyone. But my body refused to align with the objective. I couldn't move. Feet rooted to the ground. Mephisto placed his hand on my back to urge me forward.

Erin, you have to do it. He needs you to do it. Brushing my hand over my face to wipe away the remaining tears, I snatched the stake from the box and marched toward the car.

"I'll give Dr. Sumner a good death, but Landon's will be painful."

Landon answered my pounding knock, an ominous smirk curling his lips, although that disappeared when I shoved him several feet back with a strike of magic to his chest. Elon grabbed a handful of my hair and yanked me to him and had his fangs at my neck.

"Let her go," Mephisto demanded from the door, calculating eyes searching for advantage before Elon could use his fangs on me.

Elon's cool breath beat against my neck as he chuckled.

"Erin, don't make this difficult, please," Dallas provided from his position protecting Landon who was now standing, rubbing his chest where the magic had hit. Shrewd disdain scowled his face.

"The nerve," he chastised.

"Go to hell," I snapped.

"By the looks of those puffy red eyes, you seem to have been in your own personal hell. Did you believe you get to change the rules at your whim? You made an open debt that needs to be satisfied. I don't appreciate having to force your compliance."

With a flare of exaggerated movement he extended his hand to Dr. Sumner's supine form. Eyes closed, Dr. Sumner's face was drained of color. I glared at Landon and extended the contempt to Dallas who was protecting him. My nails dug into Elon's hand, causing him as much pain as possible as he waited for the word from Landon to use his teeth on me.

I was prepared to let Dr. Sumner die. It was the plan. But seeing him lying on the sofa made the decision harder.

I didn't see a vampire in transition when I looked at him. I saw my therapist and the only person who allowed me to be vulnerable in a way that I'd never known. The person I felt free to share my secrets with. The man who grew to care for me in a way I never expected. I saw my friend. And I'd take him any way I could have him. Even as a vampire.

"What do I need to do to change him?" I asked. Mephisto's lips parted to speak, but he held it.

A smile slowly curled Landon's lips and everything in me wanted to wipe it off in the most violent way possible.

"He simply needs your blood."

"Okay."

"Release her, but take the stake away," Landon directed, sneering at the stake poking out from the makeshift holder I'd made in my dress.

Making my way to Dr. Sumner, I pressed my hand to the opposite side of the bite and looked for a pulse. It was weak but present. Before I could position my body to feed him, Mephisto was at my side.

"Erin?" he said.

Looking up from Dr. Sumner, I blinked until Mephisto wasn't a blur in front of me. "I can't let him die. Please don't ask that of me."

"Erin," he pleaded.

"Don't." I looked away from the disappointment that flooded his eyes. He sighed and nodded, but his resignation spoke volumes and the promise he'd made to me. He'd protect me. Was this something he deemed I needed protection from?

Lifting my eyes over the veil of wet lashes I whispered, "Let him live. I need you to let him live, too. Please."

"I can't. You know this isn't the best for all involved, and he said he didn't want to be a vampire."

"Please. He won't be a menace. I can make this work. You know I always do. Please don't kill my friend." Tears spilled again and Mephisto cursed under his breath.

"I. Fucking. Hate. You." He spewed at Landon with such vitriol lacing every word that it sent chills through me. Unadulterated and pure hate.

Landon took a cautious step back. "Well, that's hurtful," he said in a lively melodious tone that only heightened the visceral loathing we had for him. Landon allowed Dallas to remain his shield as he approached. "My blood is sustaining him, which is why his pulse is so weak. It won't maintain this life for long. He needs to feed from you to live."

"He won't be living," I said grimly.

Landon rolled his eyes at the correction. "Live as a vampire," he amended.

"You should not have done this to her," Mephisto said in a lethal low voice that belied the consolatory touches he applied to my arm. His hate so intense nothing he did could temper it. His restraint not to act on it amused the vampires.

"She should have honored—"

Mephisto's fist slammed into the coffee table next to us, splintering it into large pieces of wood. Before the vampires could react, a piece of it had been shoved into Elon's chest and Dallas tossed into the kitchen. Landon's mouth parted although his words of caution were useless against Mephisto's quick retrieval of a knife from the butcher block that he plunged into Dallas's chest.

"That injury is going to require you feeding," Mephisto said coolly, then his eyes snapped over to Elon who would suffer true death if he didn't feed. They were no use to Landon right now, who would be left alone.

"Go," Landon commanded. Dallas dislodged the knife from his chest with a grimace. It started to heal. But a wound of that severity would require him to feed to replenish his strength.

Landon stood taller, his eyes narrowed on Mephisto, and then moved to the Obscuro Mors stake, Elon had dropped. Landon tracked Mephisto's movements, no matter how minute.

"As I was saying before I was rudely interrupted. She should have honored her agreement. Now she must." Landon worked at removing the fear from his face as he slowly made his way toward me.

"What do I need to do?" I asked.

"First, call off your ill-tempered beast." Landon was livid.

Mephisto had devolved into a primal bipedal predator in an expensive suit ready to pounce at the smallest sign of movement. A product of the Veil in its rawest form.

Mephisto's slightly tilted head and narrowed, calculating eyes made me wary. Obsidian black eyes met Mephisto's, culminating in a thunderstorm of animosity.

"A vampire existence is better than none," Landon said in an attempt to reason with Mephisto. "Look at her. Do you think she will recover from his death? Let her keep him."

Nothing about Mephisto's demeanor demonstrated that he'd received Landon's words, but Landon inched toward me as if he believed they were. He remained cautious with his movements keeping a wary eye on Mephisto.

"His heart will stop. When it does, he must feed to revive him as a vampire. I must make the first bite. The venom I produce will initiate the process." He maintained a careful eye on Mephisto as he checked Dr. Sumner's pulse, pulling his eyes away for a moment to look at me as he swept my hair aside to expose my neck.

"My wrist," I said, moving from his touch.

"It will take longer," Landon noted.

"Then it will take longer."

Landon took hold of my proffered arm. His finger gliding languidly over it earned a low rumble of dissatisfaction from Mephisto. Amused by it and feeling Landon was safe from a reaction, I hissed when he sank his teeth into my arm. It felt different when it wasn't in the thralls of sex, as it had been on the many times I'd gotten vampire bites from my ex.

Brushing away the solitary tear that managed to escape, I positioned myself so that Dr. Sumner could draw from my arm with ease. Mephisto was a haze of movement through my tear-obstructed vision as he snatched Landon from his position next to me and tossed him against the wall. I ignored the plaster that rained onto the floor. One drop of my blood and Dr. Sumner's eyes opened. His vibrant peri-

blue eyes had dulled with a gray cast over them. He closed his fingers around my arm, continuing to pull from it like a person suffering from dehydration. Once the transition was over, his eyes would be black. My tears fell unrestrained, the violence taking place between Landon and Mephisto a disturbing soundtrack that I forced myself to ignore.

Dr. Sumner fed from me hungrily. It was more obvious than ever that this wasn't the man I'd developed such strong feelings for. He was now a vampire. There was no such thing as a good death, but I'd give him the best one I could.

Using my free hand, I brushed the hair from his damp forehead. Touching his cool skin flared a level of desperation and foolish hope that made my sole goal to pull back the human that was slipping away. Malific had created life. I had created life from plants. There had to be something I could do.

The spell formed so quickly it felt innate, weaving together parts of the plant spell and modifying a spell from the Mystic Souls. It demanded to be used. I was willing to do it. Magic peeled from me, an invisible thread binding me to him. Dr. Sumner gasped, loosening his hold on my arm. Small pulses of magic moved over his body before he dropped my arm in a screech of pain. Rolling to his side, he folded into himself, his body jerking and spasming before it relaxed into a quiet ball. The fighting stopped and I glanced at the two bruised and bloodied men and the room that had fared far worse. Landon stood with mannequin stillness, his mouth parted, his ear turned in Dr. Sumner's direction. His face screwed into a scowl.

"He has a heartbeat. He. Has. A. Heartbeat. Erin, what the fuck did you do!" he bellowed. Dr. Sumner sat up. His coloring with still pallid but flushed with vigor. The midnight cast had fallen from his eyes, slowly giving rise to the peri blue.

"I stopped him becoming a vampire," I said, my voice

wavering with the uncertainty I felt despite the deep breaths Dr. Sumner took, the heartbeat Landon heard, the glow of vitality increasing with each moment.

In wide-eyed awe, Landon looked at me then back to Dr. Sumner and disappeared just as Mephisto, with the Obscuro Mors stake in hand, lunged to grab him.

Mephisto dropped his head with a sigh. "You reversed vampirism, Erin. There has never been an account of that being done. Not even by Arch-deities. I'll have to kill Landon before he kills you. Once this is known, no vampire on this side or in the Veil will allow you to live."

MESSAGE TO THE READER

Thank you for choosing *Ironclad* from the many titles available to you. My goal is to create an engaging world, compelling characters, and an interesting experience for you. I hope I've accomplished that. Reviews are very important to authors and help other readers discover our books. Please take a moment to leave a review. I'd love to know your thoughts about the book. Whether you write a few sentences or several paragraphs, your review will be appreciated.

For notifications about new releases, *exclusive* contests and giveaways, and cover reveals, please sign up for my mailing list at McKenzieHunter.com.